Dear Target Reade

Thank you so much for picking up my debut thriller, *When No One Is Watching*! I'm super excited for this book to be out in the world, and I truly hope you enjoy it. I will forewarn that this book gets tense—I made *myself* anxious when writing certain scenes, and I knew what was going to happen at the end!

Writing this kind of letter for a thriller is a bit like threading a needle; I think it's best to read *When No One Is Watching* without knowing *too* much going in. It's a thriller about gentrification and its driving forces, about history and whose stories are considered important. While I won't reveal too much, I can answer the question that I've been asked many times over the past few months: "Why did you write *When No One Is Watching*?"

I've wanted to write something about gentrification for years. I remember the first luxury condo that cropped up near my parents' home, and how each time I visited, there were more of them and fewer of the old familiar places—and faces—that had been integral to my childhood. People often don't think of urban neighborhoods as communities in the way that they do small towns, and they often see large-scale gentrification as improvement, ignoring what comes alongside it: erasure. What is a dream come true for some is existential horror for others, and for Sydney, the protagonist in *When No One Is Watching*, her shock and grief at losing her community is something that's all too real for many people.

Sydney's decision to set up a historical tour of her neighborhood is also personal to me. I love "hidden" history, in part because so much of what's been hidden are the contributions, and sometimes even the very existence, of Black Americans and other marginalized groups. In my research over the years, I've discovered so many amazing things that I should have been taught long ago—that we all should have been taught long ago—but wasn't because our textbooks and our society tend to see only a particular kind of story as valuable. The reason so much of this history falls by the wayside is that a lot of it reveals an ugly truth: oppression and greed in America have always been intertwined with the ideals of Liberty and Justice for all. That dissonance is still affecting us today. Sydney and Theo's journey in this book grapples with the secrets that lurk in the shadows of the American dream, with lots of tension, suspense, and romance thrown in for good measure.

I'm writing this letter to you in the summer of 2020—the past for you (though, as you'll see in the pages ahead, the past is always still relevant)—when many of the events currently playing out in American (and global) society are deeply interconnected with the events in this book. I hope you enjoy spending time with Sydney, Theo, and the residents of Gifford Place, and I hope that they leave you with some ideas about how to survive these turbulent times. Uplift your community by assisting those who are the most overlooked. Seek connection in a society that benefits from fracture, up to and including checking out the hot single neighbor across the street. Lastly, remember that as bad as it gets, it's been worse before, and always—*always*—there are people who fight to make things better for everyone. Be one of those people.

With Love,
Alyssa Cole

WHEN NO ONE IS WATCHING

ALSO BY ALYSSA COLE

RUNAWAY ROYALS

How to Catch a Queen

RELUCTANT ROYALS

A Princess in Theory

Once Ghosted, Twice Shy (novella)

A Duke by Default

Can't Escape Love (novella)

A Prince on Paper

THE LOYAL LEAGUE

An Extraordinary Union

A Hope Divided

An Unconditional Freedom

OFF THE GRID

Radio Silence

Signal Boost

Mixed Signals

OTHER WORKS

That Could Be Enough

Let Us Dream

Let It Shine

Be Not Afraid

Agnes Moor's Wild Knight

Eagle's Heart

WHEN NO ONE IS WATCHING

A Thriller

ALYSSA COLE

WILLIAM MORROW
An Imprint of HarperCollins*Publishers*

This is a work of fiction. Names, characters, places, and incidents are products of the author's imagination or are used fictitiously and are not to be construed as real. Any resemblance to actual events, locales, organizations, or persons, living or dead, is entirely coincidental.

HarperCollins books may be purchased for educational, business, or sales promotional use. For information, please email the Special Markets Department at SPsales@harpercollins.com.

FIRST EDITION

Designed by Diahann Sturge
Unless otherwise indicated below, emojis on pages 24, 274, 275, and 293 © FOS_ICON / Shutterstock, Inc.
Woman-saying-no emoji on page 181 © weberjake / Shutterstock, Inc.
Teen-girl-face and horse-riding emojis on page 274 © weberjake / Shutterstock, Inc.
Adult-woman-face emoji on page 293 © weberjake / Shutterstock, Inc.
Water-gun and skull emojis on page 293 © ASAG Studio / Shutterstock, Inc.
Man-with-beard emoji on page 293 © robuart / Shutterstock, Inc.

Library of Congress Cataloging-in-Publication Data has been applied for.

ISBN 978-0-06-298265-0

20 21 22 23 24 LSC 10 9 8 7 6 5 4 3 2 1

The position of my white neighbor is much more difficult. . . . The game of keeping what one has is never so exciting as the game of getting.

—Zora Neale Hurston, from "How It Feels to Be Colored Me," *World Tomorrow* (1928)

One is astonished in the study of history at the recurrence of the idea that evil must be forgotten, distorted, skimmed over. . . . The difficulty, of course, with this philosophy is that history loses its value as an incentive and example; it paints perfect men and noble nations, but it does not tell the truth.

—W. E. B. Du Bois, from *Black Reconstruction* (1935)

ACKNOWLEDGMENTS

I'D LIKE TO THANK PETE HARRIS AND ALLI DYER OF TEMPLE Hill Publishing, my partners in fictional crime for this project, as well as Erika Tsang, my amazing editor, who puts up with my tornado brain that is always leaving new ideas in her inbox (even when I'm late with another project, lol). Lucienne Diver, my agent, who always has my back and keeps me on track. Pam Jaffee, Imani Gary, Nicole Fischer, and everyone on the Harper-Collins staff who made this book possible. Special thanks to Laura Cherkas, my copyeditor, and Jeanie Lee, my production editor; their work was invaluable to this book.

I would also like to thank Suzanne Spellen, whose work popped up again and again as I researched this book, and who was kind enough to speak with me about Crown Heights and Bed-Stuy history. As with so many of my books, I'm truly indebted to the hard work and detective work of historians, especially those who center people often left off the pages of textbooks.

I'd also like to thank Rebekah Weatherspoon, Janet Eckford, Bree Bridges, and Donna Herren for chat group support—Janet, especially, for being the book's earliest reader and hype person.

Finally, I'd like to thank my parents for their love and support, and also for their stories and for encouraging mine.

PROLOGUE

Sydney

HISTORY IS FUCKING WILD.

Last fall, on a night when my ass was getting well acquainted with the uncomfortable guest chair in Mommy's hospital room, I'd numbly tapped and swiped my way to an article about a place called Black America. Not the label politicians use to place our concerns into a neat box full of worries they don't have to attend to immediately or ever, but an actual, tangible place—a slavery theme park that'd opened in Brooklyn at the end of the nineteenth century.

Slavery. Fucking. *Theme park.*

Black America, the theme park, was billed as "an opportunity to become familiar with plantation life for those of the North who belong to a generation to which the word slavery has but an indefinite and hazy meaning." This was, like, twenty years after slavery ended, mind you. I mean, I too get nostalgic when an eighties jam starts playing on the radio, but these motherfuckers really needed to reminisce about owning humans?

It was the "those of the North" part that really annoyed me. The North *does not* remember; in fact, the North has a super-selective fucking memory. As if slavery was something that happened *down there*, even though there were enslaved Africans building, planting, and harvesting in colonial Brooklyn alongside the Dutch.

People bury the parts of history they don't like, pave it over like African cemeteries beneath Manhattan skyscrapers. Nothing stays buried in this city, though.

Anyway: Black America.

White people came to Brooklyn to tour the "faithfully re-created plantation." They sang along to Negro spirituals and took refreshment as they watched Black people, free Black people, pretend to be slaves.

History.

Wild.

After I stumbled onto that article, Brooklyn history became a refuge for me. It blotted out thoughts of my failed marriage and the persistent sense memory of restraints chafing my wrists. It was something to focus on besides my mother's illness and the way everything was changing. Everything, no matter how much I wanted the world to stop spinning for just one goddamn minute.

I decided to pay for one of those expensive-ass "Historic Brooklyn Brownstones" tours. I'd lived in one of the beautiful old buildings for most of my life, apart from those few years in Seattle, but I needed a distraction, and maybe an outlet for my frustrations. A Groupon-discounted tour with a meeting point two blocks from my front door had been cheaper than therapy and a thousand times easier to get an appointment for.

I wanted to know what the tour guides said about us as they led crowds over the cracked blue slate sidewalks of Gifford Place. I wanted to know what the tourists were *ooh*ing and *ahh*ing over when they clustered in front of our houses, looking through the present inhabitants in search of long-dead grandeur.

It was a day that actually felt like autumn—the weather cool enough to wear a cute blazer and the oak trees lining Gifford Place ablaze in gold and red. I was struck by how beautiful my neighborhood was, bathed in these warm hues that contrasted so well with the brick and brownstone exteriors, how beautiful it had always been despite decades of being ignored. Neglect had shielded us, in a way, and watching strangers stroll through in their comfortable sneakers, with Nikons hanging around their necks, felt like our walls had been breached and the horde was marching in.

The tour guide, Zephyr, was pale with a brown bob and a British accent that gave her a sense of cheery authority, though it seemed like she'd just memorized some Wikipedia facts. She didn't know shit about my neighborhood, *really*, but she didn't need to. The tourists weren't there to hear about Mommy's community garden, or the time someone left a snake and some tarot cards on Ms. Candace's stoop when they thought she was talking shit about them. They didn't want an anthropological deep dive into the relationship between bodega owner and lotto enthusiast, or an oral history of stoop usage.

Zephyr was just fine for them.

She pointed down the tree-lined street and asked us to imagine the Brooklyn of old. I stared at the spots where I'd skinned my knees Rollerblading and gotten tangled up in double-Dutch ropes, but Zephyr had meant *old* old. Cobblestone roads and horse-drawn carriages and homes owned by the elite of the elite old. It was probably easy to do for the people on the tour—the street was quiet and almost empty, as if my neighbors had sensed the approach of the interlopers and retreated into the safety of their homes.

We started to walk, the leaves crunching beneath our shoes serving as the beat under Zephyr's singsong voice.

"And this is the former Gifford Medical Center, originally the Vriesendaal Sanitarium, completed in 1830 and shuttered in 2005," she said as we stepped into the street to bypass the chain-link fence surrounding the building where I was born. The architecture was still striking, even with the boarded-up windows, but I'd known it as "Murd-ical Center," the hospital where either incompetence or ghosts would fuck you up, so I wasn't impressed.

"This building has recently been the center of controversy, as it's one of the proposed sites for the next VerenTech Pharmaceuticals campus," Zephyr said. "There have been protests by community activists who don't want the company here, despite the promise of hundreds of new jobs and a revitalization of the area. Those against the campus are also upset that an opioid research center is being placed in a community that they feel was overpoliced during their own drug epidemic."

It was a bit more complicated than that—my best friend, Drea, worked for the city and had been keeping me and Mommy informed of what would happen if VerenTech chose our neighborhood, and none of it was good. Not for us.

"These people are never satisfied," a white man with graying hair grumbled.

I glared at him, and so did a few other people, but he didn't seem to care. Zephyr ignored him and ushered us on.

As we stopped in front of each brownstone, she'd carefully detail the lives of the rich white people who'd lived there a hundred years ago—what food they'd eaten, what kind of clothing they'd worn, the parties they'd thrown. That was all well and good, but as the tour pressed on, my frustration—my anger at being erased from my own life in so many ways I'd lost count—pushed my hand up into the air like the teacher's bane I'd been long, long ago, before I'd learned curiosity killed the cat. Zephyr narrowed her gaze at me for just a second, perhaps sensing my petty intentions, before saying, "Yes?"

"So the stuff about the Vanderwhosits is cool, but the woman who lives here now was the first Black female head of an engineering firm," I said peevishly.

"Oh? Thanks for that tidbit." She waved the tour onward and I followed, smirking because annoying people with history they didn't want to acknowledge was kind of fun.

We stopped in front of Mr. Joe's house, and Zephyr talked about some architect named Frederick Langston.

"The current owner is a jazz musician who traveled all over the world, playing with some of the greats," I cut in. "He gives music lessons to children now."

"That's cool. Who'd he tour with?" The question came from a tall, solidly built white guy with dirty-blond hair, a heavy brow, and ridiculous cheekbones; he asked quickly, as if purposely trying to get the question in before Zephyr could talk over me. His gaze was focused, and something about the way he waited intently for a response threw me off.

His girlfriend, a short, high-ponytailed Lululemon type, nudged him with her elbow. "Theo. Stop disrupting the tour," she chided, as if he'd just dropped his pants to his ankles instead of asking a question, then looked in my direction as if her words also applied to me.

The *I wish a motherfucker would* simmered in my veins at the familiar condescension in her eyes. For a moment, Ponytail Lululemon's face morphed into that of the nurse who'd looked me dead in the eye and said my mother didn't need more pain meds, even as Mommy writhed and wailed in the bed beside us.

"I appreciate the bonus information. It's quite helpful," Zephyr cut in, her tone showing she didn't appreciate it at all, "but this tour is about historically *important* people."

"This is a historically *Black* neighborhood, but none of the important people you've mentioned thus far have been. What does that mean?"

Her face flushed but she hit me with a customer-service smile.

"Look . . . miss. I'm just doing my job. If you have a problem with this tour, you can send suggestions to the organizers. Or maybe you should, I don't know, start your own?" she said cheerily, then smoothly returned to her script.

I pursed my lips. Nodded. Turned and crossed the street, heading to the bodega to get an egg and cheese on a roll and a coffee, light and sweet. Comfort food. Abdul was on the phone behind the counter, arguing with his landlord about how he couldn't afford another rent hike, which didn't help my mood, though playing with Frito, the store's resident cat, did.

I walked by the group a few minutes later as they learned about filigree or some shit, then jogged up the steps to my mother's house and turned the key in the lock with more force than was necessary. The advertising flyers shoved into the crack between the door and the jamb fluttered to the ground.

Sell your house for big money! We pay cash! Quick and easy sales! screamed the cards scattered around my feet. The one closest to the toe of my boot, from a company called Good Neighbors LLC, had the tagline, *We care about your future!*

Zephyr's voice faded into the background as I snatched the flyers and crumpled them up. I wanted to turn and throw the wad at the tour group, to chase them away. I wanted to call the police and report strange people who might be casing the neighborhood for a break-in, like some new neighbors had done the previous week—police had shown up and harassed a man who'd lived here for twenty years.

Logic prevailed—that shit wouldn't fly for me. I already knew how easy it was for authorities to believe someone like me was a problem to be locked away; one wrong move on my end and the vultures circling Mommy's house could get what they wanted all the sooner.

I glanced over my shoulder as I stepped into the foyer, mostly so Zephyr could see that this was *my* house, no matter who had lived here in the nineteenth century, and caught the heavy-browed guy watching me intently.

I closed the door firmly in his face.

Welcome to the OurHood app, helping neighbors stay connected and stay safe. You have been approved as a member of the GIFFORD PLACE community. Please use the site responsibly and remember that each one of us can make our neighborhood a better place!

CHAPTER 1

Sydney

I SPENT DEEPEST WINTER SHUFFLING BACK AND FORTH BEtween work and hospital visits and doctor's appointments. I spent spring hermiting away, managing my depression with the help of a CBD pen and generous pours of the Henny I'd found in Mommy's liquor cabinet.

Now I'm sitting on the stoop like I've done every morning since summer break started, watching my neighbors come and go as I sip coffee, black, no sugar, gone lukewarm.

When I moved back a year and a half ago, carrying the ashes of my marriage and my pride in an urn I couldn't stop sifting through, I thought I'd be sitting out here with Mommy and Drea, the holy trinity of familiarity restored—mother, play sister, prodigal child. Mommy would tend to her mini-jungle of potted plants lining the steps, and to me, helping me sprout new metaphorical leaves—tougher ones, more resilient. Drea would sit between us, like she had since she was eleven and basically moved in with us, since her parents sucked, cracking jokes or talking about her latest side hustle. I'd draw strength from them and the neighborhood that'd always had my back. But it hadn't worked out that way; instead of planting my feet onto solid Brooklyn concrete, I'd found myself neck-deep in wet cement.

Last month, on the Fourth of July, I pried open the old skylight on the top floor of the brownstone and sat up there alone. When I was a teenager, Mommy and Drea and I would picnic on the roof every Fourth of July, Brooklyn sprawling around us as fireworks burst in the distance. When I'd clambered up there as an adult, alone, I'd been struck by how claustrophobic the view looked, with new buildings filling the neighborhoods around us, where there had once been open air. Cranes loomed ominously over the surrounding blocks like invaders from an alien movie, mantis-like shadows with red eyes blinking against the night, the American flags attached to them flapping darkly in the wind, signaling that they came in peace when really they were here to destroy.

To remake.

Maybe my imagination was running away with me, but even at ground level the difference is overwhelming. Scaffolds cling to buildings all over the neighborhood, barnacles of change, and construction workers gut the innards of houses where I played with friends as a kid. New condos that look like stacks of ugly shoeboxes pop up in empty lots.

The landscape of my life is unrecognizable; Gifford Place doesn't feel like home.

I sigh, close my eyes, and try to remember the freedom I used to feel, first as a carefree child, then as a know-it-all teenager, as I held court from this top step, with the world rolling out before me. Three stories of century-old brick stood behind me like a solid wall of protection, imbued with the love of my mother and my neighbors and the tenacity of my block.

Back then, I used to go barefoot, even though Miss Wanda, who'd wrench open the fire hydrant for kids on sweltering days like the ones we've had this summer, used to tell me I was gonna get ringworm. The feel of the stoop's cool brown concrete beneath my feet had been calming.

Now someone calls the fire department every time the hydrant is opened, even when we use the sprinkler cap that reduces water waste. I wear flip-flops on my own stoop, not worried about the infamous ringworm but suddenly self-conscious where I should be comfortable.

Miss Wanda is gone; she sold her place while I was cocooned in depression at some point this spring. The woman who'd been my neighbor almost all my life is gone, and I didn't even get to say goodbye.

And Miss Wanda isn't the only one.

Five families have moved from Gifford Place in less than a year. Five doesn't seem like much, but each of their buildings had three to four apartments, and the change has been noticeable, to say the least. And that doesn't even count the renters. It's gotten to the point where I feel a little twinge of dread every time I see a new white person on the block. Who did they replace? There have, of course, always been a few of them, renters who mostly couldn't afford to live anywhere else but were also cool and didn't fuck with anybody. These new homeowners move different.

There's an older, retired couple who mostly have dinner parties and mind their business, but call 311 to make noise complaints. Jenn and Jen, the nicest of the newcomers, whose main issue is they seem to have been told all Black people are homophobic, so they go out of their way to normalize their own presence, while never stopping to wonder about the two old Black women who live next door to them and are definitely not sisters or just friends.

Then there're the young families like the people who moved into Miss Wanda's house, or those ready to start a family, like Ponytail Lululemon and her Wandering Eye husband, who I first encountered on the historical tour. They bought the Payne house across the street—guess they *had* been casing the neighborhood.

They don't have blinds, so I see what they do when they're home. She's usually tearing shit apart when she's there, renovating, which I guess is some kind of genetic inheritance thing. He seems to work from home and likes walking around shirtless on the top floor. I've never seen them actually interact; if I had a man walking around half-naked in my house, we'd be more than interacting, but that's none of my business.

The shrill, rapid-fire bark of a dog losing its shit pulls me from my thoughts.

"Goddammit, somebody put him in his cage before the guests arrive! Terry!" a woman yells, followed by a man shouting, "Christ, calm down, Josie! Arwin! Did you let Toby out of his cage?"

Terry and Josie and Arwin and Toby are Miss Wanda's replacements. They've never properly introduced themselves, but with all the yelling they do, I figured out their names quickly.

Toby barks incessantly while they're at work and school and whenever he damn well pleases because he needs more exercise and better training. Terry wears ill-fitting suits to work, leers at the teenage girls in the neighborhood, and doesn't pick up Toby's shit when he thinks no one is watching. Josie wears tailored suits to work, spends her weekends dividing her backyard garden into exactly sized plots, and obsessively posts in the Columbus-ly titled OurHood app about people who don't pick up dog waste.

Claude, my first post-divorce friend with benefits, used to call my new neighbors "Becky and Becky's Husband." We laughed at how they'd peek suspiciously at him through the curtains when he waited for me in his car out front, or how they'd hurry past when he stood at my front door in sagged jeans and Timbs instead of his tailored work suits and loafers.

Claude is gone now, too. He texted right before Valentine's Day:

Not feelin' this anymore.

Maybe there'd been another woman. Maybe I'd spent too much time stressing over my mother. Maybe he'd just sensed what I'd tried to hide: that my life was a spinout on a slick road and the smart thing to do was pump the brakes while he could.

When Drea had opened her apartment door and found me sniffling as I clutched a pint of Talenti, she'd hugged me, then given my shoulder a little shake. "Girl. *Sydney.* I'm sorry you're sad, but how many times do I have to tell you? You won't find gold panning in Fuckboy Creek."

She was right.

It's better this way; a warm body in bed is nice in the winter but it's too damn hot for cuddling in the summer unless you want to run the AC nonstop, and I don't have AC-nonstop money at the moment.

I notice a group of people approaching from the far end of the block, down by the garden, and scratch at my neck, at the patch of skin where a few months ago three itchy bites had arisen all in a row. *BEDBUGS* had been the first result of a frantic "what the fuck are these bites" internet search. Plastic-wrapped mattresses on the curb are a common sight now, the bedbugs apparently hitching rides on the unwashed legs steadily marching into the neighborhood. Even after weeks of steaming and bleaching and boiling my clothes and bedding, I can't shake the tainted feeling. I wake up in the middle of the night with the sensation of something I can't see feasting on me—I have to file my nails down to keep from scratching myself raw.

Maybe it's too late; maybe I'm already sucked dry.

Sure as hell feels that way.

I drop my head and let the morning sun heat my scalp as I sit hunched and hopeless.

The group I'd spotted, apparently this week's batch of brunch guests, clusters a few feet away from me on the sidewalk in front of Terry and Josie's outer stairs, and I stop slouching: shoulders back, chin up. I pose as the picture of unbothered—languorously sipping my bodega coffee and pretending sweat isn't beading at my hairline as I blatantly watch them. None of them even glance at me.

Terry and Josie come outside—her rocking an angular *I'd like to speak to the manager* platinum-dyed bob and him with a tight fake smile. They keep their heads rigidly straight and their gazes fixed on their friends as they greet them, like I'm a junkyard dog who might growl if they make eye contact.

I don't think they even know my name is Sydney.

I don't want to know what "funny" nickname they have for me.

"The place looks great," one of their friends says as they start up the stairs.

"We used the same company as Sal and Sylvie on *Flip Yo' Crib*," Josie replies as she stops just in front of the doorway so they can admire the newly installed vintage door and stained glass in the transom window above it.

Their contractors had started their early-morning repairs right after the new year, waking Mommy up each time she finally managed to get comfortable enough to rest. In the spring, I'd been jolted awake a full hour early before I had to head to the school office and smile at annoying children and their annoying parents all day—everyone was annoying when you just wanted to sleep and not wake up for years.

Or ever.

"You just would not believe how these people don't appreciate the historic value of the neighborhood," Josie says. "We had to completely renovate. It was like there'd been a zoo here before!"

I glance at her out of the corner of my eye. Miss Wanda had been of the "bleach fumes so strong they burned her neighbors' lungs" school of cleaning. Josie's a damn liar, and I have the near-death experience with accidental mustard gas to prove it.

"The other houses look nice to me, especially this one," says the last person in their line of friends, a woman of East Asian descent with a baby strapped to her chest. "It looks like a tiny castle!"

I smile, thinking about the days when I'd sit at the window set in the whimsical brick demi-turret, a captured princess, while my friends scrambled on the sidewalk out front, vying for the chance to rescue me from the evil witch holding me captive. It's cool to say the princess should save herself nowadays, but I don't think I've experienced that sensation outside of children's games—of having someone willing to risk life and limb, everything, to save me.

Mommy protected me, of course, but being protected was different from being saved.

Josie whirls on the top step and frowns down at her friend for apparently not being disdainful enough. "The houses look nice in spite of. No amount of ugly Home Depot plants can hide the neglect, either."

Oooh, this bitch.

"Right," her friend says, anxiously stroking the baby's back.

"All I'm saying is that I can trace my ancestors back to New Amsterdam. *I* appreciate history," Josie says, turning to continue into the house.

"Well, family trees have a lot of missing leaves around here, if you know what I mean," Terry adds as he follows her inside. "Of course they don't appreciate that kind of thing."

Maybe I should hop over the banister of my stoop and give them a lesson on the history of curb stomping if they like history so damn much.

The chastised woman's gaze flits over to mine and she gives me an apologetic wave of acknowledgment as she files into the house. The door closes firmly behind her.

I was already tired, but tears of anger sting my eyes now, though I should be immune to this bullshit. It isn't *fair.* I can't sit on my stoop and enjoy my neighborhood like old times. Even if I retreat to my apartment, it won't feel like home because Mommy won't be waiting upstairs. I sit trapped at the edge of the disorienting panic that strikes too often lately, the ground under my ass and the soles of my flip-flops the only things connecting me to this place.

I just want everything to stop.

"Hey, Sydney!"

I glance across the street and the relief of seeing a familiar face helps me get it together. Mr. Perkins, my other next-door neighbor, and his pittiehound, Count Bassie, stroll by on one of their countless daily rounds of the neighborhood. Mommy had gone to the ASPCA with Mr. Perkins after his wife had passed a few years back, and he's been inseparable from the brown-and-white dog ever since then.

"Morning, Sydney honey!" Mr. Perkins calls out in that scratchy voice of his, his arm rising slowly above his bald head as he waves at me. Count lets out one loud, ridiculously low-toned bark, a doggie *hey girl*; he loves me because I give him cheese and other delicious human food when he sits close to me.

"Morning!" I call out, feeling a little burst of energy just from seeing him. He's always been here, looking out for me and my mom—for everyone in the neighborhood.

He's usually up and making his daily rounds by six, stopping by various stoops, making house calls, keeping an ear to the ground and a smile on his face. It's why we call him the Mayor of Gifford Place.

Right now, he's likely on his way to Saturday services, judging from his khakis and pressed shirt. Count usually sits at his feet, and Mr. Perkins jokes that when he howls along with the choir, he hits the right note more often than half the humans singing.

"You gonna have that tour ready for the block party next week? Candace is on my behind about it since you put it on the official schedule."

I want to say no, it's not ready, even though I've been working on it bit by bit for months. It would be so easy to, since I have no idea if anyone will take this tour, even for free, much less pay for it, but . . . when I'd angrily told Mommy what Zephyr had said to me about starting my own tour, her face had lit up for the first time in weeks.

"You always did have the History Channel on, turning to Secrets of World War II *or some mess while I was trying to watch my stories. Why shouldn't you do it?"*

It became a game for us, finding topics that I could work into the tour—it was something we could do while she was in bed, and it kept both of us occupied.

"This is the first time I've seen that old fire in your eyes since you got home. I'm glad you're coming back to yourself, Syd. I can't wait to take your tour."

"How's your mama doing?" Mr. Perkins calls out, the question causing a ripple of pain so *real* that I draw my knees up to my chest.

"She's doing good," I say, hating the lie and ashamed of the resentment that wells up in me every time I have to tell it. "Hates being away from home, but that's no surprise."

He nods. "Not at all. Yolanda loved this neighborhood. Tell her I'm praying for her when you see her."

"I will."

Count lunges after a pizza crust left on the sidewalk, suddenly spry, and Mr. Perkins gives chase, bringing the painful conversation to a blessed end.

"Come to the planning meeting on Monday," he calls out with a wave as he walks on. "I've got some papers for you."

He could just hand them to me, but I think he's making sure I show up. He knows me well.

I nod and wave. The window of Josie and Terry's living room slams shut, punctuating our conversation.

I take a sip of my coffee and hear the slapping of two sets of feet against the sidewalk.

"Good morning!" Jenn and Jen say. They're holding hands as they stride down the street in sync, matching smiles on their faces. Even their flourishing plots in the garden complement each other: Jen's bursting with flowers and Jenn's with vegetables.

"Morning! Have a good day, you two," I say as they march past, sounding like an auntie even though they're probably only a few years younger than me.

I'm not faking my pleasantness. I want them to know that if their presence bothers me, it's not because they're holding hands. It's because of everything else. I wish I didn't have to think about everything else, but . . . Miss Wanda is gone. The Hancocks. Mr. Joe.

Sometimes it feels like everything rock-solid about my world is slipping away, like the sand sucked through my fingers when I'd sit in the breaking waves at Coney Island.

I suddenly remember one of our mother-daughter beach days, when I was four or five. Mommy had treated me to Nathan's, and a seagull swooped down and snatched a crinkle-cut french fry out of my hand right before I bit into it. The biggest fry. I'd saved it for last. The sudden shock of the fry theft, the unfairness of it, had made me start wailing. Mommy shook her head and laughed as she wiped my cheeks with thumbs gritty from sand and smelling of ketchup. "Baby, if you wanna keep what's yours, you gotta hold on to it better than that. Someone is always waiting to snatch what you got, even these damn birds."

I'm trying, Mommy. And I hate it.

A shiver runs down my spine despite the heat, and when I look up, I see Bill Bil coming. His name is William Bilford, real estate agent, but I call him Bill Bil because it annoys him and why should I be the only one suffering? I'm alone, my new neighbors are assholes, and this con artist is roaming the neighborhood, trying to bring in more of them.

I grimace in his direction. He's wearing jeans that are too thick and too tight for the heat index and the amount of walking he's doing. There are sweat stains around the armpits of his tight gray T-shirt, hinting at the swamp-ass horror show that must be playing below. His face sports carefully contoured stubble and eyes that are red-rimmed from too much booze or coke or both. His light brown hair is carefully styled, though, so he's not entirely a mess.

"Hey, Ms. Green," he says with a wink and a grin that probably goes over well in a dive bar in Williamsburg but has no effect on me at all.

"Hey, Bill Bil," I chirp. His shark's smile doesn't falter but the brightness in his eyes dims. I pick up the loosie and lighter I bought from the bodega and make a big production of holding the flame to the tip of the cigarette. The smoke that floods my mouth is disgusting—I can *taste* the cancer, and hey, maybe that's what makes it enjoyable—but I've been smoking one with my morning coffee every now and again anyway.

"That's bad for your health," he says.

I exhale a cloud of smoke toward where he's standing at the bottom of the stairs. "Nothing has changed from the last ten times you walked by here. We're still not selling the house. Have a blessed day."

His shark smile widens. "Come on. I'm just being friendly."

"You're just trying to create a false sense of camaraderie because you think it'll make me trust you. Then you can convince me to sell so you can pocket that sweet, sweet commission."

"You really think that?" He shakes his head. "I'm out here trying to *help*. A lot of people don't even know that they could earn more than they've ever had in their entire life, just by moving."

"Moving where? Where are people supposed to go if even this neighborhood becomes too expensive?"

I suck at my cigarette, hard.

He sighs. "The struggle is real; I feel that. Why do you think I'm out here hustling? I have bills to pay, too, but I don't have a house to sell for a huge profit. If I did, I could pay off school loans, medical bills." He shrugs, like he couldn't help but point out those two specific things.

"Well, there are plenty of vultures circling, so if I do give up on the neighborhood, I have lots of realtors to choose from." My hand shakes as I lift the cigarette to my lips again, and I try not to fumble it.

He drops his affable shark mask.

"You act like I'm some scumbag, but you just proved my point. There are lots of realtors interested in this area, especially with the VerenTech deal as good as done. It's the hottest emerging community in Brooklyn right now."

"Emerging community?" I tilt my head. "Emerging from where? The primordial ooze?"

His brows lift a bit, and I know it's not because he's registered my question but because the motherfucker is surprised I can use *primordial* in a sentence.

"Look." He runs a hand over his hair backward and then forward, not messing up his look. "I'm not some villain twirling my mustache and trying to push people out onto the street. I'm not even one of the buyers carrying around bags of cash and blank checks to tempt people into taking bad deals. I'm just a normal guy doing a normal job."

Just doing my job. How many times have I heard that while arguing with people over my mother's health, money, and future? Everyone is just doing their job, especially when that job is lucrative and screws people over.

"And I'm just a homeowner who's told you repeatedly that I don't want to sell," I say.

"You don't have to sell," he says, walking off in search of someone more receptive to his bullshit. "But you can't stop change, you know."

I don't think he's even trying to be threatening, but I mash out the cigarette against the bottom of my flip-flop and stand, suddenly full of nervous energy. After stepping into the hallway to grab my gardening bag and slip on sneakers, I lock the door and make my way to Mommy's community garden. I could never manage to keep even a Chia Pet alive, but I'm doing my best. I go every day; I put in work, even if I don't have much to show for it.

It keeps me close to her, and that dulls away the sharp edges of the guilt that's always poking at me. I sigh deeply, then pull out my phone and call her—it goes to voicemail. And when I hear her voice say, "You've reached Yolanda Green. I'm away from my cell phone or otherwise indisposed. Leave a message, unless you're asking for money, because lord knows I don't have any," my throat goes rough as usual.

"Hi, Mommy," I say after the beep, even though I usually don't leave messages. "Things are hard, but I'm holding steady. Just wanted to hear your voice, but I'll see you soon. Love you."

Gifford Place OurHood post by Ashley Jones:
For anyone who hasn't seen it, here's an article about VerenTech Pharmaceuticals choosing the old medical center as the location for their U.S. headquarters and research center.

Asia Martin: *sigh* I'm sorry. I know you, Jamel, and Preston were out there protesting every week. The drug research center is nice, but I wish we could have had something like that instead of getting locked up and having our babies taken away.

Candace Tompkins: Speak on it.

Jamel Jones: Don't get me started. Apart from that, mad shady shit went down at the community board meetings. One rep basically told us "fuck yo community." 😤 The wildest part is the city is paying THEM to come here! To "revitalize" the area. Meanwhile, they been ignoring us for years.

Candace Tompkins: Revitalize their pockets more like . . . eminent domain soon come.

Kim DeVries: We should all be happy that this drug crisis is being responded to with kindness and compassion. It will be great for the neighborhood, too. Look at how much nicer downtown Brooklyn has become since the Ratner deal.

Drea Wilson: 🙃

Candace Tompkins: 😒

(75 additional comments . . . see more)

CHAPTER 2

Theo

THERE'S AN EMPTY BEER CAN POKING INTO MY RIB CAGE when I wake up and a photo album laid flat open across my chest. A warm wet spot under my armpit reveals the beer can hadn't been empty when I passed out last night. When I shift, there's the crunch of chips breaking and a bag crumpling, and shards of Cool Ranch Doritos stab into my back.

Really living the dream here, bud.

My body hurts as I stretch, the ache of too much booze, too much salt, and the crushing stress of my life falling apart. The beer can tumbles to the floor, but I hold the photo album to my chest protectively. After a few seconds of letting the bleariness fade, I lean it back to see what page it's open to—a picture of "the grandparents," an elderly couple with dark skin. He's bald, and her hair is silver-white and close-cropped. In this photo, developed on heavy stock paper and with a white frame around it, they're dressed in their Sunday finest outside a big church that looks like the one a few streets over.

The pictures are mostly from this neighborhood. *My* neighborhood, I guess—mine and Kim's—even though I mostly feel the way I do with this photo album: like a creep looking in at other people's lives from the outside.

The pictures are old—most spanning the forties, fifties, sixties, seventies. The people are Black, like most of my neighbors, and they wear neatly hemmed dresses and stylish suits, with their hair flat and shiny in some photos and puffed out in Afros in the later pages. A wedding photo showing the grandparents before they were grandparents. Young grandpa going off to war. Laughing with young grandma upon his return. Babies upon babies. Friends and family. Beach trips.

It's kind of weird, how often I flip through this album of other people's memories I found atop a pile of trash while walking the streets in the middle of the night, but the people in these photos look perfect, happy, and full of love. It's the closest I've gotten to any of those things in a long time, maybe ever, but it was so unremarkable to someone on this street that they left it out on garbage night.

The hammering that awakened me starts up again—absurdly relentless, as if a Looney Tunes character broke in and is banging a mallet against a wall for the chaotic joy of it. It's a homing beacon giving the location of the person I once thought would bring me perfection, happiness, and love. I press my palms against my ears, trying to drown out what's become my millennial version of "The Tell-Tale Heart"—"The Renovation-Crazed Girlfriend."

Or ex-girlfriend?

It's complicated.

The idea that Kim and I once thought we liked each other

enough to buy a home together makes me cringe. The fact that I thought she'd never figure out *I* was the kind of item to be left out on garbage night, something no one should pick up, bands shame across my shoulder blades.

I climb out of bed and take a few heavy steps over to the window. One good thing about being stuck in this shitty apartment? It gives me a great view of half the street—the whole street if I shove my head out. I can see who comes and goes, what patterns people fall into without realizing it, and when I'm really bored, what my neighbors do in the privacy of their own homes.

Mr. Perkins, the nice old guy from across the street, shuffles past a window in his living room. He's one of my favorite people on the street to watch: he's out there every day, reliable and friendly. Consistent. It's around the dog's feeding time, and in a few minutes Mr. Perkins will take him out for the first of many walks. I admire his ability to stick to a strict schedule while also seeming to be puttering around at his leisure. He always chats when our paths cross, even inviting me to local events that I never attend because it would be awkward to go without Kim.

My gaze drops down to the whir of motion I've been saving for last—*she's* sweeping the sidewalk in front of her house. The woman from the brownstone tour. The Interrupter.

Until a few weeks ago, she'd leave her house in business casual every morning, and then return in the afternoon. Now she has a cup of coffee on her stoop before heading to the community garden down the street with gardening supplies—maybe she's out of a job, too. Because her curtains are so sheer when she turns on her lights that they're basically useless, I know she often enjoys a glass of wine and, sometimes, twerking in front of the mirror in her living room.

After a few glasses of wine, the twerking sometimes dissolves into tears. I avert my gaze more often than not when that happens, but I've raised my beer bottle in silent solidarity, too.

I've made up countless backstories for her. She's taking online classes, since she's often tapping away studiously at her laptop, and once she graduates she'll find a job that makes her happy, if such a thing exists. She's a dedicated gardener because she's the kind of person who loves making things grow—a nurturer.

I make up things about the future, too, like what might happen if I ring her bell the next time she starts to twerk—or to cry. Concocting a fantasy where I save a beautiful damsel in distress, or have sex with her, is way more satisfying than dealing with reality.

Outside the window, three neighborhood kids speed past on their bikes and she calls out greetings to them, followed by a warning to watch out for cars in the intersection as they continue on.

Terry, the shithead who lives next door to the Interrupter, walks out of his house with his shithead dog. It bounds down the stairs while barking at the kids on bikes and gets caught short by its leash because the Interrupter is bending over to pick something up and Terry's busy ogling her ass.

The hammering restarts in earnest downstairs.

Sweat beads on my temples, my chest, my back, and when it rolls into my ass crack, I sigh deeply and peel my arm from the chipped paint of the window frame. I'm pretty sure whoever owned this house in the past cooked meals up here in the summer because this apartment also functions as an oven.

And you're the turkey that voluntarily stepped into it.

I leave the apartment with a change of clothes and three-in-one body wash, shampoo, and conditioner rolled up in a towel, then trudge through the wallpaper-stripped hallways and down two flights of yet-to-be-varnished hardwood stairs.

My shower hasn't worked for weeks. My first Brooklyn summer has mostly been spent sweltering in this attic apartment, marinating in beer fumes and hangover funk until I'm grody enough to slink downstairs for a shower.

I could try repairing it, for the tenth time, but somehow each time I do, a new problem appears. I was the man of the house growing up, in between Mom's boyfriends, and I've worked construction jobs between more lucrative gigs. And yet . . .

"Must be gremlins," Kim had shouted over her shoulder a week ago as she took a power sander to a brand-new table to make it look old. "Or maybe you're actually fucking things up when you think you're fixing them?"

Story of my life.

The path to the bathroom on the main floor is clear since Kim is currently busy with her demented hammering, so I slide into the shower and wash quickly, efficiently, like I'm in a prison shower and can't drop my guard.

Afterward, no longer smelling like stale IPA and flop sweat, I steel myself and walk into the kitchen.

Half the cabinet doors are off their hinges and a thin layer of sawdust covers the floor and the other flat surfaces. Kim is wearing a ratty but expensive tank top and yoga pants with cat paws all over them, even though she thinks cats are parasites; her hair is up in a messy bun on top of her head, and her expression is solemn and focused. For a second, it feels like a year ago, before things had gone bad, when I found her "concentration" face so damn sexy she had to shut the door on me while scrolling through real estate listings.

A lot can change in a year. Not the door shutting in my face, though now it's more like three doors and two stories.

She has her iPad holder with the extensible neck clamped to the counter, and she's squinting at the screen, scrubbing her finger up and up and up over the smooth glass, leaving trails in the sawdust.

I can guess what she's looking at. Two apps were clocking the most usage on her devices last time I was privy to that info: OurHood, a kind of virtual neighborhood watch that's fascinating in its ability to turn any activity into something sinister, and Boomtown, the home renovation and decoration app for people like us—or like her, rather. Wealthy millennials who buy and DIY for fun and profit because they plan to sell the houses they buy on the cheap in "emerging communities."

When we'd scored an advanced viewing for this place, I told her I liked the vintage feel of the kitchen, with its dark wood cabinets and stained-glass windows. Apparently, what I thought was cool, she considered gauche.

This is the third time she's repainted the cabinets, the last attempt a hideous peach color buffed with rose gold. Half the house is in various stages of "work in process," and I'm no longer consulted on projects.

Her interest in me dropped drastically over the course of the home-buying process, though she kept insisting things were fine. Me losing my job shortly after the move was the cherry on the shit cake that's our relationship now. That she doesn't know the real reason for my unemployment? I guess that's the decorative icing; it spells out *At least you tried.*

I should be glad things didn't turn out worse than my relationship foundering on the rocks, but I've never been one to focus on the brighter side.

"Good morning." I try to sound pleasant, not like someone who's considered gathering up all her expensive gold jewelry and touring pawnshops in the tri-state area.

We're linked by the house, after all; separating would be a clusterfuck. I'd lose thousands of dollars and have to scramble to figure out where to go and what to do. Plus, we did care for each other once, not even that long ago.

When Kim doesn't respond to my greeting I say, "Wow. HGTV city in here, huh?"

She glances up from her screen and the mild contempt in her gaze is like her fancy ceramic knife slashing across my gut. She perks up a moment too late and gestures to the mess scattered across the kitchen. "Sorry about the noise. I couldn't sleep and figured I should be productive instead of lazing around."

The way the corners of her mouth turn up into something like a smile pours salt along the gut wound.

This house was a *bad* idea.

Everything between me and Kim over the last year was a bad idea.

Band-Aids over Band-Aids over Band-Aids, so we didn't even know what pus-filled wounds they covered, or if there was even anything left beneath the scab.

"How did you sleep?" she asks, her attention back on her iPad. She doesn't care how I slept. The question is just noise to fill the silence between us, like the drilling and the hammering and the power sanding.

"Okay," I say cautiously—her question was benign but that doesn't mean it can't lead to another pointless argument. "It's getting way too hot up on the top floor, though. I need to upgrade from the box fan to an AC."

"Summer's almost over. You really can't ride out a few more weeks?" There's that expression again—not so much a sneer as the absence of the ability to pretend to care. "Besides, I saw you with a new camera. Maybe you should've spent that money more wisely."

I grunt, ruffling my hair with one hand.

Kim has a top-of-the-line AC unit in her bedroom, where she sleeps on the three-thousand-dollar mattress she purchased shortly before banishing me upstairs.

She sleeps in comfort on the first floor while I sweat in the attic, with all of her reasons for our separation-in-deed-but-not-name populating the two floors between us:

She was scared I'd cheat on her, and that hurt her.

She still had feelings for David, whom she'd actually fucking cheated on me with, and *that* hurt her.

She couldn't be sure I wasn't using her for her money.

She couldn't rely on me.

She needed time to figure things out.

I'd swallowed my frustration as I carried my stuff upstairs, almost breaking my neck three times and unsure if she'd care if I did.

I hadn't pointed out that she'd been the one who pushed for homeownership to begin with—who'd talked about the house as an investment for both of us, as a way to reconnect and reaffirm her commitment after the David situation. She'd insisted that we were going to get married anyway, despite everything, and also pressed that prices wouldn't stay low in this neighborhood for long.

I'd stayed with her and gone along with the house purchase in part because, hell, no one had ever pursued me like that, and in part because she was the one from a wealthy family and she was going to take care of all the hard money stuff.

God, it all seems so stupid when I lay it out like that. She didn't trap me; I was just an idiot with something to prove. I had no fucking idea what buying a house entailed—Mom and I had moved from apartment to apartment, outrunning evictions and the fists attached to her bad decisions.

I had no idea what a good relationship was supposed to look like, either. Mine and Kim's seemed so *normal*, like in sitcoms where the wife nitpicks and the husband is slightly dismayed with the state of his life and that's fine. That's just how things are.

Now, as I look at her, there's a challenge in her eyes. One that says she knows she's hurting me with her late-night and early-morning renovations, with her jabs about my unemployment, and she enjoys it.

Maybe this *is* normal.

There are worse things. Black eyes and bruises and holes in walls made by fists instead of hammers, for instance.

I walk over to the coffee maker sitting on a barstool and rest my knuckles against the carafe to see if it's still warm.

"There might be some paint dust in there," she says in that tone between playfulness and contempt.

"You didn't use lead paint, right?" I joke.

She rolls her eyes and it's almost like old times, which makes me wonder whether the old times were ever really that good.

I brew a new pot.

AN HOUR LATER, I've wrangled the kitchen into some semblance of order while she's painted cabinet doors in the backyard. It feels a little bit like when we used to do things as a couple, without the hair-trigger contempt that led to our upstairs/downstairs living arrangement.

When she steps back inside, her face flushed and her expression serene, I get hit with the sudden, naive belief that we can get back to how we were before.

I think we can.

Maybe?

I don't know. But some part of me, probably the self-destructive hopefulness that I inherited from my mother, drives me to say, "There's a new brunch place three blocks down, where that

Dominican restaurant used to be. I heard they make this amazing vegan steak and eggs scramble. Wanna try it?"

Her shoulders draw closer to her ears as she tenses in annoyance. "Look, Theo—"

"It's just food," I say, then wave toward the space where the oven is supposed to be. "You have to order out anyway."

"You need me to pay or something?" she asks coolly, as if me demanding to pay for things wasn't one of our longest-running petty fights.

"My treat," I say, not rising to the bait. "Or we can just go to the corner store. They have vegetarian options."

She nods, but there's no excitement or interest in her eyes. She grabs her phone, unlocking it and scrolling as we head out of the house.

We used to go for long walks together all the time, just because. Kim used to go on runs. Now? She has a treadmill in what was supposed to be my game room and she Ubers everywhere.

It started a few weeks after we moved in. She came home with tears in her eyes, saying a group of teenagers had followed her out of the train station, harassing her, after she'd told them to stop laughing so loud in the train car. I'd wondered why she hadn't just put on her sound-canceling headphones, but she'd been shaking when she walked in, so it hadn't been the right time to ask.

"It was terrifying! And I looked around and realized everyone was . . . I don't know if anyone would have helped me," she said. "There's just so few of us here."

I was confused. "Us?"

She pulled her head back to look at me and I realized that she wasn't shaking with fear. She was furious.

"You know what I mean," she snapped. "The neighborhood better change as fast as the realtor said it's going to, because I'm not gonna put up with a bunch of—"

She sucked in a breath.

"I was perfectly within my rights. And their response showed that they were dangerous."

"Yeah." I'd rubbed her back, a weird feeling in the pit of my stomach.

She'd stared into my eyes, still angry. "You would have done something, right? If you were there and they tried anything?"

"Like what?" I'd asked.

She'd pulled away from me and stormed off.

Kim has a framed portrait of Michelle Obama in our living room, so she's not . . . you know. She was shaken up, that was all, and at that point our relationship was held together by dollar-store glue. I didn't want to push. Maybe I didn't want to know what she would've answered.

Now, as we walk to the corner store, there's a foot of humid air between us. It's already super hot, and the sun hasn't even reached the highest point in the sky. Air conditioners drone in every window we pass under, the sound mocking me, but I find it hard to be annoyed when I'm walking down our street.

Maybe it's because I grew up in shitty small towns filled with falling apart single-wides, but the rich pigment of the brownstones, the slate gray of the sidewalks, the brick and concrete and flora that thrives in the minutest speck of dirt . . . of course I went along with moving to this place.

Our house feels like a prison, but our neighborhood is like something out of a movie. When I walk around Gifford Place, or even just watch from my window, I don't feel crushed by the multi-car pileup of stupid decisions I've made. I feel like maybe this is a place I can belong, eventually. If I'm honest, that's why I'm walking with Kim to the store, why I'm even trying—I don't want to move. I guess the fact that I love our house more than I love her at the moment makes me kind of an asshole.

I look over at her; her fingers are tapping at the screen of her huge smartphone as she texts someone. I see the words *roach-infested corner store* and look away, my gaze landing on a high-end Range Rover I haven't seen in the neighborhood before.

Mr. Perkins and his dog stroll in our direction, both looking this way and that for a neighbor to greet or for anything that's amiss.

"Hey there," Mr. Perkins says as our paths cross. "Having a good weekend?"

"So far, so good." I lean down to pat the old dog's side, sure my hand will come away smelling of corn chips. "Who's a good boy?"

"Not this dog," Mr. Perkins says affectionately, mock-glaring down at the hound. "Count stole the pork chop I was marinating last night when I nodded off in front of the TV."

The dog drops his gaze to the ground, as if he knows we're discussing his misdeeds, and we both laugh.

"Oooh," Kim coos at the dog from next to me. "You're going to get trichinosis because your owner was irresponsible!"

"Kim." I knew she was an asshole to me, but this is different.

"I'm just joking," she says.

"Right," Mr. Perkins says, his usually friendly gaze wary. "I just wanted to tell you in case you didn't see on OurHood, we'll be having our annual Labor Day block party next Sunday. The final planning committee meeting is tomorrow night at my house at seven or so."

"Sure," I say. "We'll come around—" I turn and realize that Kim has already walked away. I make a face of contrition, something I've mastered over the last year. "I'll be there," I finish, and when he nods and waves me off, I jog to catch up to her.

"What was that about?" I try to keep my tone light, but the fact that we can't even walk a few yards without drama is pissing me off.

"I thought you were hungry." I feel any semblance of goodwill she'd extended make a decisive retreat. I immediately regret saying anything. Now she'll ice me out even harder, and the tiny step forward this walk was supposed to symbolize has taken us ten steps back. One day, one of those steps back is going to be right over the edge of a cliff.

"Yerrr, Preston!" a young man's voice calls out.

The clicking spokes of bike wheels behind us follow the shout, and Kim turns with wide eyes, startled.

I glance back and see a familiar teen—husky, dark skinned, sporting that Gumby-type haircut that's popular again—pull up on his bike in front of one of the houses. The door opens and the kid I usually see at his side, this one lighter skinned and skinnier, steps out.

"I told you, Len, Moms don't like it when you yell in front of the house," the boy named Preston says in a quelling tone.

"Sorry, Mrs. Jones!" Len calls out with typical teenage obnoxiousness, and Preston lets out a long-suffering sigh.

I like this aspect of the neighborhood: families and friends. Normal families who know each other and catch up at night after work, look out for each other's kids, not just neighbors you hear arguing through your thin condominium walls.

It reminds me of one of my favorite parts of my own youth, when I spent a summer with my grandparents in Michigan. They asked if I wanted to stay with them and signed me up for the local high school in the fall. There were kids my age who didn't hear my mom getting knocked around at night, who hadn't seen her bad makeup and so couldn't single me out as either too different or too similar and thus someone they couldn't be friends with. The group of boys in the neighborhood had loaned me a bike and we'd ridden around backwoods roads, laughing and joking.

Just before school started, my mom got dumped again and decided I need to come "home" to be with her, promising I could go back to my grandparents the following summer. I looked forward to it all year, but Mom got into another situation and my summer was lost in the fallout.

Most of my childhood was spent floundering in the wake of my mother's turbulent decisions. The apple really doesn't fall far from the tree, I guess.

Falls there and rots.

Kim starts walking faster. "They're so fucking loud. Jesus."

She still has her phone, cradled in her other hand, open to the OurHood app and begins tapping awkwardly with her thumb.

I pull open the door to the corner store and a blast of ice-cold air slaps into me, and Middle Eastern music drifts out. The place was still a little shady, but they were slowly trying to adapt by getting a better beer selection and offering vegan sandwich options and stuff. They don't have a bulletproof plastic screen with a little merry-go-round for you to put your money on and get your food from, like the liquor store and the Chinese restaurant two blocks over.

Frito, the spotted white store cat, trots over and twines his round body around Kim's feet.

"This has to be a violation of the health code," she mutters as she toes him away.

I ignore that and walk over to the grill portion of the store.

"One tofu scramble on a roll with vegan cheddar and veggie bacon, and one ham, egg, and cheese, American, with salt, pepper, ketchup on a hoagie," I say when the guy working the grill turns to me.

He doesn't smile, just nods and gets to work.

The dude behind the register is the people person, chatting with customers, wishing people luck as they buy their lottery tickets while likely talking shit about them to his coworker in their own language.

There are a few people milling around the store, and I move past them as I head to the refrigerators in the back, grabbing a six-pack. I need to cut back on the booze, but sometimes it's like I can feel Kim's disdain seeping up through the floorboards of the house, even though she spends most of her time ignoring me. When I'm not out of the house trying to make quick cash, a beer and a video game help create a force field of apathy. I'm focused on choosing between an IPA and a refreshing amber ale, something I used to make fun of people for before I met Kim, when the conversation at the front of the store gets louder.

"Are you really gonna pull the tears out? Over this?" A woman's voice. I recognize it—smooth, controlled, even in her annoyance.

I hustle down the aisle and find Kim staring up at the woman from across the street, a familiar anger etched into her expression. "I told you I didn't see you standing in line and—"

"—and I pointed out that I am wearing bright yellow and I'm pretty hard to miss."

I should side with Kim, but the other woman is right. There's no missing her, even without the yellow bandanna around her hair, yellow T-shirt, and denim overall cutoffs that should have looked like a ridiculous farmer costume but really, *really* didn't.

"What are you trying to say?" Kim's eyes are wide and her lips are pressed together and oh hell, that expression never precedes anything good.

"I'm saying that even if you didn't see me, when you realize you've made a mistake, you don't ignore me and continue making your purchase. You move away and let me make mine. Like a civilized person."

Kim's face is pink now. "You need to stop attacking me."

The woman tilts her head in confusion. "Attacking?"

"You're making me feel unsafe, and if you don't stop, I'll—I'll call the police." There's a malicious glee on her face as she says it, like when she knows her renovating work has woken me up. An expression that says, *I'm fucking with you just because I can.*

Everyone in the bodega has gone still, and there's sudden tension in the air that's as stifling as the humidity outside. The people who've been in my peripheral vision come into focus. An older man holding a lottery ticket form, gray haired and blank faced as he looks at Kim. A woman in her thirties with a teenage boy almost taller than her. Her arm has gone around the boy's shoulder, and there is anger in her eyes. A Hispanic teen covertly recording the interaction with his cell phone, his lips twisted with amused disdain.

The employees are also still. The cheerful guy behind the counter has a neutral expression, but his eyes suddenly flick to mine, pleading.

"Got the beer!" I say with aggressive cheeriness as I step forward, the same tone my mom used to distract from the bad concealer that covered her bruises.

Kim's head whips toward me, her vicious expression crumpling as she does. Tears suddenly spill down her cheeks and she runs into my arms. I feel both relief and confusion as her warm breath breaks against my chest in bursts. I haven't held her in so long and I'd forgotten that it made me feel good. Needed.

"Theo, she was saying the most awful things to me!"

The woman sucks her teeth and grabs her bag from the counter. "Bye, Abdul."

"I threw something special in your bag. Have a good day, *habibi*," Abdul says, looking at her regretfully.

"Too late for that."

Kim peeks past my arm, eyes narrowing as the woman heads out of the store.

"Can you believe that?" There are no more tears in her voice, just anger. "Just because I didn't see her! These people are always looking for a reason to be angry."

I disentangle myself from her, feeling the weight of the other customers' gazes.

I pay quickly, my face hot. I think of the last time Kim cried to me, and the boundary she laid down.

Us.

Them.

Gifford Place OurHood post by John Perkins:
The annual Labor Day block party is next weekend! We'll be having our final planning meeting this Monday evening at my house at 7:00, or whenever you can make it before Law and Order comes on at 9:00. Refreshments will be served. :-)

Amber Griffin: We might be late bc we have dance practice for the West Indian Day parade, but we'll be there!

Candace Tompkins: Get it, young ladies! If you're lucky, I'll show you some moves at the meeting.

LaTasha Clifton: X__x

Jen Peterson: Yay! Looking forward to hanging with Count!

Jenn Lithwick: Super excited to help plan our first block party!

Kavaughn Murphy: I'll be there after the community board meeting. Folks are seeing if there's anything we can do about the VerenTech deal but looks like it's too late.

CHAPTER 3

Sydney

MY PHONE VIBRATES IN MY POCKET AS I WALK THROUGH THE front door of the house.

I switch the plastic bag containing chips and salsa to my left hand and tug the slim rectangle out. My stomach flips when I see the label MOMMY'S LAWYERS pop up. I never updated the contact to Gladstone and Gianetti, which would be easier on my nerves every time they called. I consider sending them to voicemail, but Mommy needs me to handle this shit since she can't.

"Hello, this is Sydney Green," I say in a pleasant voice as I turn to the mailbox hanging next to the door. I haven't checked it for two weeks, and a quick flip through the envelopes shoved into it makes me wish I hadn't. Scammy credit card offers; collections notices from hospitals, ones here and in Seattle; the water bill; the electricity. The latest bill from the retirement home, too. I'll have to try to figure out a payment plan next time I force myself to go out there.

"Hi, Ms. Green." The cool, familiar voice of the receptionist at the lawyers' office. "I'm sorry there's been such a delay in getting back to you about your mother's case. I hope she's doing well?"

I flip the mailbox lid shut and start down the stairs.

"She's hanging in there. She's about as tough as they come," I say. A peek over the railing shows that no one is early for the meeting at Mr. Perkins's and lingering within earshot. "Any news about the situation?"

"As you've been told, with cases like this there often isn't any recourse. But Ms. Gianetti has found some things that she'd like to share with you and your mother that might be helpful moving forward. Can she give you a call on Thursday morning at eight thirty?"

"Yes! Yes, that would be great. I'm—I'm really hoping we can get this figured out. It'd make Mommy so happy, especially with everything else going on."

"Will she be on the call?" the receptionist asks.

"We'll see how she's feeling," I say.

"Of course," the receptionist says, followed by an awkward pause. "There's the matter of the payment . . ."

I scoff. Chuckle. Some combination of the two sounds. "Don't worry about that. I sent the next payment by check, so you should be getting it in the mail soon."

"Right," she says. "Great. Talk to you Thursday at eight thirty."

"Thank you."

I slip the phone back into my pocket with shaking hands. Okay. Thursday. I try not to get my hopes up, but if it was bad news they would've told me, wouldn't they? This isn't a medical diagnosis.

I take a deep breath and head next door.

The garden-level entrance to Mr. Perkins's house is shrouded by the leaves of the plants that fence his windows—they started as clippings from my mom, like so many of the plants in flower boxes and pots lining this street. The leaves brush my face as I walk in, soft and smelling like Mommy's green-thumbed hands.

The door is unlocked and ajar, and I huff an annoyed sigh as I step inside. "How many times do I have to tell you to lock this door?"

No response, apart from the low murmur of television announcers and the drone of the air conditioner.

More familiar scents greet me, even if Mr. Perkins doesn't—Folgers coffee grounds, newspapers as old as me and stacked as tall, moldy carpet, though the old carpet had been pulled up at last after Hurricane Sandy.

When Mrs. Perkins was around, she called this part of the house City Hall because people would pop in to talk about neighborhood business like local elections, how to deal with troublemakers of both the criminal and police varieties, and who needed help and wasn't asking for it.

It still serves that function, but with so many of the original neighbors gone and the new ones skittish, it's more town hall than city.

The walls are still covered by the dark wood paneling of a bygone era, and there are still boxes full of papers, books, and lord knows what else stacked along the walls. He's not quite a hoarder, but Marie Kondo would advise him to let some of this stuff go.

I know why he doesn't. Mommy's room is still how it was the day she left, minus her favorite blanket. I thought she'd want to take that with her, to have something familiar. When she'd been at the hospital the first time—well, the first time after I came back from

Seattle—she'd complained about the cold and kept reaching for the crocheted blanket that was usually at the foot of her bed at home.

An odd draft passes through the hallway, cool in a way AC can't replicate. "Mr. Perkins? Count?"

I walk into the darkened den, with its hodgepodge of couches and chairs picked up from the Goodwill over the years. The blackout curtains are drawn, and Mr. Perkins is napping on his torn and duct-taped La-Z-Boy. Count snores at his feet, the most useless guard dog ever. The light of the television, tuned in to the Home Shopping Network, shifts shadows over both of them, but after a second I realize that what I'm seeing isn't just the play of light creating an illusion of motion or my sleep-deprived brain playing tricks on me.

Mr. Perkins is jerking in his sleep—small, isolated movements all over his body. Count is doing the same at his feet. Unnatural twitches and spasms that I might have confused for a seizure if it wasn't moving through both of them. If it didn't spark a sudden fist of nauseous worry that presses against my diaphragm.

Count whines and growls as his legs twitch.

"Mr. Perkins?" I try to call out, but my voice is a barely audible whisper, like in a bad dream. Like when I walked in and found Mommy . . .

No. No.

Clammy sweat dampens my skin and anxiety fizzes through my body like an Alka-Seltzer tablet made of fear. I fumble for the light switch, forgetting where it is even though I've seen it a thousand times. My shaking hand passes over dusty paneling for a frantic moment that goes on for far too long, until the webbing between my thumb and index finger finally bumps up under the switch. I slide my palm up to flip it on.

I clear my throat. "Mr. Perkins?"

He startles awake, finally, eyes wide as they turn to me. For the briefest moment, there's no recognition, just terror, and then he places a hand on his chest and exhales.

"*Lord*. You ever have one of those nightmares where something is just standing over you, watching, and you can't move?" He rubs his hands down his arms, smoothing away goose bumps. "Like your arms and legs are just locked up?"

Mommy used to call that the devil at your elbow, and that same devil has been visiting me for months now. Drea says it's anxiety and gave me some Ambien to make me sleep, but that made it worse.

"You're okay now, though, right?" I ask.

He glances at me and smiles reassuringly. "I'm fine. Shouldn't have had roti for dinner, that's all. Too heavy on my stomach."

"Hard to resist good Trini food," I say as I scratch at my shoulder. I glance down to make sure there are no new bites. "How many people do you think will show up tonight?"

"Maybe ten? Not like it used to be, when this whole den would be full and Odetta would make her sweet lemonade . . ." He trails off, hand gripping the arm of the chair as he stares at the floor. His shoulders rise and fall and then he nods decisively. "Let me go get the refreshments from the kitchen upstairs."

"I can get it."

"Sydney, you tryna make me feel old? I got this." He smiles, seemingly having shaken off the remnants of the nightmare. "Count'll help me out."

Count hefts himself to his feet with a *wuff* and follows him, bumping into Mr. Perkins's legs when he stops short and turns back to me. "Oh, I found some papers for you that might help with your tour, in Odetta's things. In that folder over there."

His wife had been a librarian who'd loved doing programs about the history of the neighborhood. I know it must have been hard for him to look through her stuff to find this for me, but he'd done it to support this dumbass plan of mine.

"Thanks," I say.

He and Count trot off, and I replace the accordion folder on top of the TV with the bag of snacks, pull open the curtains to let in the evening light, and settle into one of the room's mismatched armchairs.

Neighborhood Things is scrawled in Mrs. Perkins's handwriting on a white label in the corner of the folder.

I undo the stiff string wrapped tightly around the tab and gently tug out the paper at the top. It's a reproduction of a pamphlet that was probably made on an old crank-style copy machine, given how yellowed with age it is.

Newes from America. 1638. By John Underhill.

I shall according to my abilitie begin with a Relation of our warre-like proceedings, and will inter-weave the speciall places fit for *New Plantations*, with their de-

> scription, as I shall find occasion in the following discourse, but I shall according to my promise begin with a true relation of the new *England* warres against the *Block-Ilanders*, and that insolent and barbarous Nation, called the *Pequeats*, whom by the sword of the Lord, and a few feeble instruments, souldiers not accustomed to warre, were drove out of their Countrey, and slaine by the sword, to the number of fifteene hundred soules in the space of two moneths and lesse: so as their Countrey is fully subdued and fallen into the hands of the English: And to the end that Gods name might have the glory, and his people see his power, and magnifie his honour for his great goodnesse I have indevoured according to my weake ability, to set forth the full relation of the Warre from the first rise to the end of the victory . . .

It takes a bit to make out the wacky spelling, but this seems to be a straight-up *Check out how many indigenous people we killed and stole land from* brag, like an old-school version of a terrifying online confession. I start to put it away, but a second underlined phrase catches my eye.

The truth is, I want time to set forth the excellencie of the whole Countrey.

Underhill—it strikes me that this is probably the man Underhill Avenue, a street I'd meandered down countless times in my life, is named after—goes on to list all the attributes of the lands from New England down to New Jersey. The good soil, the perfect places for docking English ships, the beautiful land that isn't appreciated by its inhabitants, though sometimes as he rambles on about how move-in ready it is, he speaks as if it isn't inhabited at all.

Goose bumps spread in a wave down my arm and I quickly tuck the booklet back into the accordion folder and place it on my lap. This isn't the kind of thing I'll be talking about on the tour, but every bit of history is useful in some way.

I try to imagine how Gifford Place must have looked to the people who lived here back then. Big-ass trees and thick underbrush. Darkness unbroken by streetlights. And in that darkness, the sudden arrival of men who'd decided the land was theirs . . .

. . . slaine by the sword, to the number of fifteene hundred soules in the space of two moneths and lesse . . .

"Hey."

I jolt, shaken from my thoughts that had been segueing into a dream because I'm so damn tired.

When I look over, Ponytail Lululemon's man is standing in the doorway, his hair messy, short beard trimmed neatly, and blue eyes bright with a particular kind of curiosity.

"Hi." I imbue my voice with every ounce of *don't even fucking think about it* I can muster.

He sits down on the old plastic-covered couch across from me, seemingly not picking up what I'm putting down because he smiles at me. He's kind of odd-looking, with several prominent features instead of one or two, but it works for him. "Ugly-fine" is what Drea might call him.

"We meet again," he says.

"We've never actually met before. You're a strange white man who wandered into my friend's house." I tap the folder in my lap. "Given what I'm reading about your people, maybe you're here to claim it as your own."

He shrugs. "The only thing I'm trying to claim is unemployment, and I'm barely managing that."

I press my lips together to avoid giving him the satisfaction of my smile.

"Let's officially meet now," he says anyway, then holds out his hand and leans forward, stretching his arm and body long so I don't have to move from my seat if I choose to meet his hand. "I'm Theo. I live across the street from you. I haven't been very neighborly, and I'm looking to change that."

I reluctantly reach out to give his fingertips a quick shake, but he closes his hand over mine, holding on for a bit longer than is necessary. I almost let him, because the attention-starved part of me has the nerve to enjoy it, but then I pull my hand away.

No more panning in Fuckboy Creek, and most definitely no climbing Cheating White Guy Hill.

"Is your delightful wife coming? Or is she busy threatening to call the cops on other innocent Black people?"

"We're not married. It's—complicated." He leans back into the couch and runs his hand over his beard. When he speaks again, there's wry humor mixed with frustration in his voice. "Kim isn't coming. I do want to apologize about what happened in the store yesterday. She's not . . . not usually like *that*. Things have been weird since we moved here, I guess."

"Mm-hmm" is all I say in response. I'm not his therapist and don't care about his relationship.

"Maybe I can make it up to you somehow?" His eyes brighten. "Do you like coffee? There's a new place a few blocks down."

I stare at him, trying to discern if this dude is really trying to shoot his shot *while* discussing his wild-ass significant other who already tried to call the police on me.

"Neighborly coffee," he adds, leaning forward in a way that's somehow nonthreatening even though it brings him closer to me. "Nothing more. When we did that tour you—"

"Um, *hi*." I look up to find Drea glancing speculatively between me and Theo. Her hair is slicked back into a puff ponytail, and she's changed from her work clothes into a T-shirt and shorts.

"Theo, this is my best friend and housemate, Drea. Drea, this is Theo from across the street. He lives in the Payne house." Because I'm mean and want to deflect, I add, "His girlfriend is the one who threatened me at the store yesterday."

"Oh. *Oh*." She perches on the arm of my chair and fixes her gaze on Theo. Drea is all of five feet tall and currently wearing a purple T-shirt with a unicorn on it, but her death stare is terrifying—it was why no one had fucked with me from grades five through twelve.

"Hello, Brad," she says. "Wonderful to meet you."

"Oh, it's Theo." His flirtatiousness is gone and his body is tense, as if Drea herself has a unicorn horn and might gore him.

Good.

Drea claps her hands together, then drops them between her knees as she leans forward. "You do know this is the planning meeting for the annual block party and not the Police Benevolent Association fundraiser, right?"

"Drea." I laugh. "Be nice."

"Fine." She gives Theo an evil look. "But tell your girl that if anything happens to my Sydney, or one of my neighbors, because she wants to call 911 for no reason? Then we're gonna have a problem. She don't want no problems with me."

She leans back and spreads her arms, and when she speaks again, her voice is light and chipper. "Welcome to the neighborhood!"

Theo swallows. "Thanks."

The room has started to fill with other neighbors: Asia Martin and her son Len, who's a foot taller than me now, somehow, even though he was at my shoulder when I moved away. Jenn and Jen, who brought homemade dog treats for Count and homemade hummus for us humans. Tiffany, LaTasha, and Amber, the head of the neighborhood's teen dance troupe. Ashley and Jamel Jones, without their son, Preston, who's probably at one of his fifty-leven college-prep extracurriculars. Ms. Candace, who's stepped up to help with the organizing since Mrs. Perkins passed away. Their chatter fills the den as they pour soda into plastic cups and grab handfuls of chips; even with so many people here, there are noticeable gaps where so many of the old familiar faces used to be.

Theo ends up perched awkwardly on the edge of the couch next to Len, whose back is to Theo because his focus is on the three girls demonstrating dance moves for Jenn and Jen. Theo looks nervous, out of place, but trying to be cool. It was how I felt living in Seattle and never quite fitting in at all of Marcus's work functions and sports events and happy hours. I eventually stopped trying.

"Hot damn, ho, here we go again," Drea mutters, breaking the unfortunate direction of my thoughts.

I whip my head up to find her looking down at me, judgment a divot etched between her brows. "What?" I ask innocently.

"What?" she mimics in annoyance, then leans over and whispers in my ear, her voice sharp and singsong. "Why are you staring at Theodore like you've spotted fool's gold, yet again?"

I raise a brow. "Do you propose I just ignore the strange white man at our gathering? Have you read a newspaper lately? This is surveillance. I'm trying to make sure I don't need to take his ass out."

She stares at me.

I hold up my index and middle fingers and covertly gesture from my eyes to Theo's general direction. "Sur. Veil. Lance."

She just looks at me, a glimmer of frustration in her eyes, then she shakes her head. "You have theeeeee worst taste. The worst. Though . . ." She glances over at him. "He does look a little *spicy*, with them thick-ass eyebrows. He at least puts paprika on his chicken, I'm guessing. Maybe even some Lawry's."

"Drea! If you don't stop—"

"Stop what? Predicting your dumbass behavior based on a lifetime of observation?" She says it jokingly, but she's right—she's always been there to warn me when I was about to slip up, and to catch me when I ignored her and inevitably fell. When my nightmares weren't about the devil at my elbow, they featured Drea walking away from me and my neediness—like Marcus had.

She touches my shoulder lightly. "You're lucky I love you."

"I am." I lean into her a bit, letting myself rest against the familiar warmth of a side that has propped me up countless times over the years, through failures and bad decisions, marriage, divorce, and . . . everything since I came back to Brooklyn. Drea would do anything for me—like, that's a fact and not a supposition.

My lips turn up at the corners and I sigh, comfort sliding over me like a weighted blanket. The beginning of a bangin' nap, this one not marred by weird half dreams of colonial destruction, starts to pull me under.

Drea nudges me with her elbow, jostling me away from the edge of sleep. "I talked to work bae in the contracts department about the VerenTech stuff you were complaining about."

"You didn't have to ask," I say grumpily. "I didn't tell you about the rejected information request so you could do the work for me."

She rolls her eyes. "Well, I did. And it's too late to tell him never mind, because then he's gonna be mad at me since he's already going out of his way for me since there's all this extra security around this project."

That was the thing with Drea: a simple question can turn into her going ten blocks out of her way to get something you didn't ask for, or, in this case, having her coworker do possibly illegal searches for info that'll probably be useless to me.

I feel the urge to snap at her, but catch myself before stepping on that particular Lego of regret. Drea . . . has really been there for me. *Really* fucking been there, and held me down when anyone else would've let me go to pieces. I've been asking a lot of her while being too empty to give back, and yet here I am about to cop an attitude because she's being too helpful.

"Thank you, Drea Bond," I say, reminding myself how lucky I

am. I know what it feels like to not have the kind of support Drea excels at, and I never want to feel that way again.

She strikes a pose with a finger gun and winks at me. "I got you."

"I'm calling this meeting to order," Ms. Candace says loudly, her voice cutting through the noise to silence everyone. "Now, we have a week until the block party. Almost everything is set, but . . ." She looks around and shakes her head in annoyance. "At least four people on my list aren't here."

"Maybe the mole people got them!" Tiffany says in a creepy, raspy voice that imitates an announcer on a kids' Halloween special.

"I heard they been snatching people up all summer! The news is ignoring it, though." LaTasha shakes her head.

"Are you serious?" Jen asks, eyes wide. "I thought the neighborhood was supposed to be safe."

"They're joking, honey," Jenn says with a smitten roll of her eyes.

"See, that's why they don't talk about it," LaTasha says, sounding just like her mom, who she probably heard this story from. "Nisha's aunt went missing and somebody said they saw her get pulled through a subway grate."

Amber looks between her two friends skeptically. "I don't believe that story because—deadass?—who walks on subway grates? Even if there aren't mole people, you can't be walking on no subway grate."

She's right. Nobody with an ounce of common sense is trying to fall through a weak subway grate, a busted manhole, or a janky metal cellar door outside a bodega.

"Where is Kavaughn at?" Ms. Candace calls out. "He volunteered to help Sydney with the last of the research for her tour *that she snuck onto the agenda at the last minute*. Did the mole people get him, too?"

The room doesn't go quiet again, but voices lower as people look around, searching for Kavaughn's familiar Mets cap.

"Oh." Len snaps his fingers. "I think maybe he went to visit his family in North Carolina? Since his summer session ended. He goes down there for a few days every summer, and it's so country they don't even have internet!"

"No internet?" Tiffany, LaTasha, and Amber cry out in horror, turning to look at him.

Len freezes, unprepared to be the center of attention of the three girls he's been trying to work up the nerve to talk to. Theo nudges him—quickly, encouragingly—pushing Len into action. The boy throws his hands up, grins. "I'm saying! 'Can you hear me now?' 'No, bruh, get Fios!'"

Tiffany, LaTasha, and Amber burst out laughing and Len's posture slackens in relief. I, on the other hand, am shit out of luck.

"So my assistant just up and left? Cool." Maybe this is a sign I should just give up on this idea, even if it would feel like disappointing Mommy.

"I can help," Len says. His gaze flicks over to the girls to make sure they're listening, then back to me. "I'm taking AP classes at LIU and working at the YMCA camp, though, so I'm pretty busy."

The girls start whispering and his chest puffs out a bit.

Then Theo raises that big hand of his and says, "I can help, too."

"Don't you have better things to do?" I ask.

"Absolutely not." He runs a hand through his hair with that

look of practiced innocence white men use when they're on some bullshit. "Unemployed, remember? And no AP classes, either. Tests aren't my strong point. What do you need help with?"

"I'm planning a historical tour of the neighborhood," I say. Theo was there when Zephyr told me to make my own, and I feel like I'm revealing some dirty secret, but his expression doesn't change. "I want to do a demo run during the block party."

"Because she'll have a captive audience," Mr. Perkins calls out, and everyone laughs.

I ignore him. "I need help with some historical research and with the tour overview."

Theo's eyes brighten. "I'm good at research. And I wanted to explore the neighborhood and get to know my—our neighbors. I could do that and help you at the same time."

And just like that everyone but Drea is looking at me like if I don't say yes I'll be kicking a dog in the ribs. The worst part? I don't think any of them even realize it.

"I have a camera," he adds.

"Everyone has a camera, man," Len says, joking because he apparently likes Theo enough to do that now. "It's called a cell phone?"

Amber laughs, and Len's chest puffs up even more.

"And I bet your tour will be way better than the brownstone one. If I can help with that . . ." He shrugs. "That'd be cool."

"Sydney, you're the one who put this on the schedule last minute," Ms. Candace says in her no-nonsense tone that reminds me she spent years managing a bank. "You need help. Our neighbor has offered to help. What exactly is the problem?"

I cross my arms over my chest and glance at Theo.

"I was gonna pay Kavaughn, but I'm not paying you," I say. "If you really want to help, you can think of this work as reparations."

There. A little twitch at the corner of his eye. But when he opens his mouth all he says is "Great. Just let me know when and where."

The meeting moves on and I tune it out, glancing at Theo as he interacts with these people I've known all my life. I have no idea why this man is so invested in helping me, or is suddenly all up in the neighborhood Kool-Aid, but I guess I'm about to find out.

Gifford Place OurHood post by Josie Ulnar:

This evening when I was walking home from work, I noticed a group of men in hoodies riding their bikes slowly up and down the street. I'm not sure if they were casing houses or if it's part of the gang initiations that apparently happen at this time of year, but I did call it in to the police.

Ashley Jones: That was my son Preston, who is 17, babysitting his cousins, who are 8 and 11 years old and thus only allowed to ride their bikes from corner to corner on this street, WHERE THEY LIVE. (-__-)

Josie Ulnar: I was just being vigilant. Crime has been on the rise and it's something we all need to keep an eye out for.

Kim DeVries: I'm with Josie. There have already been several break-ins over the last few weeks and gangs plan robberies for three-day weekends, when people are away and no one is really paying attention.

Ashley Jones: www.nyccrime.gov/crimerates Crime in our neighborhood is at the lowest it's been in decades, but go off sis.

(14 additional comments . . . see more)

CHAPTER 4

Theo

VOLUNTEERING TO HELP SYDNEY WAS A DUMB MOVE—I'M supposed to be blending in enough that people will think I'm nice. Normal. Not being the center of attention. But something about my neighbor leads to ill-advised decisions.

Before this evening, she was "the woman from the tour" and then "the woman I watch from my window." My run-ins with her had either been abrupt and awkward, or from a detached distance, like watching a character in a *Sims* video game go about her business. Now she feels . . . real, I guess. All of the neighbors I spoke to do.

I hadn't thought of them as real people. Even when I'd chatted with Mr. Perkins, even when I'd watched from my window or observed people during my walks, I hadn't really been *seeing* them. It's a startling realization, but to be fair, I've spent most of my life having to quickly categorize people as either threat or . . . something else. That doesn't leave much room for having to think about their past or their feelings, or whatever.

Now I want to know more. And Sydney—I might want more than that.

Hold your horses, buddy.

Volunteering for her project is just a way to kill time until the ax over my head drops or miraculously disappears. While Sydney makes for a nice fantasy, my reality is being stuck in a co-owned house with a woman who barely acknowledges my existence, let alone our relationship.

I intend on going right up to my cramped attic studio and looking up some history stuff so Sydney doesn't realize I know nothing about history, before heading out again. Kim has been staying out later and later anyway—which probably means exactly what I think it means, so I've been spending my nights out and about—but I hear music floating through the closed windows of the living room as I jog up the front steps.

The low, sorrowful notes sound like one of Kim's classical music albums, which I call her "cultured entertaining soundtrack" since she usually listens to Taylor Swift when she's alone; she must have guests.

Anxiety punches me in the belly as I imagine her parents behind that door, the rich, judgmental pieces of work who'd made it clear from the beginning that I wasn't good enough, but they'd tolerate me temporarily because what Kim wanted, Kim got.

One Easter dinner at their place in the Hamptons, they'd told the story of how Kim had always begged for a new bunny every Easter and they'd obliged her, to the point that they'd started to run out of bunny names. When I'd attempted a joke about them recycling the same rabbit and renaming it every year, the table had fallen silent and her father had laughed in that tone someone uses when you've mispronounced your entrée at a French restaurant.

"You don't keep replaceable playthings for longer than necessary," he'd explained, and there'd been contempt in his eyes that had seemed disproportionate to a discussion about Easter rabbits. At the time, I thought he was making a sly jab at Kim's affection for me, but now I think maybe he'd really been disgusted that I'd been gauche enough to suggest they couldn't simply buy what they wanted, dispose of it when they were tired of it, and get a new one when the mood struck again.

Deep male laughter sounds through the door to the first-floor apartment, followed by Kim's flirtatious giggle.

Maybe it isn't her parents. Maybe it's the asshole who sat across from me at brunch almost exactly a year ago, talking to me about his 401(k) like he hadn't fucked Kim in the hot tub just hours earlier.

If David had been smug or had seemed like he was needling me, that would have given me something to really hitch my rage trailer to. But no. He'd been bland and boring before, and he'd been bland and boring after, and apparently that was what Kim preferred over me. And instead of leaving, I'd stayed and tried to make things good again, like it was another challenge and I'd win some kind of prize.

I really was my mother's child.

The music suddenly grows louder as I stand on the bottom step, indecisive, and I turn to see Kim standing in the open doorway and looking at me like she's glad to see me. The invisible anxiety fist gets in a few more jabs somewhere around my chest region. Or maybe it's just heartburn from the chips and salsa I shoveled into my mouth while standing around after the block-party planning meeting had finished because I didn't want to go back to my sweltering attic room.

"Theo?"

Kim says my name how she used to. Before we moved. Before she detached so hard she took a chunk of my flesh with her. Before almost exactly a year ago when she'd walked up to the brunch table where I'd listened to David drone on, sporting a low-cut top that nonchalantly displayed a hickey that I hadn't given her, like we were in some kind of teen drama.

"What's up?" I try to sound cool, but it comes out sounding surprised, which is a completely honest reaction for once.

"Want to come have a nightcap with us?" she asks politely, inclining her head toward the noise in her living room.

"Who's 'us'?" I steel myself to just walk up the stairs if she says David's name, which seems in the realm of possibility, given the last few months.

"The neighbors from across the street. Terry and Josie. Remember, they had us over to try some of Terry's craft beer right after we moved in?" She pulls the door open and I see the neighbors who live on the other side of Sydney smiling at me expectantly like we're old buddies about to catch up. Terry's beer had tasted like piss, and both their dog and their son had bitten me, so of course I remember our visit.

"Sure," I say, trying to muster if not enthusiasm then hospitality. I *should* be happy Kim seems to be trying. "I'll have a quick drink."

"Quick? You have something else to do?" Kim's nose wrinkles a bit, but she holds on to her smile and ushers me in.

"Hey," I say as I walk in and take a seat on the weird angular couch Kim bought last month. The room smells like fancy cheese, so like ass, mixed with the tart scent of wine.

"Theo. Buddy!" Terry reaches over the coffee table littered with the remains of their appetizers and gives my hand a hard squeeze. He's sporting an expensive Rolex on his wrist, and I imagine how he'd react if I slammed it down onto the edge of this ugly but sturdy coffee table.

"Long time no see," Josie says, then holds up the bottle of white wine in her hand. It's so huge it looks kind of like a novelty, but I'm sure it's expensive and delicious. "Want some?"

Kim slides onto the couch beside me. "Dad brought it back from his trip to France," she explains, casually placing a hand on my knee. A little shiver passes through me at the familiar press of her fingers. It feels more intimate than if she'd called me in here to fuck.

"Come on, look at this guy!" Terry's words are a bit blurry around the edges, but he seems like a guy who comes home every night and hits the wet bar before taking off his jacket, so he's possibly more than a little drunk. His face is wide, and, right now, the center third of it is flushed red and mottled like he got hit with the problem-drinker stick. "Wine? What does he look like? He's going to have some bourbon, right?"

"I—"

Terry thumps his chest. "Bourbon. Man's drink! Thatta boy."

Terry is maybe ten years older than me, tops, but he's clearly taken on the role of pushy drunk uncle at this gathering. I decide to roll with it. I take the glass from him as he hands it across the table, and feel the weight of three gazes settle on me as the smoky heat of the first sip warms my throat and chest.

"So, how was it?" Kim asks, squeezing my leg.

"How was what?"

"The meeting," Josie says, leaning in conspiratorially. "About the block party."

"Oh. It was fine." I take another sip and run my tongue over my teeth.

"That's it? Fine?" Kim asks, squeezing my leg a bit harder. "What'd they talk about?"

Part of me wonders if she knows I spoke to, and maybe flirted a bit with, Sydney. If she knows I volunteered to help with the tour instead of busting down doors looking for a job opportunity that's not going to happen.

I use my free hand to gently pry her clawlike grip off me. "It was a party-planning meeting. The most exciting thing was when these two women started trash-talking each other's macaroni and cheese."

I shrug and take another sip, but Josie's gaze narrows. "They didn't talk about anything else?"

There's something odd in how her gaze has gone from diffused friendliness to sharpened interrogation, despite the same pasted-on smile. I gulp the rest of my drink and plonk the glass onto the coffee table. "How about you just ask me what it is you want to know? Clearly I'm missing something, and I don't have time to play guessing games."

Kim's breath brushes against my ear just before she whispers, "Don't be rude."

"Aren't you unemployed?" Terry asks pointedly as he leans over to pour me more bourbon. "I'd say you have plenty of time."

All three of them laugh, that rich-fuck giggle, and I turn to Kim with both brows raised.

"What's up with this?" I grit out.

"Don't be upset, we're all friends here," Josie says. "We saw the party-planning post on OurHood and our private group decided to have a meeting of our own."

"There are private groups in OurHood?" I ask.

Josie gives me a look and continues. "We started wondering what exactly they were getting up to. We need to know whether there's anything to worry about. Safety-wise."

"You think a bunch of people sitting around planning activities to enrich their neighbors' lives is a safety threat." I laugh a little but no one else does. I know I probably have a somewhat different view of safety than these three, given my background, but this is so comical I need to know more. "Are you actually worried that our totally harmless neighbors are plotting against you?"

"They're not totally harmless," Kim says. "One of them tried to attack me at the corner store. You saw that. I don't know what she would've done if you hadn't stepped in."

She squeezes my arm.

I don't say anything.

"Come on, buddy," Terry says. "Don't tell me you haven't noticed how they look at us. Felt it. Like *we're* the ones who don't belong here."

"If you were in our private group, you'd see that some of the other emerging neighborhoods around us have been dealing with . . . unpleasantness." Josie presses her lips together and lets the word settle, as if unpleasantness is the worst thing ever.

Terry makes a weird sound in his throat. "There have been package robberies from doorsteps. Expensive items. Two homes that were featured on Boomtown were broken into and had jewelry stolen, family heirlooms that had been passed down for generations."

"And?" I hold his gaze. "People get robbed all the time. This is Brooklyn."

"A couple was mugged five blocks over by some thugs last week, too," Josie continues. "A couple like you two. Like Terry and me. They were told that it was 'reparations.'"

Sydney had said something similar to me, but we'd laughed afterward because it was a joke.

"Well, I'm sure that wasn't funny for the people being robbed, but it clearly wasn't a mission statement."

I wait for them to acknowledge how ridiculous this is, but no one does.

Terry shakes his head. "There have been a lot of issues popping up since the VerenTech deal was floated for this neighborhood. Troublemakers having meetings, planning things, trying to make sure the deal doesn't go through by any means necessary, as they say. Now that it's been approved, we're worried about . . . escalations, especially because Josie works there."

Kim rests her hand on my leg again, and the weight feels cloying now. "They see the VerenTech deal, and us, as a way of, I don't know, taking what's theirs or something. So we thought—"

"Wait. Wait, wait. You guys are serious?" I look around the room and see that they are. "Christ, Kim. It was literally a bunch of neighbors hanging out and planning something fun for everyone, and you're acting like it's leading up to Harpers Ferry." I place my glass on the table and stand up. "All three of you might consider deleting the OurHood app because it's clearly making you paranoid. This is—"

"This is what?" Terry's voice is low and angry, following the typical drunk-bastard cycle. "Ridiculous? You think because you went to one meeting with those people that you're *down* now?"

"You keep saying 'them' and 'those people' when you mean our neighbors who were just now nefariously choosing time slots for who was going to oversee the bouncy castle," I say slowly. "So, yes. It is ridiculous."

Terry smirks at me, a mean and familiar curve of his mouth upward, and I realize he doesn't mean "our neighbors." He's thinking something much worse. "Calm down, Theo. We're just looking out for you. Kim told us you've been having problems and we thought maybe—"

"You told them we've been having problems?" I ask Kim.

"I told them *you've* been having problems," she clarifies. "I have a job and pull my weight around the house."

I haven't missed any mortgage payments, thanks to the gigs I've picked up here and there over the last few months, but I wonder what she's told these people.

"VerenTech will be hiring soon, and—" Jodie says.

"We're just trying to help," Terry cuts in. "We have to look out for each other. We're just trying to foster good neighborly relations because we need to depend on each other. To know we have each other's backs."

I look down at Kim and think of the day she came home upset. *"There's just so few of us."*

"When you're depressed and jobless, it's easy to fall in with the wrong kind of people—" Josie adds, but they're all talking to my back now because I'm heading out the living room door.

I consider going upstairs, but the thought of being boxed in by Kim and those weirdo neighbors makes me pivot out the front door. I'm agitated and annoyed and I really shouldn't be, because everything they said was ridiculous. Still, while they'd been worried I was attending some kind of anarchists' meeting, they'd been having their own kaffeeklatsch about what a loser I was.

I stand outside on the stoop for a minute; it's dark out already, but still hot and humid. Kids are heading home in groups of two, three, and four. The whir of bike wheels and flash of spoke reflectors speed by. Sydney's house is dark—she's probably still at Mr. Perkins's place with her friend who lives upstairs from her.

I do what I always do when I'm frustrated: I walk. For blocks and blocks, I wander down streets with names I can't pronounce, with housing styles ranging from squat two-story colonials, to grand brownstones with all the bells and whistles, to old prewar tenements with dozens of apartments, to housing projects. Lots of new construction, too, in the same bland "modern" style. I'd worked on a few sites for condos like these—and after dating Kim, had been friends with people who could afford to live in them. These were the kind of people who called people trailer trash in one sentence and complained about leaks and thin walls in the next—the same problems that'd plagued the trailers I grew up in. My mom now lives in a beautiful trailer that beats most of these condos, and it didn't cost half a million bucks, either.

I'm always hyperaware of my surroundings, but tonight I'm on edge, tuned in to how people in the neighborhoods I walk through look at me. A group of dudes my age, all Black, sitting on their stoop, nudge each other, and one of them laughs like jicama going over a grater. A couple of streets down, an older woman eyes me cautiously and gives me a wide berth, as if she can tell there's something dangerous about me, though she nods a greeting when our gazes meet. As I pass another group, boys and girls in their late teens all sitting on a park bench in one of those green spaces that pop up randomly around here, one of the boys calls out, "Have a good night, bro, have a good night." I can't tell if he's buzzed and feeling overly friendly or making fun of me. Maybe both.

I reply with "You too, man," and keep walking, trying to shake the weird feeling I've had since I left the house. I'd been in a good mood for once after leaving Mr. Perkins's, like I could be part of this neighborhood and create some snapshots for my own personal photo album, but Kim, Terry, and Josie have gotten into my head so I'm walking around paranoid and jumpy.

I have to wonder if this is what Kim feels like all the time. Constantly suspicious and thinking that everyone is out to get her for no reason. I do have reason, but none of the people I've passed are a source of worry for me.

I decide to make my way toward the bar a few blocks down

from our house, where they sometimes have jazz on Monday nights, across from one of the pawnshops I've been to a few times. When I arrive, it's quiet outside, so I head in and take a seat. It's darker than I remember, a polished and cleaned version of the dive bars I used to frequent, and instead of jazz, an old Radiohead album is playing. Each stool is occupied by a white dude with a beard. They all turn and look at me as the door slams shut behind me.

The bartender saunters over to the end of the bar, a cute short girl who I recognize as the college kid who rents from Mr. Perkins.

"Hey, neighbor," she says, batting her lashes at me. She seems to be going for the smoky-eyed manic pixie dream girl look tonight, and personality, too, judging from how she leans invitingly over the bar. "What can I get you? Beer? Bourbon?"

"I actually came for jazz," I say. "But I think maybe I have the wrong bar?"

There's something about the way this place seems manufactured, like a hipster Hard Rock Cafe, that makes my skin itch. Even the customers fit a mold: every guy at the bar is dressed in the same variation of graphic tee and dark denim, slouched over a beer or phone with the same curve of his back. It's weird.

"Oh, that was the last place," she says. "They closed down a couple weeks ago."

"That sucks."

She quirks a brow. "Does it? We don't have to go all the way to Fort Greene to find a chill place now."

I thought the old place was more chill than this prefab dive bar, but I'm annoyed and don't feel like talking to this kid anymore.

"Right." I scrub a hand through my hair, nod, then point at the door behind me. "I'm going to head out."

She leans forward a little more, and the heads of the dudes lining the bar swivel to check out her ass. "See you around."

I heave a sigh and walk back, the humid air clinging to me along with an even crappier mood. I'm not drunk, or even buzzed, but the two glasses of bourbon paired with the disappointment of the night were just enough to leave me feeling sullen. I glance into dark windows as I walk, noticing how almost all the newly renovated places I pass have cameras pointed at their front doors now. Kim had wanted to get one of those systems, too, but I'd told her I didn't want her to be able to monitor when I leave and enter the house from the comfort of her phone—though I doubt she cares enough to bother.

I'm passing by the old hospital, and stop to casually look through the fence surrounding the building—there's all kinds of construction equipment littered around the place, and I wonder what's inside. Had they already cleared everything out? I hear a noise like scraping metal and lean closer.

The building is dark and the weak yellow-orange glow filtering from the streetlights barely illuminates the area past the fence. The windows are nothing but uniform black, but then a thin line of light flickers somewhere in the depths of that darkness, on the floor that's slightly lower than ground level. I blink a couple of times and lean closer, squinting to try to catch sight of that weird flicker again . . .

A hand clamps down on my shoulder and, a second later, is followed by a heavy weight slamming me into the fence.

A body.

The chain link rattles as instinct kicks in and I struggle to pull my hands out of my pockets to fight back, but my attacker is big and wraps me in a bear hug. Thin strips of warm, grimy metal press a diamond shape into the side of my face as the weight slumps against me, a heart hammering against my shoulder blade and breaths coming fast and shallow.

Whoever it is smells like pissed pants and body odor, and I suck in breath through my mouth to avoid gagging.

"M-m-mo—" A deep voice stutters in my ear, but the end of the word is clipped as a violent shudder passes through the person, vibrating through me and the chain link.

I force myself to relax, sagging into the fence, then push back hard as soon as the grip loosens in response, catching them off balance so they stumble away from me.

When I turn around, already squared up and with a rage in my veins that I've avoided for years now, I see a heavyset Black guy in a T-shirt and jeans reaching for me as he sways on his feet. He grasps at me a few times, but comes away with palmfuls of air as I step out of reach.

I imagine Kim giving me a smug look and telling me she tried to warn me. I knock his hands away as he reaches for me again.

"What the fuck, man?" I grit out.

He lists sideways, then struggles to right himself, the streetlight glinting in his dull eyes. It's then that I notice how delayed his motions are, how his dark irises have been eaten by the blown-out black of his pupils.

He squints at me and slurs something that sounds like "Mummy."

"What?"

He thrusts his hand toward me, closing and then opening it, and I finally understand.

"Money?" I snort a laugh of frustration, and he shakes his head, then nods. "Sorry, pal."

He talks again, still sounding like he's speaking around a mouthful of marbles. "Bring money. Help me, man."

I sigh and drop my guard a bit. "You can't just grab people like that. And sorry, I can't help you."

His eyes widen in confusion, shining with tears. "Please. *Please.*"

He really isn't in good shape.

"Do you want me to call an ambulance? Get you to a hospital?"

He stares at me for a moment, his eyes briefly focusing, and then he grabs me by the collar and slams me against the fence again.

"No! No! No!" he shouts directly into my face, so close that I can tell he hasn't brushed his teeth for days just before his spittle lands on the corner of my lip.

I'm about to land a blow to his kidney when the sudden high-pitched warning blip of a siren down the street drags his attention from me. When red and blue lights wash over us, he lets me go and tears off running, ungainly and stumbling.

A black sedan, an undercover car, pulls up to me as I'm adjusting my collar, and the man in the passenger side, a white guy with a beefy face and a buzz cut, rolls down his window. The barest hint of cold air passes over my forearm as I step closer to the car.

"You see a big, crazy crackhead around here?" he asks. "Giant Black guy? We got some reports of a man hassling people."

His partner, an Italian-looking guy with a mustache, leans forward and fixes me with his stare.

I point down the street and see that my hand's shaking from the adrenaline rush. "He went that way. Attacked me when I wouldn't give him money."

"Is that so? Can't help themselves, I guess." The buzz-cut cop chuckles mirthlessly and gives his head a shake. "All right. We'll bring him in."

He reaches for a walkie-talkie.

"You know it's dangerous for you to be out around here this late, right?" the mustache cop says. "Give it a year or so."

They blip the siren again and then take off fast down the street in the direction of my attacker.

My heart is thumping furiously in my chest and my legs feel shaky from delayed adrenaline as I walk toward the house, but I keep thinking about the attacker's eyes. Even when he had his hands at my throat, he didn't have the look of someone who wanted to kill me. To hurt me. To be honest, he'd looked . . . scared.

Addiction is a hell of a disease. I can't even feel good that the cops showed up because jail won't help that guy, either. I regret letting them know he attacked me and sending them after him, though maybe I've saved the next person the guy might have encountered.

I'm a few yards away from the house when I see Kim sprint down the stairs into a car waiting at the curb, an overnight bag on her shoulder.

I don't call out her name. I just take the additional gut punch, though it feels like a light tap at this point.

After the car pulls away, I walk up the steps. As I unlock the door, I look up and to my left, into the black square lens of a doorbell camera. *What the hell?* I head to my apartment, scrub the hell out of my face and hands with hand sanitizer, and stare out the window.

Across the street, TVs flicker in various windows, a checkerboard of blue lights, and in the distance, a police siren wails.

Gifford Place OurHood post by Derek James:
Anyone been feeling the ground shake at night sometimes? Feels like when I used to live on Nostrand over the A train line. You think all this construction is messing with the already fucked up infra-structure? I'm not tryna die by sinkhole.

Angie C.: Does it always happen at 2 am?

Derek James: Yes!

Angie C.: That's the witching hour, my guy. Get you some holy water and some sage and you'll be straight.

CHAPTER 5

Sydney

AS I BRUSH MY TEETH WITH ONE HAND, I HAVE MY PHONE IN the other, web browser open, scrolling through search results for "why does it feel like my bed is shaking when I fall asleep?"

My other searches this morning have been "earthquake + Brooklyn" and "do demons shake your bed," so whichever NSA Brad is collecting my Google searches is probably having a good laugh.

I, on the other hand, am so tired I want to throw up.

The only nonsupernatural explanation in the results is that high stress levels and overconsumption of caffeine can create the sensation that your bed is shaking, like how you sometimes feel like you're falling even though neither your body nor your bed has moved.

I place the phone on the edge of the sink and finish brushing my teeth.

My phone buzzes and a text message pops up: Hello Ms. Green, we're messaging you with a lucrative offer on your house! Please contact us at 212–555-CASH.

I trash the message, minty-hot rage zinging through me as I spit and rinse my mouth.

These vultures can even harass you by text now? It's like real estate psychological warfare—they bombard you with flyers, blow up your phone, have people showing up at your door, and now can show up in your text inbox. How many people do they wear down, or catch in a moment of weakness or desperation?

Bastards.

I apply my undereye concealer with shaking hands, not wanting to deal with questions at the hair braiding shop. Five hours of someone tugging at your scalp is bad enough without every other person who comes in commenting on how tired you look.

I head into my room and open the sealed plastic bag that contains my clothes—after the first couple of bedbug scares, I'm not taking any chances. I check the baseboards of the apartment and the furniture every few days, too. Drea says I'm being crazy, which isn't my favorite descriptor after what happened in Seattle, but she's seemingly immune to them. She doesn't have clusters of cocoa butter–resistant scars marring her neck and ankles. She doesn't start itching every time she sees a tiny dark mote from the corner of her eye. And she doesn't lie in bed at night wondering why the mattresses out on the curb are quickly being followed by moving trucks.

I do.

I lock up the house, cringing as Josie yells at her kid, or her dog, or her husband, and head to the community garden to make sure everything is good.

By the time I get there, I'm already sweating through my T-shirt. It's hot and humid and there's no way I'm walking all the way to the salon in this heat.

Ms. Candace is in there with Paulette. She's picking some tomatoes, lettuce, and peppers from her plot, dropping them into a basket in Paulette's lap. Paulette's dark eyes lock on me as I stop at the entrance, but she doesn't say anything. Her gaze strays toward the toolshed, then she looks down.

You're imagining it, I tell myself, though more beads of sweat pop up along my hairline. The shadows of the sunflowers sway back and forth over the two women.

"Everything good? You need anything?" I ask.

Candace looks up at me and gives me a warm smile. "Everything's good. We're getting some salad makings for the Day Club Crew's lunch later, isn't that right?" She glances at Paulette, who doesn't respond, then looks back at me. "What you up to?"

"Heading to the beauty supply, then the braid shop," I say. "And then working on the tour some more."

She rests her hands on her knees, examining me, and I know the concealer isn't doing its work. "Stay safe, okay?"

She's told me this countless times since I was little, but this time it seems like an actual request.

"I will."

I look over the garden one more time before I turn to leave; all the plots, except the one I'm tending, are thick with green and red and orange foliage. Honeysuckle climbs over archways, shading the gravel pathways. Sunflowers, Mommy's favorite, stand tall and heavy-headed along the back edge.

The three-block walk to the beauty supply to pick up my hair feels like I'm moving underwater. It strikes me when I'm walking that several of the stores on just this short stretch are new. The West Indian fruit and veggie store is still here, as are the patty shop and the nail salon, but the pet store where I got my first goldfish is gone. The barbershop where older men used to congregate and play jazz records is now a home goods boutique. And the halal market is a thrift shop that has price tags more expensive than neighboring stores that sell brand-new items.

I start walking faster, pushing through the fatigue as a single terrifying thought possesses me: What if the beauty supply is gone? I passed it two days ago, but . . .

I speed walk that final half a block and feel a sense of disproportionate relief when I catch sight of the pink awning with BEAUTYLAND written across it in bold white letters.

I step into the air-conditioning, out of breath and out of it. I wander through the aisles, my pulse racing for absolutely no reason and the panic trying to get a tight hold on my sweat-slick body, but eventually it loses its hold on me.

"Hey. You okay?" the older woman behind the counter asks as she rings me up, then gestures toward the fridge near the register. "Want to add a Red Bull?"

This store has been here for years, and this woman has never asked me how I was doing. I must look a mess, but Red Bull is the last thing my jackrabbit heart rate needs right now.

"No, thank you. I'm fine."

She nods, though her expression shows she disagrees.

The salon is a fifteen-minute walk from the beauty supply since my stylist moved to a cheaper storefront, and I decide to do myself a favor and order an Uber. I'll have to wait . . . six minutes for Terrel in his Nissan Altima, but it's hot as balls and I already feel dizzy from the short walk to the main drag of stores.

My phone vibrates and I check it.

Terrel has canceled the ride.

"Okay, fuck you too, Terrel," I mutter, wondering if I really need my hair braided. Then, in what feels like a miracle given the general bullshit that has been my life lately, I immediately get a new alert.

Your driver is arriving in 1 min. Look for Drew in a black Ford Crown Victoria.

Someone lays on the horn, and I jump and look up to see the Crown Vic idling at the curb in front of me. He honks again, then again, and I hurry over and pull open the rear door.

"Drew?"

An older white guy wearing a Red Sox cap and reflective aviators looks back over his shoulder at me. "Yup. Sydney?"

I get in and he jerks into traffic, making me almost fall to my side before I can finish getting my seat belt on.

I snap it into place and shoot him a look in the rearview mirror, but he's staring resolutely ahead and his aviators reveal nothing. My annoyance starts to grow as I realize there was no damn reason for him to be honking like that when he arrived.

I look around the car's interior. It's old, with no decorative accents. Instead of the usual air freshener scent, it smells . . . antiseptic. The hairs on my arms rise. When I glance at him again, I notice how the hair at the back of his thick neck is cut—shaved close to the skin with brutal efficiency, like a crew cut.

"Man, things have changed around here," he says as we roll to a stop at a red light, pointing to a billboard for an upcoming luxury condominium. The ad features a white woman with sleeve tattoos relaxing in a luxurious bathtub, and the BVT Realty logo that can be seen on most new builds around here is stamped in the corner.

"Yeah," I say tersely, wishing I'd had time to put in my earphones.

"You don't like the change?" he asks.

"I grew up here. I don't like people getting pushed out of their homes by rising rent and property tax," I say, even though I should keep my mouth shut.

"Ohhh," he says as the light turns green and he starts driving again. "Were you one of the people who protested?"

"No."

He laughs. "Good. It didn't get them anywhere, did it?"

Everything about this conversation is making me regret my life choices, so I decide to bury myself in my phone. When I try to navigate away from the app screen my phone doesn't respond. I stare at the picture of the man in the driver photo—if it's my current driver, he's put on a lot of bulk since the picture was taken. There's a license plate on the screen, but I realize I didn't have time to check if it matched, since he'd hurried me into the car.

"The way I see it, it's just . . . Darwin," Drew says easily. "Survival of the fittest. You can't protest that shit."

The click of the doors locking echoes in the car as a punctuation to his statement and my hands reflexively curl into fists.

"Why did you lock the doors?" I ask.

"Those are the child safety locks, they kick in automatically after a while," he says.

I glance through the window, willing myself to calm down. This feels wrong, all wrong, but after we pass this corner we'll be just a few blocks away and it's a straightaway on a busy Brooklyn thoroughfare. I've been extra jumpy lately and I had an unprovoked panic attack over a beauty supply shop. I'm probably just being paranoid.

"You find something nefarious in everything," Marcus's voice echoes in my head. *"Then you wonder why I call you crazy."*

Drew suddenly whips a left onto a side street.

"What are you doing? The beauty shop is straight down this street."

"My GPS said there was an obstacle on Fulton, so I decided to take another route. Don't worry about it."

There's no damn GPS in this car. It has a radio with a cassette deck and his cell phone is facedown in the cubbyhole below it.

"Pull over," I demand in the steadiest voice I can manage.

"We're almost there," he says in a *calm down* tone. "But like I was saying, it's survival of the fittest. This part of Brooklyn has been riddled with crime for decades: drugs, shooting, theft. We don't have those problems where I live because we understand the order of things. We follow the law. Back when I was a cop, I hated patrolling this neighborhood."

"Pull. Over."

I search for the lock on the door next to me, but there's a hole where it should be sticking out. Sick fear pools in my stomach as I jiggle the handle, but Drew keeps talking.

"I always thought it would be a great place to live if there were just more . . . civilized people. Right?"

He makes a right and the car glides down a street with barely any traffic that's lined with garages, industrial buildings, and half-erected condos.

My phone's screen is still frozen and I try to force restart, but the app stubbornly resists.

We pass a couple who've stopped to kiss in the middle of the sidewalk and I bang on the window as we fly past them, but when I look back they're laughing and she's giving me the finger. They didn't see that I was trying to get help, not judging them for their PDA.

"Back in the day people didn't take romantic walks over here. It was a good place to chat with people who didn't understand civility, and *make* them understand." He laughs, as if he's reminiscing about something benign. "But I guess that's the stuff people call brutality these days. People who don't know what it takes to keep a community safe."

I'm digging in my purse for my keys. I'm gonna have to jab one into his neck on the right, and then reach past him on the left for the master lock. I am *not* dying in a motherfucking Uber, at the hands of a Sox fan no less.

I slide the keys between my knuckles and flex my fingers around them, my heart thumping and my hands tingling, preparing myself to strike, but then the car pulls to an abrupt stop and I jerk forward and then back.

My keys puncture the leather at the back of the driver's seat, leaving two small rips.

Drew looks back over his shoulder at me. "Location is a block over but this street is one-way. Hope you don't mind walking a little, Ms. Green."

The doors unlock and I push out of the car and jog off on wobbly legs, not bothering to close the door.

Up ahead, I see the flow of human traffic on Fulton Street and jog toward it. When I stumble out into the middle of the sidewalk, stopping short of one of the subway grates, people look at me funny but flow around me without saying anything.

I fumble with my phone, trying to take a screenshot of the frozen page with Drew's info, but when I look at the screen, it shows the message letting me know that Terrel canceled the ride.

Shit. *Shit.*

I look behind me and the street is empty.

Did I imagine that whole ride? No. I can't have. A wisp of seat stuffing is still clinging to my keys.

I think about Seattle, and Marcus looking at me quizzically

when I asked him about the texts I'd seen pop up on his phone and telling me he had no idea what I was talking about.

I shake my head and compose a text message to send to Drea.

Just had a wild ass Uber ride. I thought the motherfucker was gonna kill me. He knew my last name somehow?

I look at the last message Drea sent me, in the middle of the night when I'd texted to see if she was awake after my latest nightmare.

I know you're not feeling therapy after what happened in Seattle and everything else, but I can't be the only one carrying this with you. I love you, but I'm stressed, too.

I delete the message I was about to send her and pull myself together. Okay. The car ride was scary but I have no evidence and nothing happened in the end—I don't need to worry Drea, and it's not like I can get the police involved. I'll send a report to Uber and be more careful in the future.

I'm okay.

I'm not okay.

I call Mommy and feel a bit of relief go through me when her voicemail message plays. I don't hang up after the beep.

"Something scary just happened," I say as I begin to walk. "I was ready to use my keys how you taught me, though. He really had the wrong one. I'll—I'll see you soon, okay?"

I get to the shop and stand in front of the window covered

with glossy posters of Black women of all shades sporting different braided styles, and see myself reflected, phone pressed to my chest to still my racing heart, expression wild and unfamiliar.

Breathe, Sydney. Get it together.

A white couple walks past behind me as I take deep breaths while pretending to choose a style.

"Uh yeah, guess we're never going in here," the dude says as their reflections pass behind mine. "Can you imagine?"

"What are you talking about? Maybe I'll get some of those Kardashian braids," his girlfriend says. They laugh, and then their reflections are gone.

Survival of the fittest.

I go inside.

FOUR AND A half hours later, Sandrine, my hair braider, taps me on the shoulder for probably the fifteenth time and I jerk awake.

In the background, the low shouts of drama as a Real Housewife of Somewhere flips over a table on the television filter through the small, clean three-chair salon.

"Here." Her Malian accent softens the *r* in the word. She presses a cup of coffee from the nearby Dunkin' Donuts into my hand. "The mailman who always flirts picked it up for us. Yours is light and sweet with hazelnut flavor."

"Thank you." I lift the cup to my mouth to cover my yawn, then work at the plastic lid. "I'm sorry I keep falling asleep and making it harder for you."

I take a sip and let the impending sugar crash flood my taste buds. I'd vaguely mentioned not sleeping and having a bad experience with my driver when she'd noticed how shaken I was earlier. I'd fallen asleep because I was tired, but also because I had kind of shut down after the adrenaline rush.

She laughs softly as she separates some strands from the pack of brightly colored hair I picked up. "If you're so tired you can sleep through getting your scalp pulled, then you must need the rest. I'm almost done."

I raise my brows dubiously. "I'm not falling for that. You'll have me getting all excited to get out of this chair, then start splitting the same one-inch tuft of hair into fifty braids."

She sucks her teeth playfully, which doesn't ease the pain as her knuckles dig into my forehead as she starts to braid one bit along my hairline. I wince and send up a prayer to the god of edges that she doesn't fuck my shit up.

When my teeth are no longer gritted I say, "Thanks again for fitting me in."

"It's all good. But I have to give you my new number because next week I'm moving to a new shop."

I glance at her reflection in the mirror to gauge whether this is a good thing or a bad thing. Her fingers move with a rapid efficiency that's its own art form as she weaves the Kanekalon hair with my own, forming thick braids that ombré from black at the roots to teal at the tips. Her expression is tight and her lips are pouted out in a frown that isn't her usual expression of concentration.

"Is it the rent?" I ask, already knowing.

She nods. "Landlord suddenly wants us out. He's selling the

building, and the new owners don't want any tenants to deal with. I believe they'll knock it down and make one of those ugly condos."

"Doesn't he have to give you time?" I ask her.

"Probably. He told me if we had a problem with it, he could call ICE to do the job for him. I'm still waiting for my green card and I don't want any problems."

I pass my coffee cup from hand to hand. "I'm sorry, Sandrine."

"It's okay. I'm going to rent a chair at the barbershop around the corner. They have a little room for me to work in, so that will mean you don't have five dudes in your face watching you get styled." She tries to laugh, but it comes out more of a sigh. "How's your mother doing? Did you ever call my friend, the home health aide?"

I regret how much I used to share with Sandrine during the hours and hours I passed in her chair.

"We actually decided on an assisted living home," I say, the words heavy in my mouth. "It hurts, not seeing her every day, but it's what she wanted. I visit her as often as I can."

"You made the choice that was right for you both. Don't feel guilty."

I take in a shaky breath and dab at my eyes.

"Need a tissue?"

"No. You know I always tear up when you do my edges. I'm fine."

Sandrine is quiet after that, and there's nothing but the sound of rich people acting up for the reality TV cameras until the shop doorbell rings.

Sandrine pauses to look over her shoulder, sighs, then says, "Can you push the button?"

I press the unlock button on the underside of the counter in front of me and hear the jingling bells hanging from the door, followed by the scrape of flip-flops as someone shuffles into the room slowly without lifting their feet.

"Hey, Sandrine. And is that Ms. Green's daughter?"

I see why Sandrine sighed. "Hi, Denise."

Denise knows my name is Sydney. She just likes trying to start mess and has for years.

"Girl, you look like shit."

"Did you wash your hair this time, Denise?" Sandrine asks, in a tone that's much different from the one she uses to speak with me.

"My appointment is in half an hour, I'm going to wash it now," Denise snaps. "I popped in because—"

Sandrine sighs. "I'm almost finished with Sydney. How long do you think I will wait?"

Denise draws her head back to look down her nose at Sandrine. "You'll wait just like I have to wait for you every other time I come here."

I can't argue with that, even if she does get on my nerves.

They stare at each other for a long moment. Sandrine loses and goes back to focusing on my braid.

"Anyway, I *popped in before washing my hair because* the police swarmed up on Gifford Place a little bit ago."

My hands grip the edge of the seat.

"Is that what all those sirens were?" Sandrine asks casually. She doesn't live there. Only knows me and a couple of people who are her clients.

"Yup. They rolled up to Jamel and Ashley Jones's house and stormed in. Pulled up the floorboards in Preston's room. The boy was moving weight, apparently. Felony weight."

My stomach turns. "Preston Jones? That doesn't make sense."

I'm not gonna pretend I know anyone's secrets, but his family is solid, does all right for themselves, and he seems to have a very definite idea of how he wants his life to turn out.

I can't reconcile "moving felony weight" with the nerdy boy who regularly showed up at my door over the winter to see if I needed help shoveling, and who always has his face in his books. It isn't that he's "too smart" to sell drugs, but if he is involved in that, he's too smart to be holding an amount that would jeopardize his future or put his parents in danger.

Denise shrugs. "Not a bit of sense. And no one was in the room when they found the drugs, either. Don't change the fact that they arrested him a little while ago. He was crying like a baby. His mama is a mess."

Part of me wants to get up and swing on her, going around telling the Joneses' business to anyone who'll listen. But when I glance at her in the mirror and see the red flush under her light brown skin and her wide eyes darting back and forth, the urge fades away. What is the proper response to seeing a child arrested? *Another* child, the umpteenth child, when you've lived here long enough. And worse, arrested for something you can't be sure they actually did, even if they get found guilty?

Denise and Sandrine continue talking, but their conversation fades into the background as my breath starts to come fast and shallow.

The police came for *Preston.*

The knowledge that it can happen just like that, that they can show up and ruin your life, feels like an itch in the middle of my back that I can't reach.

Sandrine rests a hand on my shoulder, stilling me. When she speaks, her voice is gentle. "I'm almost done."

After what seems like eternity but is likely about twenty minutes, I'm out of the chair and marching back to Gifford Place.

When I get there, people are congregating in front of Mr. Perkins's house.

"Do we know where Preston is?" Gracie Todd asks in her crisp Masterpiece Theatre accent. She's pushing eighty and wearing a simple blouse and slacks, but with her elegant gray bob and fine bone structure, she looks like an aging Black starlet. "There's no more cash bail, right? I saw that on the morning news show. Shouldn't he be home soon?"

Mr. Perkins shakes his head. "They can still add bail for what they call major traffickers. And apparently whatever they found makes him a major trafficker, being held at major-trafficker bond amount."

Rumbles of anger and disbelief roll through the small crowd.

"Were they wearing body cams?" I ask.

Mr. Perkins sighs heavily and Count whines at his feet. "Apparently, they forgot to turn them on."

"Preston didn't mess with no drugs, John," Ms. Candace says, fury in her voice. "We all know that."

"Yes, we all know that. Maybe the police know that, too. Doesn't change a thing." Mr. Perkins's lips press together.

"How will they pay the bail?" I ask. "Can we raise money or something? GoFundMe?"

"When I left, they were on the phone with someone talking about the equity of their house."

"That's why 223 sold, you know," Gracie says. "The husband got caught up in some charges, assault or something, before the bail reform. He was exonerated eventually, but they had to sell the house to pay for all the legal fees."

Goose bumps rise on my forearms even though the midday sun is scorching and the humidity is strangling. I rub my palms over my arms as I worry my bottom lip. Something about this whole thing nags at me, but grief is running interference on my thought processes. Preston hasn't died, and people are already coming together to figure out what to do, but this very well could be the wake for the boy's future.

My chest hurts and my head is pounding from the tight braids and the sadness. Without saying anything, I step back from the crowd and head back to my apartment, wondering whether it's too early to have some wine.

The answer is no.

Gifford Place OurHood post by Josie Ulnar:
I am not going to post about this again. Not picking up your dog waste is a fineable offense. I've filed reports and the police say they will be patrolling the area to keep an eye out for offenders.

Candace Tompkins: We have bigger issues in the neighborhood right now, like young men being falsely arrested. Why don't you talk to your husband about this at home and keep it offline?

Josie Ulnar: I don't need to talk to him. I know Terry feels the same way.

Candace Tompkins: smh

Asia Martin: welp

(17 additional comments . . . see more)

CHAPTER 6

Theo

WHEN I WAKE UP IN THE EARLY AFTERNOON, I LIE IN BED ONLY slightly hungover but mostly wondering if the night before, after the meeting, was a weird dream. Kim, Terry, and Josie's paranoia, the attack outside the old hospital.

One thing I didn't dream was seeing Kim get into an Uber with an overnight bag. I should care where she went, but I really don't. A relationship on the rocks is one thing, but paranoia that Mr. Perkins and the rest of our neighbors are plotting against us is entirely another. I can't exactly use my mom's technique and run off to a new town with this house partly in my name, though, so for now I have to wait and hope that this is just some weird phase Kim is going through, like when she became obsessed with hot yoga.

When I look out the window, there's a cluster of people in front of Mr. Perkins's house. This isn't unusual, but their somber mood is. There aren't any kids playing on the street, though at this time they might be at day camps or doing whatever else it is kids do at home in the summer. I spent most summers watching TV and waiting for my mother to get home from work.

I slip on shorts and a shirt, grab the duffel I usually take with me on my night walks, and shove my shower stuff into it with a change of clothes after placing the flashlight and gloves under my bed. I bypass Kim's portion of the house without checking to see if she's inside.

Instead of participating in the shower of shame, I decide to walk over to the local YMCA, where the annual membership I bought when we first moved in has been languishing for months.

When I cross the street to say hey to the group of neighbors, which includes several older people I've seen around the block but haven't ever spoken to, the conversation goes quiet. Mr. Perkins gives me his usual hello, but his gaze isn't as bright as it usually is, and worry brackets his eyes.

I leave.

I spend an hour on the treadmill, watching the various people in the gym: young kids heading to the pool for lessons, middle-aged guys lifting weights with friends, a group of older women heading into a fitness class. The guy on the treadmill next to me forgets his iPhone X, and jogs back to grab it right as my treadmill cooldown finishes.

I have to wear flip-flops when I head into the shower, but I also don't feel as if the pounding spray is reminding me what a loser I am. If I needed a reason to start hitting the gym daily again, I guess I've found it.

Or maybe you're trying to lose the dad bod for a certain neighbor.

I ignore inconvenient thoughts of Sydney while showering in public, then towel off and head to my locker. The elastic of my boxers has just snapped around my waist when I whip my head to the right, my body reacting to some disturbance in the force before my mind does. There's a guy sitting farther down on the bench where I've laid out my clothes, looking up at me with a goofy grin—he has trendily messy hair and thick stubble that makes me itchy just looking at it.

I look away from him and grab my gray sweatpants.

"Hey, bro," he says. "You live on Gifford, right?"

I glance at him out of the corner of my eye and realize I've seen this big head and square jaw before. "Yeah. You worked at the real estate place, right?"

"Right." His smile grows wider. "I was just office staff back then. Made copies of your papers and stuff while you were closing on the house. Full-fledged agent with all the benefits now, though."

I slip on my T-shirt, partly to mask what is probably a look of pure WTF on my face. That was one of the things Kim had liked about me at first that had later grown to annoy her when we went to her fancy work parties. *"Can't you even pretend to be interested? You're so bad at faking! Like, god, have you ever even won a poker game?"*

I'd turned my face away from hers without answering, and she'd assigned her own personal meaning to that, as people generally do. Who needs pretending when people do your work for you?

"Um, good for you," I say to my weird locker room buddy who's making me reassess my newfound fitness goals. "Congrats."

"You like your job, man?" he asks.

"I like it well enough," I lie.

"If you're looking for something on the side, I can get you in at my agency. We have the lockdown on this neighborhood, and with VerenTech moving in? It's gonna change everything." He mimics an explosion with a loud *kaboosh.* "You ever see pictures of an atomic bomb drop? Not the mushroom cloud, but that energy rippling out, completely changing the landscape? That's what VerenTech's about to do here."

"You know that isn't a good thing, right?"

He chuckles. "Depends on who you ask. Get in now if you want that good money, bro. I can hook you up."

He hands me a card, which I take with pinched thumb and forefinger because he's sitting here in tightie-whities and I don't know where he pulled it from.

The card has a weird font that's supposed to be trendy but just makes it hard to read: *William Bilford, Real Estate Master, BVT Realty.*

"Yeah. Thanks. I appreciate it."

A couple of Black dudes walk in from their shower and William Bilford turns back to putting on his clothes, winking at me as he does. I guess this is what happens when you stop skulking in your room or walking the streets when no one is around—you run into some really weird people.

I tuck the card into the pocket on the side of my gym bag, then make my way back toward Gifford Place, walking slow and taking everything in. It's slightly less humid than when I went in—the telltale puddles show it rained sometime during my workout, and there's a light breeze coming down the street, cool on my wet scalp. The sounds of this larger street amplify whatever feel-good hormones the treadmill has pumped into me: the squeal of a bus's brakes as it screeches to a halt down the street, the flap of a pigeon's wings as it takes off after stealing a bread crust from a small brown bird, the roll of tires on wet asphalt.

I almost stop walking as it really hits me: I'm in a good mood. Despite the weird night I had and the fact that my maybe-ex-girlfriend/co-homeowner is clearly stepping out on me. The basic facts of my life haven't changed, and even if I don't feel like shit, I'm still a piece of it, but I don't really care about that right now. Because—

I spot Sydney through a gap in the foliage that clings to the chain-link fence in front of the community garden that I've passed countless times. I'd checked out its value, wondering how it still existed in an area where houses would soon be on the market for a million-plus, but now I really see all the bright beauty of it. Sydney is on her hands and knees, her hair styled in long, thin teal-tipped braids cinched in a twist atop her head and her ass encased, barely, in denim shorts.

I should keep walking, but I turn into the open gate of the garden. Instead of approaching Sydney directly, I take a little turn around the place, checking out the various plots and what people are growing. Lots of tomatoes and leafy greens. A half-built henhouse. Flowers galore, and rows of cuttings waiting to be planted. I'm not super interested in plants, but it feels weird to walk up on her from behind. Now, as I make my way around a plot that seems to be growing some kind of frizzy lettuce, she glances up at me.

I thought gardening was supposed to be a relaxing hobby, but her mouth is turned down in a grimace so pronounced that it's almost comical. Her gaze is hard, underscored by dark circles beneath her brown eyes, and it doesn't soften when she sees me. She takes a deep breath and stands, revealing that her shorts are the overalls she was wearing at the corner store, with both straps buttoned over a black T-shirt. She strips gloves from her hands and throws them onto the ground next to the box she's been working in.

"Your hair is different," I say.

"Is it?" she asks, then pats at her head and makes an expression of smug shock. "Wow, I didn't notice. I guess it just did that by itself. Magic!"

She smirks at me.

Oh boy.

"Did a rabbit steal your carrots or something?" I walk a couple of steps closer to her. "You have a real Farmer McGregor vibe going right now."

She rolls her eyes, but the hardness softens a bit in the millisecond it takes her to do it.

"We have raccoons here, not rabbits. And they have nothing to steal from my garden because I'm killing everything edible."

There's strain in her voice in that last sentence, even though she tries to play it off as a joke.

"That sucks. Is it the weather or just a bad season? Those happen sometimes."

I have no idea what happens sometimes in gardens, but that sounds about right.

She shakes her head and bends down to grab one of those travel coffee mugs—from the clink of ice cubes I'm guessing there's iced coffee inside.

"I'm not my mom. That's the problem." She sips almost angrily. "She started this garden when I was a teenager. I was so mad when I had to waste weekends toting trash and helping set up plant boxes while my friends were outside the gates riding bikes, or off at the beach or doing other fun shit. But now . . . well, she's not here to take care of things now. So I have to do it. And I'm the worst."

Her mom owns a prime piece of land plus that fantastic house? I try not to be envious of what that kind of security must feel like.

"I would offer my gardening services in addition to my research services, but I'm not really good at stuff like this." I glance at the plot where she's been working. It does look a little less vibrant than the others, but it's not a total loss. "That seems to be growing well, whatever it is."

"It's a weed," she says miserably, then laughs a little helplessly. I recognize this laugh, the one you make when you feel like you're just caught up in life's gears, slowly getting ground to dust.

My envy retreats. Mostly.

"Some weeds are edible. Dandelions? You can make salad with that."

"Are you some kind of prepper or something?" she asks.

"No. Just something I picked up as a kid. I was briefly fascinated with things you could eat for free."

Great. I guess that's one way to reveal you grew up poor and hungry.

"Look," she says on a sigh. "You don't have to do this research thing, you know. I got it. It was nice of you to offer, but—"

"Are you firing me?" I place both hands over my chest. "Wow, kick me when I'm down."

"You haven't started yet," she reminds me. "A lot of this week's research is focusing on . . . shit that's going to make you uncomfortable. For example. All this land originally belonged to indigenous tribes, right?"

"And then they sold it," I say automatically. I know this history. "For some beads."

"Not really. Land sale didn't work the same for them. Mostly colonizers took what they wanted. And that's what keeps coming up as I research." She bites her bottom lip, releases it. Sighs. "I don't wanna have to worry about your little white feelings, okay?"

"Wait. Do you think I'm racist or something?" My body tenses and my cheeks go hot, and Sydney throws a hand up in the air.

"See? This is what I'm talking about. It doesn't matter if I think you are—even if you aren't, you're gonna need me to reassure you about it. Like, Preston got arrested this morning. I don't have the energy to make you feel better."

"Okay. Okay, I get that." I *don't* get the connection between a teenager getting arrested and me helping her, but I can deal with that later. I look at her, try to figure out her mood. I smile. "I still want to help. I'll try to keep my white feelings, which aren't little, in check."

She purses her lips, and I can tell she's trying not to laugh. "Fine. Whatever. But we need a safe word."

"Do we?"

She looks at me sharply.

"A safe word for when you're being dangerously white," she clarifies.

I grimace, but say the first thing that pops into my head. "Hmm . . . how about 'Howdy Doody'?"

Her laughter comes out in a peal that makes her face scrunch up and her eyes close tight. I don't even care if she's laughing at me. It sounds so much better than the being-ground-by-gears sound, and I want to make her laugh like that again.

"Perfect," she says. "I was gonna go with 'mayonnaise,' but let's be real, Miracle Whip really hits sometimes. 'Howdy Doody' it is."

The sounds of squealing children interrupt us and then she shrugs and points at the group of young kids streaming in through the gate, followed by Len, who waves at us. "Day camp kids, here for a visit. Can you come to my place at like five o'clock? We can go over what I have so far."

"Your place?" I feel like I just stepped off the treadmill all over again.

She tilts her head. "Yeah. Directly across the street from you?"

"Sounds good. See you then."

I head back to the house I live in, I guess what most people would call home. Kim isn't there, but I wave at the new camera as I go inside. My phone vibrates in my bag, and when I pull it out it's Kim.

Make sure you lock the front door. You didn't when you left last night. I know you think these people are harmless,

but Josie's friend a few blocks over said someone tried her doorknob a couple of days ago, and her tenant left his window open and had his photography bag stolen right off of his windowsill.

I sigh and turn off the phone.

Gifford Place OurHood post by Kaneisha Bell:
The video graphic with this article on gentrification is alarming. Look at the way the brown dots disappear and get replaced with pink dots in historically Black and POC neighborhoods. Harlem, Jackson Heights, Bed-Stuy.

Fitzroy Sweeney: Frightening!

Kim DeVries: Gentrification literally means an area that was once in disrepair being improved upon. Why does it matter whether pink or brown dots are doing the improving?

Jenn Lithwick: Hey, Kim, there're a lot of studies about the harmful effects of gentrification on neighborhoods like ours. Jen and I read a lot about it before buying here, and we have links if you want.

Kim DeVries: I don't need to study sociology to be a good neighbor. And if I posted an article saying all the brown dots are bad for the neighborhood, I bet that would go over well!

(30 additional comments . . . see more)

CHAPTER 7

Sydney

THE PAPERS MR. PERKINS GAVE ME ARE SPREAD OUT OVER THE kitchen table's scratched and scuffed surface. I'm casually leafing through them like Theo isn't sitting there, waiting for me to explain the project.

This all feels a little childish now. Mommy always treated me like I was so smart I could be anything. Could do anything. Instead, I'm a thirty-year-old divorcée working an admin job I hate and wasting time on a bootleg history tour sparked by pettiness.

"So, whaddaya got?" Theo finally asks. I glance up, try to act like I hadn't zoned out.

"Sorry."

He shrugs, though his gaze is probing.

"Are you going to talk about the history of the houses at all, like on the brownstone tour?" he prods. "Or are you going to talk about people who live here now, like you did?"

"A little of both." I tug a printout from the pile of papers and hand it over. At the top is an image showing an aerial view of Gifford Place from Google Earth—our street looks mostly the same for now, though the area around us is missing all the new condos and storefronts. There are numbers written in five colors of Sharpie labeling several houses. Beneath the photo is a key, giving a brief explanation for each color and number.

"These are the 'stops' I have so far," I say. "The green outnumbers everything because they're the easiest—it's what I did before, talking about some of the interesting neighbors we have *now*, instead of only the white people who lived here a hundred years ago.

"I went to the Brooklyn library and found specific information on some of the white people who lived in the houses, and if they had anything to do with Black Brooklyn, good or bad." I tap a pink number on the Jens' house. "An abolitionist lived here in the old days. Things got so heated that they had to move, because a mob of angry men showed up and tried to kill him and his family."

"Whoa," Theo says. "Here in New York? In Brooklyn?"

"Yup. Here in Brooklyn."

"Okay," he says. "So . . . what happened to the white people? Are you gonna talk about that? I've been wondering about that since the tour, actually. The tour guide talked about all these wealthy white families, but eventually the neighborhood became . . ."

"Black?" I fill in.

"Poor," he corrects me. "I mean, everyone wasn't poor. But whenever I used to hear about Brooklyn it was people warning me not to come here because it was dangerous and—"

"Black?" I cut in again, and this time he runs a hand through his hair.

"Well, they didn't say *Black*." He shifts in his seat. "I mean, it's rude to just say it. But that's what they meant, I guess."

"Rude. Rude?" I lean forward a little as something dawns on

me. "Oh. Oh shit! Is that why you guys always whisper it? Like, 'My friend is dating a—'" I look around furtively and then lean closer to Theo and whisper, "'*Black* guy'?"

He shrugs, embarrassed amusement dancing in his eyes. "You aren't supposed to point out stuff like that. That's what my mom told me, at least."

I bust out laughing, imagining white people chastising their kids for literally describing a person's race. I guess if you think being Black is an unfortunate affliction, of course it would seem rude. I could push and ask why so many of them are eager to say the n-word if *Black* makes them squirm, but I'm not trying to have to ring the Howdy Doody alarm while alone in my apartment with him.

"Okay, to answer your question. My tour is about Black Brooklyn, but I do go into why the *white people*," I whisper the last two words and he laughs, "left. In more recent times, it was white flight to the suburbs. But back in the day, there was the Panic of 1837. Basically, the bottom fell out of the slave and cotton market, and then all the rich people had to sell their land to recoup their losses."

"Why would slavery affect people in Brooklyn?" he asks. I can't even hate because I only learned this shit recently myself.

"Slavery ended in New York ten years before the panic, but not completely. And New York was the banking capital of the U.S. Slavery was a business. Cotton was a business. Rum was a business. Sugar was a business. Banks handle money for businesses. So . . . boom. That's why."

He has the nerve to smile.

"What's funny?" I ask, straightening in my seat.

"I think your tour is going to do well. I never learned any of that, anywhere. And now I know, and I want to know more. And anyone who comes on your tour will know and want to know more. That's pretty amazing."

"Oh." I get a warm feeling in my stomach. Honestly, so much of this project has been fueled by pettiness and escapism, by a need to reclaim what should have been mine, that I'd forgotten there's a joyful side to sharing knowledge, too.

"Thanks." I clear my throat and then tap the printout. "Anyway, pink text represents Black Brooklyn history topics. The purple numbers and text are things specific to Gifford Place. There's stuff I got from my mother, and my own memory, but I want to talk to some older people in the neighborhood. And Gifford Place used to be part of a historic Black community that sprang up after the panic, so I need to look into that too. There's a heritage center not far away I've been meaning to visit."

He nods, and I wonder if he's judging me for not having done all this sooner. I thought I'd already done so much research, but it feels like there is so much to do in just a week if I don't want to embarrass myself.

"Want to go tomorrow?" he says. "To the heritage center?"

I raise my brow. "Did you forget you're the assistant and not the boss?"

He grins. "Sorry. I'm just excited now. You only have yourself to blame."

This flirtatious motherfucker. I narrow my eyes at him. "We're going to the Weeksville heritage center tomorrow. Bring your camera. If you want something to do in the meantime, look into the Dutch West India Company. They were the ones who funded the Dutch coming here, and played a big part in the formation of Brooklyn, but I haven't done a deep dive on them yet. If you find anything relevant to the tour let me know." He nods again, his eyes scanning over the paper I handed him.

"I'll email this to you, too, if you write your email address down," I add. I'm kind of enjoying this tiny bit of authority—it's been so long since anyone listened to me without giving me any shit for one thing or another. "You can take these papers and see what else you come up with. I just want to make it interesting for people."

I lean back in my chair as he jots down his email. My face is still kind of warm despite the fact that by next week Theo will go back to being a neighbor I occasionally peep through his window—except maybe not even that, because I'll probably recommend he get some blinds.

"I doubt you'll have trouble with that," he says as he slides over the paper. His phone number is on there, too, even though I didn't ask for it, and it's underlined. "You're interesting even when you're not being all passionate about history."

He smiles at me in that curious way again.

Nope.

"Okay, we're all set here," I say, hopping up from my seat and walking toward the apartment door.

"Yeah, cool. Cool." He gathers the papers up, but when I pull the door open, he stops at the threshold and looks down at me. "I appreciate you letting me help with this. If you need anything else, just text me."

I don't think he's flirting this time, but he's staring at me like I'm fascinating, and I don't have time for the way my body responds to that.

"I'm not trying to air-condition the hallway," I say, ushering him out.

A flush spreads over his cheeks so quickly that it's almost startling, but he steps out into the humid hallway and doesn't stop until he's outside. He jogs down the stairs, then turns to wave and trips over a raised corner of slate sidewalk and it's cute.

I look away so I don't watch him head into his house. Somewhere nearby a jackhammer is breaking up solid ground, and the whine of construction machinery floats through the air. A Black woman with high cheekbones and a brown-skinned Asian woman walk down the street, chatting in accented English; each pushes a stroller with a white child tucked inside. They nod at me in greeting, and Toby starts up his barking as they pass by.

As I close the door, I hear the phone ringing upstairs. All the way upstairs. In Mommy's apartment.

It could be a telemarketer—every time I bother to answer, it's someone warning about auto insurance default for a car I don't own or trying to scam me with questions about tax evasion.

Those threats are nothing compared to the call I'm dreading, and I can't keep avoiding said calls because that could lead to worse consequences. I bolt up the stairs, pull the key from my pocket as I round the banister, and fumble the door open.

"Hello?"

I pray for the automated click of a recording trying to sell me something or scam me, but a man's voice says, "Hello, is this Yolanda Green?"

A lifetime of lying to bill collectors enables me to lie smoothly and without hesitation. "She's out right now. May I take a message?"

"She gets out a lot for a woman in her condition," the man says.

"Can I take a message?" I repeat, putting a little steel in my tone. These weasels had found her number at the hospital, trying to find out her condition. Getting her into the retirement home had felt like a spy mission, even if it had gone to shit in the end.

"No message. I'll call back at a better time. Which would be . . . ?"

"Actually, I have your number here, I'll have her call you back. Does that work?"

He chuckles. "Sure."

With that I hang up and walk out of the apartment, feeling like I'm wobbling on stilts, my head spinning like it's in the clouds. My heart is still hammering from my dash up to the apartment, and I sit down in the middle of the staircase and drop my forehead to my knees, forcing myself to breathe deeply. The air is humid and thick in the stairwell, and my nose itches from dust because I haven't swept up here in a while, but I don't get up.

I can do this. I'm my mother's daughter. I can do this.

I pull my phone out of my pocket and text Drea.

Are you busy? I'm sorry to bother you every time but they called again.

I'm at work. We can talk about this later.

Okay. <3

I put the phone down and just breathe. I start to nod off a bit, the heat and the soul-deep fatigue threatening to pull me under. I feel too heavy, and the thought of carrying this body all the way down to my apartment is overwhelming.

My eyes are drifting closed when Toby starts barking next door. I try to ignore him like I usually do, since he barks at damn near everything, but his bark is so insistent and almost desperate that I drag myself to my feet. This isn't how he sounds when demanding a walk or barking at whoever walks by outside. I stumble down the stairs, still in a pre-nap fog, cursing Josie and Terry for not putting him into the new doggie day care that they can certainly afford.

When I get to the main landing, the front door of the house is wide open, and I freeze on the bottom step. Hadn't I closed it after Theo left? I was in a rush and I haven't been super sharp lately, but closing and locking the door is instinct for me. Second nature.

Mommy drilled that shit into me, especially because I'd sometimes be home alone during the time between when I left school and she got home from work. It was muscle memory now.

I peer over the banister into the hallway, which is dark even in midday because Drea always turns off the light as she heads out to work, another habit instilled by my mother.

Toby is still barking wildly, but I stand on the bottom step like a kid afraid to hang their foot over the side of the bed because they expect a monster to pull them down into the darkness. I don't see anything, but fear gathers at the nape of my neck as I stare because I feel like someone, or something, is looking back.

I think of Drew the Uber driver's calm as he ignored my demands that he stop. How he knew my last name and there was no trace of him on my phone, and I haven't even told anyone what happened.

The shadows near the door shift and my heart slams in my chest. Someone is there.

"Sydney?"

I jump, and damn near piss myself, but the voice is coming from outside. Ms. Candace, gripping her cane and peering in.

"You okay?"

I nod, even though tremors of fear are running through my body, a light thrum against my constant tension.

"I was like, 'Did this child forget to lock the door?' and instead you just standing there looking like you saw the boogeyman." She laughs.

I step firmly down onto the hardwood floor, forcing myself not to look behind me into the dark end of the hallway. It's only a few wobbly steps to the doorway, and then I flip on the hall light.

There's nothing there but the heavy wooden apartment door, closed tightly. Did I close it before walking Theo to the door? Yes. The air conditioner is on. Of course I did.

"Girl, you need a nap. You always did turn into a bobble-headed little thing when you was tired, and I see that's still the case."

I shake my head and step out onto the stoop, where it's slightly more humid than the hallway and about fifteen degrees hotter. "I'm fine."

"Here, take this," she says, reaching into the plastic bag hanging from her arm to hand me a round aluminum container with a plastic lid. As I reach for it, the smell of plátanos and rice and beans from the Dominican spot on the corner makes my mouth water. I try to remember the last thing I ate and come up blank.

"No, that's o—"

"Take. It," she says firmly. "I have enough here to feed ten people instead of two, anyway. Gonna take some over to Ashley and Jamel, too. We're all we got."

The reminder of my neighbors, who are dealing with every Black parent's worst nightmare, puts my own problems in perspective. I can't just fall back into the hole of self-pity.

"You're right. Thanks." I blink and inhale deeply. "Are you doing okay?"

She shrugs. "I'm old, my body hurts, but my brain is sharp as ever, even though *some* people wish that was otherwise."

My fingers press into the sides of the aluminum container. "Who?"

She sucks her teeth. "These fools playing on my phone, trying to trick me into selling my house like I didn't spend thirty years processing loans at Apple Bank and wasn't blessed with two helpings of good sense."

Some of the sauce from the beans dribbles out onto my fingers and I loosen my grip. "The real estate people?"

She nods. "Been coming to my door, too. Telling me all kinds of bullshit, thinking if they talk fast I'll go along with it." She sucks her teeth again, holding it for longer this time to show the true depth of her disdain. "My hair is gray, but my gray *matter* is still functional, thank you very much."

"It's terrible," I say woodenly. "But they can't get anything over on you."

"Not today, not tomorrow, not in this lifetime, baby," she says with a laugh. "Let me get going. I'll see you later. Make sure you get that tour ready."

She says it the same way she used to say, "Make sure you do your homework" when I was a kid, except when I go into the kitchen to do my work now, there won't be a bologna sandwich and a cup of SunnyD waiting for me.

"Yes, Ms. Candace," I reply. I linger a bit, take a deep breath, then head back into the apartment, checking every possible hiding place before grabbing a fork, pushing a stack of papers aside, and making myself eat.

Gifford Place OurHood post by Jamel Jones:

Thank you everyone who has stopped by, called, prayed, or sent a message. Ashley and I are hanging in there, but we talked to Preston on the phone and he's not doing too great. We're figuring out financial stuff, and we're treading water for now, but as much as I hate this, I have to ask if anyone has worked with BVT. We have some questions. When it comes to our son, we're willing to do anything.

Josie Ulnar: I highly recommend them.

Kim DeVries: Same. They're extremely professional.

Jamel Jones: Thank you both. I am looking for people in the neighborhood who've used them to sell a property quickly or have heard from any of our neighbors who sold.

(0 additional comments)

CHAPTER 8

Sydney

"WHY ARE YOU DRESSED UP?" DREA ASKS, GIVING ME ELEVAtor eyes as I stand up from beside my mother's garden plot.

I'm sweaty, my tomato vine has withered, and I'm so tired that my mind is playing tricks on me. I'm *not* in the mood to be judged for my damn outfit.

I point my trowel at her, and she dodges the clump of fertilizer that flies in her direction.

"I'm wearing a T-shirt from our junior year of high school, cutoff shorts, and I have horse crap under my nails from trying to save this tomato plant," I say with an annoyed shake of my head. "I am *not* dressed up."

Drea looks me up and down again. "Yes, an old T-shirt and shorts, but this T-shirt is the one that makes your titties look fantastic and those Daisy Dukes are the ones that show just the perfect sliver of ass cheek. You really think you can fool me?"

"Whatever." I change the subject and hope she gets the point. "Did you get the VerenTech info from work bae?"

I probably don't need it, but the way Theo had looked at me yesterday is going to my head a little. I start thinking about how I should include some of this new stuff, too, even if it isn't history;

it's important, and now that the project has been approved, it will lead to big changes. It wouldn't hurt to take a look.

She sucks her teeth. "Yes. I got you. I slipped the envelope under your door before I left today."

"Thank you. I love youuu," I croon into the trowel.

"Damn right you do." Her eyes crease at the corners when she smiles at me, which makes me smile even more widely. "I didn't look at the files, but he said VerenTech got some kind of special dispensation from the city. Same one BVT Realty gets and probably got it the same way—paying off these commissioners so they look the other way as they're stamping contracts. Meanwhile I can't even get a business loan."

"You got rejected again?" I ask. "Maybe you can do a GoFundMe, or . . ."

"Don't worry about it," she says. "Here comes your little friend." She squints and tilts her chin at something over my shoulder. When I turn, I see Theo approaching.

His hair is damp and messy and his stride is confident; he has a coffee cup in each hand. A camera hangs from a strap around his neck, bouncing over a black T-shirt emblazoned with three bold words in white: BLACK LIVES MATTER.

"Good morning," he says, holding out one of the brown cardboard cups toward me.

I snatch it, then gesture at his shirt with my other hand. "Howdy Doody! Howdy Doody!"

He plucks at the shirt. "Really? This is Howdy Doody?"

Drea looks back and forth between us, hand over her chest as she laughs. "What is happening right now?"

I narrow my eyes at Theo. "Why are you wearing this?"

He blinks a few times. "I saw the posts about Preston on OurHood. I wanted to let people know that I support—"

"Can you change out of that? Please." I run my hands over my braids, gently because my scalp is still tender. "I don't want to be known as the woman walking around with the white dude with a BLM shirt on, okay?"

I expect him to push back, but those harsh features of his kind of droop all at once, like a dog that's being yelled at but doesn't know why.

"I appreciate the sentiment," I add.

He nods stiffly, places his coffee down on the chair next to me, then the camera, and yanks his shirt up. It's nothing I haven't seen a dozen times through his window, but it hits a little different now that he's right in front of me. My neck and chest go hot in a flash and I look away.

I should just start building my cabin alongside Fuckboy Creek because obviously it's where I intend to spend the rest of my days.

"Sydney, was this all a devious plan to get him to take his shirt off?" Drea whispers, and now it's Theo who's getting her elevator-eye treatment. "Well played, well played."

"Dre." I give her a *if you don't cut it out* look, but she's busy pretending to run her hand over Theo's chest hair while the shirt is up over his head. She jerks her hand back when his head pops out of the shirt's neck.

He turns the shirt inside out and pulls it back on. "I'm just gonna hide this important social justice message that seems to be embarrassing Sydney."

His tone is a little . . . persnickety.

"Was I supposed to *thank you*? Appreciate it and give you a cookie or two?"

He looks down at me, his face flushed from embarrassment and his gaze wounded as he tugs the shirt down around his waist. "I know you don't *need* my help, but do you want it? I thought you were just giving me shit for fun, but if you seriously don't want me around, let me know now."

"You know, that's very thoughtful of you to ask, Brad," Drea says in a surprisingly friendly tone, grabbing my coffee and taking a sip, then returning the cup to my hand. "Sydney does need the help. She's not a super detail-oriented person."

"My details for the tour are oriented, thank you very much," I say as I turn to glare at her, but she has her phone out and isn't paying me a bit of mind.

I take a deep breath, lowering my hackles and trying not to be the person Marcus always told me I was. "You got a date lined up or something?"

"Line up in progress. There's this cutie working at the new Jamaican-Mexican fusion restaurant and he slipped me his phone number with my beef patty taco. Might as well make the most of the changes gentrification has wrought, right?"

She wiggles her brows, glances at Theo, and then blows me a kiss as she walks off, navigating around raised garden beds while her eyes seem to be glued to her screen. After I put my tools away and wash my hands, Theo and I head for the heritage center, marinating in the full-on August heat and humidity, and the awkwardness shared by a person who's committed a faux pas and the person who corrected them.

He slows as we pass the medical center, looking up at the huge sign on the fence with a 3-D rendering of what the VerenTech campus will look like. "What do you think of the VerenTech deal? I used to pass the people protesting, and talked to a few of them, but I didn't really get why people wouldn't want it in our neighborhood when other states were dying to have VerenTech choose them."

I bristle at his use of *our* but don't snap at him.

"Well, a big part of it is how people addicted to crack were treated back in the day." I sniff and start walking. "People acted like *those* addicts were soulless zombies, or jokes, or problems to lock away and take their babies from. Now white people get hooked on something, and we're building fancy new facilities to research how to fix things."

He has the nerve to give me *a look*. "Do you think Black people are immune to opioids? I've seen all kinds of people hooked on them. I mean, the other night, in this very spot a guy who was high out of his mind—"

I roll my eyes. "Yeah, some drugged-up Black dude from Gifford Place is exactly who's making the cover of magazines and news reports when people discuss the opioid problem."

"The alternative is not helping anyone, then?" he asks.

"The alternative is not dropping the research center and the adjoining headquarters of a major corporation dead in the middle of a community that still gets overpoliced based on War on Drugs bullshit. It's gonna be like seeing a middle finger every day for some people. Oh wait, it won't be, because none of us will be able to afford living here by the time it's done."

He doesn't say anything for once and we keep walking.

"It used to be an asylum, you know," I say eventually, feeling guilty for snapping. "Before it became a hospital. People always used to say the place was haunted. Like, bad haunted. Ghosts-tryin'-to-kill-you haunted. Supposedly, that's the real reason for all the malpractice lawsuits they got."

Theo flashes me a grin—he's not mad at me. Good.

"I'm sure the doctors backed that theory."

"Yup. And when I was a kid, there was a rumor that if you stayed out too late, the men in the white coats would get you and you'd never be heard from again."

Theo looks up at the building, old and with dead vines clinging to the sides of it but still imposing. He rubs at his arms.

"Creepy. Was that like the clown-van-kidnappers urban legend?"

"The what?" I cut my eyes at him.

"When I was growing up, they used to say clowns drove around in a white van and tried to lure kids in. I heard it in, like, six different states. There has to be some truth to it."

I laugh and shake my head. "That is *the* worst kidnapping plot I've ever heard. Dress like something that will send kids running and screaming from you and try to lure them into your clown *van*? Not even clown car for consistency? Come on now."

"Well, it makes as much sense as kids getting kidnapped by hospital ghosts." His lips are all tooted up like I didn't respect his clown story enough.

"Well. At least one person who had a relative killed by the Tuskegee experiment lives on our street. It's not that hard to figure out where the fear of hospital kidnappers might come from."

"Yeah."

Awkward silence descends upon us again and I sip my coffee, trying to figure out why I keep dunking on him like this. I want to have a conversation, but I'm annoyed at literally everything this perfectly nice and normal man is saying.

Marcus's voice pops into my head. *"You're just too difficult. Why would anyone put up with it?"*

"So," Theo says. "What do you do for work?"

"I work at an elementary school." There. I was able to respond without snapping, finally.

"A teacher? I should have known."

"Why?" I ask.

"Because you like sharing knowledge and you enjoy disciplining people," he says.

"No I don't. I'm actually very nice to most people."

"Okay. Then you just like disciplining me. Even better." He grins, then keeps it pushing before I can object. "Also explains why you haven't been working for the last couple of months. I thought maybe you'd gotten laid off, too."

I glance at him out of the corner of my eye. How did he know I haven't been working? Though I've been all up in his window like it was prime reality TV, so I have no right to be weirded out.

"I work in a school office. Admin stuff. My mom knows a lot of people there, and she got me a job after I moved back here."

What am I gonna say next week when school starts? I wonder. *What am I gonna say when I get back and people start asking harder questions than "How's she doing?"*

"Your mom?"

When I sip my coffee and fall back into silence, he quickly gets the point.

"Why'd you move back?" His choice of subject startles me—I didn't even realize I'd told him that but, yeah, I did. He's maybe a little too observant for his own good. Or for mine.

I stop and lean back to look down my nose at him. "Why are you all in my business?"

He brushes some of the sweaty hair sticking to his forehead away.

"Because I'm curious about you. Breakup?" He bites his lower lip, studying me, then nods once. "Breakup."

"I look like the dumpable type or something?" I turn and start walking faster, like I can escape the shame of his accurate guess. The reminder of what I'd put up with and how I hadn't even been the one to put an end to it.

He catches up to me in a couple of long strides. "You don't look dumpable, whatever that means. You have the eyes of someone who's been treated worse than they should've been, that's all."

Okay, yes. He's way too observant.

"It was a divorce," I say.

"Divorce isn't the end of the world, you know. I'm not judging you. In fact—"

"Drop it, Theo."

"Dropped."

I look down at the cracked sidewalk, up at the bottom of the LIRR tracks on the bridge that runs along Atlantic Avenue, at the short squat houses, and postwar tenements, and brown-brick projects with inspirational murals curling along their foundations.

Anywhere but at this man who apparently can tell I'm hurting with a look into my eyes. I'm not into that shit and I forgot to bring sunglasses.

He starts talking about painting a mural at one of his high schools, even though he's a terrible artist. How he'd been in charge of painting a wolverine, the school's mascot, and how it'd come out looking like a zombie cat creature. I nod my response, and he segues into a story about how he once lived in a town with a coyote problem. He's not trying to force interaction, I realize; he's giving me background noise so I don't have to talk if I don't feel like it.

By the time we reach the center, an incongruous glass-and-metal structure, we're both soaked in sweat. Theo's breathing a little heavy and the one-sided conversation has tapered off; we make a mutual sound of pleasure as we enter the air-conditioned welcome area, then laugh.

I glance at him, and he's looking at me like he always does, with that wide-eyed interest. No pity. No scheming to use my obvious loneliness against me.

I tilt my head to the reception desk and then walk toward the woman sitting at it, while Theo heads over to the huge glass windows lining the other side of the lobby, looking out at an open field.

"Hi, how can I help you?" the young woman at the desk says just as Theo calls out, "There are tiny houses out there!"

The woman grins in response to his excitement, her smile scrunching up the freckles on her light brown cheeks. "Those houses have been here since the 1820s. They were regular-sized back then. We give tours of them, but our tour guide is on summer break so those restart next week."

I wilt a little with disappointment. This is what I get for putting things off for months instead of walking a few blocks to do my research. "Oh. That's . . . fine."

"Sorry." She actually looks like she means it. "You can explore outside around the houses if you want. And our exhibits are open if you want to check those out. We have three pretty great ones right now."

"That works for me," Theo says, walking over with a wad of cash. "I'll pay the entry fee. And how much are those T-shirts?"

HALF AN HOUR later Theo is decked out in an olive-green T-shirt with the old houses screen-printed onto it in black, courtesy of the gift shop. We've gone through the exhibitions, which actually were useful.

The first exhibition room we entered was an overview of how Weeksville had been founded—by Black men buying property during the Panic of 1837 so that they could be afforded the right to vote. It also talked about laws that hampered the Black community in Brooklyn, like an eighteenth-century law preventing

Black people who managed to buy property from passing it on to their descendants.

I'd taken pictures of useful stuff, like a map of the old neighborhood and information about some of the historical figures who had been part of it.

The next exhibition was an overview of historic race riots in New York, starting with the slave uprisings of 1712. Apparently, fires kept breaking out in Manhattan, and instead of dealing with the reality that a town made of wood structures was gonna have some fires, someone decided they were being set by enslaved people fomenting rebellion—leading to death and dismemberment for dozens of Black New Yorkers, free and enslaved. I'd immediately thought of Kim threatening to call the police on me because I didn't let her cut me in line, and wondered if all those people died because of the historical equivalent of a Bodega Becky.

The final part of the exhibition talked about the Draft Riots of 1864, where the Irish began hunting Black people through the streets of New York, killing indiscriminately and burning down an orphanage. The people of Weeksville had taken in and protected Black New Yorkers who'd made it across the East River.

Theo's face had been pale during that exhibit, and we had split apart at one point, the awkward historical fact that white people really seemed to enjoy hunting Black people whenever the whim struck them making chitchat just a bit strained.

We'd reunited at the last exhibition; it featured photographs of people from the Weeksville neighborhood over the course of its history. Black families posing in front of fireplaces. Black teachers teaching at the African school. Barbershops and restaurants and a whole thriving nineteenth-century neighborhood, and it had just . . . disappeared.

Now I sit on a bench while Theo snaps photos of the old houses outside, and I scroll for answers to a nagging question that none of the exhibitions answered.

"Where did the people of Weeksville go?" I ask. "They'd worked hard to buy property and gain the right to vote. They'd spent decades building a community, only to pick up and leave?"

"Maybe there were better opportunities someplace else?" Theo guesses, turning his camera on me and fiddling with the focus on his lens.

"Some people would leave because of that, but not everyone. It's not like it was easy for them to just move. They weren't welcome most places and had a hard enough time holding on to what they already had," I say, trying to keep the snap out of my tone, because it's not him I'm frustrated with. "You don't just give away everything you busted your ass for."

I'm scrolling blindly now, trying to maintain my cool.

"But, look at our neighborhood—"

"I'm gonna go sit in the AC." I head back toward the reception area, fighting against the sudden pressure at my tear ducts.

I head to the bathroom, splash water on my face, then grab a cold water from the vending machine and a seat at one of the round tables scattered around the lobby. After taking a few sips, I hold the water against my neck and just breathe. I can't keep going off on Theo. It's not fair to use him as my emotional punching bag—I know what it feels like, everything you say pushing some invisible button in a person you're just trying to get along with.

He isn't even getting paid for this shit. And even if he is pushing my buttons, even if his presence does make things awkward sometimes, it's nice to have some company. It's particularly nice that said company can ask questions about my past but doesn't actually know anything about it. I can breathe a little more freely with him, even though he probably thinks I'm an uptight heifer, mostly because even while feeling freer I'm acting like one.

The door from the outside opens and Theo strolls over to the woman at the desk. I watch as he makes goofy small talk, the way she slowly looks away from the computer screen and turns her attention to him. Smiles. Gets drawn into conversation.

It's not flirtatious, exactly, it's just Theo. There's something about his openness that makes you want to let him in.

After a few minutes he strides over and sits down next to me, but I keep my eyes averted since I still feel foolish for storming off.

"Eastern Parkway," he says.

When I glance at him his gaze backflips away from where condensation is running from the water bottle down into the valley between my breasts. I pull the bottle from against my neck, take a sip, and try not to look smug. Drea was right—this shirt does make them look great.

"They built Eastern Parkway through the Weeksville cemetery," he says, then moves his hand in a horizontal motion. "Just kind of razed right through it, apparently. Some people left after that. Others left after they started putting the streets onto a grid system, which again meant more razing and change." He sighs and starts fidgeting with the camera. "And then white—well, white now—immigrants started moving in. So maybe I wasn't so wrong about it being like our neighborhood. But you were right, too. People don't just leave en masse for no reason."

He suddenly turns and snaps a picture of me.

I lower the water bottle from my lips. "What the eff, Theo?"

"Sorry," he says, looking at the camera's display screen. He's not sorry. "Couldn't resist."

He turns and shows me the photo of myself with the bottle held near my mouth, lips moist and slightly parted. My braids are pulled up from my face, showing the smooth stretch of my deep summer-brown skin over my cheekbones and the darker circles under my eyes.

I look . . . attractive, I guess.

But tired.

I look like my mom.

"So what's the plan, boss?" he asks as he pulls the camera back and glances at the screen one more time before turning it off. "How does all this fit into the tour?"

"Well, I don't think we'll walk all the way over here during the block party, but I want to mention this neighborhood, since it overlapped Gifford Place at its peak. But I'm probably gonna start way before that with the Native Americans who lived in the area—"

"That's a pretty broad lens."

"—and then talk about the enslaved Africans who helped the Dutch build their initial farm holdings on the land they stole from the Algonquin."

"The Dutch? Not the British?"

"Weren't you supposed to look up the Dutch West India Company?" I ask, shooting him an annoyed look.

Theo's eyes are warm. "I didn't get around to it. But I'm kind of glad I didn't, because I like when you pull out your ruler, especially now that I know you only do it for me."

He stands up and walks away, like he's just pulled some smooth move and I'm supposed to sit here all flustered. I scoff. If this is his idea of flirtation, he better hope I never actually decide to give in to my curiosity, because he's not ready for this jelly. The only reason I feel this buzzy sensation is because I need a nap. And the fluttering in my stomach is because I need food.

I get up and follow him, and as we head out the woman at the entrance calls us over. "You know where you can go if you're looking into the history of the neighborhood? The AME around the corner. Our archivist is always tapping their historian on the shoulder for something or another. Kendra Hill is her name. She's basically a walking encyclopedia of this area."

"I know Ms. Hill," I say through a pasted-on smile. "She's a friend of my mother's. I can call her and set things up." I turn to Theo. "Wanna head there tomorrow if she's free? And if you're free."

I wince internally; just like that and I'm already assuming he'll be there to help. I haven't learned my lesson at all.

"I'm free," he says. "I said I'd help. So I'm going to help."

I scramble for a snarky response, but the only thing I come up with is a quiet "Thanks."

I'm tired.

I need help.

I'll take it.

Gifford Place OurHood post by LaTasha Clifton:
OMG, check out this Secret New York article! It's about how there used to be secret tunnels under the Medical Center!

Amber Griffin: Wut?! The mole people are real??

Candace Tompkins: No mole people. The hospital was a factory for a little while after the sanitarium closed down, and there were underground passageways. They were used to transport shipments back in the day.

LaTasha Clifton: What kind of shipment needs to be carried underground??

Candace Tompkins: They didn't want to bother the rich people who lived in the neighborhood.

Amber Griffin: I don't buy it. MOLE. PEOPLE. PERIODT.

CHAPTER 9

Theo

WHEN I WAKE UP FROM A BOREDOM-INDUCED NAP, THE LATE-evening light is throwing shadows that highlight the raging boner tenting my boxers.

It feels wrong having this thrum of excitement in my veins for the first time in months, and not for Kim, but not as wrong as it should.

I shouldn't be popping wood over Sydney. She's just my neighbor. The end.

My dick jumps and I heave a frustrated sigh, then roll groggily out of bed and head to my bathroom on autopilot. When I turn on the tap in my shower it makes a sound like a smoker's hacking cough followed by a clang somewhere—still no water, of course.

I crack my front door and drop my head as I poke it out, half from defeat and half listening for any of the usual sounds that bounce up from downstairs when Kim is home.

Nothing.

My body unclenches at what the silence signals: No tiptoeing around. No waiting for the anvil I'd thought I could evade to finally drop out of the sky like in the old cartoons Mom would put on, volume high, to keep me busy when her latest boyfriend came over. Sometimes in the cartoons, the heavy objects falling out of the sky were unavoidable acts of malice. More often, the character about to get walloped had set his own anvil-smashing in motion through some combination of greed, hubris, and stupidity.

Yeah. I guess I hadn't paid enough attention to that part.

I wrap a towel around myself and head downstairs to shower off my sleep sweat—it's still hot as fuck in my room and I feel sticky and sluggish.

I'm relieved at the thought that Kim is gone, again, even if she is with someone else. Maybe I should be raging and trying to win her back, but all I can think of is how nice it will be to cook dinner on the stove tonight, like a grown-up, instead of eating Cup Noodles rehydrated with water heated on the hot plate in my studio. Maybe I can turn on her AC, relax, and finally look up this Dutch West India Company stuff I told Sydney I would research.

When I step into the living room, I realize I was wrong.

Kim is there, wearing cute little khaki shorts and a silky white shirt that shows she's still an adherent of "freeing the nipple" and hers are basking in said freedom. Her hair is down around her shoulders in loose waves.

She looks great, all beachy summer fun, but when her gaze passes over mine, it's coldest winter. The room is freezing, too—she's gotten an additional air conditioner after giving me shit for wanting one.

I would laugh, if my balls hadn't drawn up into my body from the look she gives me when her head swivels in my direction.

It's blank; no happiness, or even disdain. If I'd been a mouse that scampered in, she would have shown more feeling about my presence.

"Hey," I say awkwardly, tightening the towel around my waist. I glance at the rolling suitcase she's carefully zipping up. "Going somewhere?"

"My parents said I should come out to their place in the Hamptons," she says. She has to clarify because they also have a place in Martha's Vineyard and one on the Carolina coast. "They said it would be smart to get there early before all the Labor Day traffic. It's super hot there, too, but at least there's an ocean breeze."

"Oh. That's cool." I hadn't thought we'd spend the holiday together, but I'd assumed we'd both be miserable separately but in each other's general vicinity, like we'd spent the last holiday. Miserable is the last thing she'll be, up in a big fancy house with catered food, a sea breeze, a pool, and—

I really am an asshole. My girlfriend is leaving suddenly, probably cheating on me, and I'm jealous of the lobster rolls and amenities she's going to enjoy.

"Is he going to be there?" I ask.

"David?" She tilts her head. "That doesn't really matter, does it? Because when I get back, you'll be gone."

She says this so casually I almost don't catch what she means.

I'm getting kicked out.

I should do something. Get angry. Make a scene. Instead, my hands grip the towel at my waist and I kind of just freeze there like a roach when you turn on the kitchen light.

"What the hell, Kim? Just like that?" I ask, but it's not really a question, and in reality *just like that* has been coming on for months.

She sighs, shakes her head. "Look, there's no point to dragging this out. We clearly have different values and our relationship has been stalled for months. From before we even moved in. We're both relatively young and—"

"Where am I supposed to live?" I cut her off. My face is hot and I feel ridiculous and exposed: broke, jobless, and half-naked, about to be kicked out of my own house. "I threw most of my savings into moving into this place with you, I'm on the mortgage, and now you think you can—"

"I can kick you out? Yes," she says, standing her bag up. "I know you're about to mention tenancy laws or equity or something tedious, but only one of us has a parent who's a high-powered attorney with detailed knowledge on the matter."

"You aren't even going to offer to buy me out?" That's the real blow. She can afford to do that. She can more than afford it—she doesn't even need my contribution to the mortgage, but I'd wanted to prove to her that I wasn't just using her for her money.

I'd wanted to provide, but I'd been the caveman bringing an emaciated hare to our campfire when her family had already downed and preserved a herd of woolly mammoths.

She laughs, one sharp *ha.* "Why should I? Dad never did like you anyway. I'm sure he'd love a reason to fuck with you some more."

"*You* liked me once, though," I say.

She looks at me like she's the harried heroine in a romantic comedy and I'm the Joe Blow standing between her and happiness.

"Things change." A horn honks outside and she shrugs. "Look, I'm giving you a week. It shouldn't be that hard to find a room somewhere."

Not when you're rich and can pass any background check, I imagine.

"Thanks for the last few years. They were good, mostly. But they're over now, and I'm doing what's best for me. My therapist told me that I'll be much happier once my living situation is free of toxic people, so there's no reason to put it off any longer."

With that, she strolls out of the living room and out of my life, too, I guess.

"Oh!" Her voice rings out in the hallway. "You can have the leftover wine in the fridge, but don't fuck up any of my belongings or I'll make your life hell."

Then she's really gone.

I head into the shower, or my body does while my mind starts running through possibilities. I don't have any friends I can crash with—before her I'd been new to the city and friendless, hanging with my roommates out of convenience. Other than that, I'd mostly had acquaintances I'd lost touch with or who may or may not be in jail somewhere. Mom has never been able to help, so that's not a possibility.

The chances of ever getting another job like the one I got to make Kim happy are slim to none, and besides, it was too much work. I have other ways of making money fast, which is why I'll be able to afford a couple months' rent, but I'd convinced myself I was just making do while times were tough. Am I really just going to fall back into that life again?

When I was young, I'd get so mad at my mom for always making the same stupid mistakes. Now I wonder if there's any avoiding that pattern. I tried hard as hell to break it, and look where it's gotten me.

After a few minutes of standing under the lukewarm spray, the panic and anger get shunted away like they have all my life—probably compacting into a tumor in some dark corner of my body—and I turn off the water and calmly step out.

I have a week. I'll be fine.

We often moved with way shorter notice when I was a kid—I know for a fact that you can pack up everything you really need to get by in half an hour. A week is golden.

Everything will be fine.

She's probably giving David a handie on the LIE right now.

Whatever.

I head to her fridge, pull the fancy stopper out of the wine Josie had been trying to get me to drink the other night, and take a huge swallow of the too-sweet liquid. Leftovers from the fancy Italian restaurant we used to go to when we were renting in Manhattan sit on the shelf below, and I grab the box out of sheer spite.

Given the short notice, I'll probably end up in some illegal living room rental with an IKEA curtain for a wall. I *deserve* this leftover vegetarian lasagna—that's what she always orders.

I know those kinds of things about her, and she knows nothing about me. Nothing. And not just the stuff I hid from her.

I take another swig of the Riesling—which has gone bad but will still get me buzzed—then carry the box to the microwave and open it.

It's shrimp scampi.

Well, would you look at that.

After warming the food, I carry the bottle up to my studio and sit at my desk to start searching for a place. I drink. I send a text asking an old contact I'd been trying to avoid slinking back to if he has any work for me, hoping the number is still in service. I drink. I look at more places, and email a couple of them.

I'm still in whatever numb state is preventing me from being really pissed off at Kim—I'm mostly mad at myself.

I'd known she wasn't my type when we first met at that happy hour—she'd clearly been slumming it at dollar shots night while I was actually trying to save a buck. Our first dates had been in the summer, full of free concerts, train rides to the beach, and cheap beer. It was only when she'd taken me to a fancy restaurant to meet her friends four months in that I'd realized how different our bank statements, and our everyday lives, really were. But at that point it had been an ego thing—the hot rich girl liked *me*.

She was vibrant, and independent, and she didn't *need* me.

Her family was old money and they'd be passing it on to her.

I had to keep her.

Jesus, it's pathetic in retrospect, and really fucked up on my end. Had I liked her for more than the fact that she liked me when she shouldn't? That she didn't mind picking up the tab, after all? That she liked putting my life in order and pushing me to reach for things a guy like me would've never even known about?

When she'd told me I needed to get a better job . . . I'd reached a bit too high. Part of me resents that that particular Jenga block was tugged from the bottom and brought everything crashing down only *after* the ink had dried on the deed for this place.

The *ping* of an email response sounds from the computer—one of the rental ads has already responded because it's a scam. I delete it and the previous email fills the screen.

Tour Basic Overview

I click the link to the shared document Sydney sent earlier, her research opening in a new tab on my browser. A circle floats in the right-hand corner of the screen, a picture of a cartoon string bean. When I hover over it, sgreenbean@mailmail.com pops up. I try not to be goofy about the fact that she's on the other side of my screen in a way. I just get to work.

I scroll past the pages she already showed me and go to a section entitled "Black home ownership."

> Owning property was seen as pivotal to obtaining full citizenship status; abolitionists and activists over the course of Brooklyn's history have suggested that efforts to block home ownership and/or devalue property in Black communities can be seen as an attack on Black citizenship and general well-being.

I'm not sure if these are Sydney's words or someone else's, but it occurs to me that all those nights I saw her taking notes on her couch, between crying bouts and glasses of wine, this is probably what she was working on. Even though she's been acting like this is something she's doing on a whim and hasn't given enough attention to.

I open another tab and type "Dutch West India Company + Brooklyn" in the search bar, then skim through the preview text that pops up for each hit, seeing if anything catches my eye.

> After the establishment of New Amsterdam, the Dutch set about what would be one of their most lasting contributions to the five boroughs—the importation of Africans to work on farms and public works.

The preview text for another site reads: . . . with the end of slavery in Brooklyn, many of the Dutch West India Company slave owners turned their eye to a new industry: banking.

I snort. Yeah, having just been fired from a bank job, I know why some lazy asshole would turn to that business. Easy money, made from other people's hard work.

I should keep looking for a place, but instead, I grab the bottle of wine and start to read.

I COME TO with half my body slid off my office chair, the low grunt and moan of porn buzzing from my headphones, which lie across the desk. Some *weird shit* that I can only assume is the result of autoplay and someone else's eclectic video playlist is happening on my screen. I don't remember pulling up any porn. I don't remember anything after staring at an ad for a shitty basement apartment in Mill Basin. The giant bottle of wine is mostly empty, but my head is spinning like I don't regularly crush a six-pack a night by myself.

I reach out to slam the laptop screen down, but my motion is slow and unsteady, so I just tap pause and try to get my bearings.

I hit tab to change the screen and end up in the document. I blink and watch as a gap opens up between Sydney's single-spaced paragraphs, white space eating the screen. Fear tingles up the back of my neck for some reason, until I realize my own hand is resting on the space bar. I lift it with some effort . . . and the white space keeps eating the page, then suddenly stops. The cursor blinks there in the whiteness, then words start to type:

Not feeling too hot, are you?

Sydney?

No. When I look into the right-hand corner, the cartoon bean is gone, replaced by a black circle. Someone else is in the document.

Too much wine'll do that to you, whoever it is types.

I manage to get the screen down even though my arms feel numb, but when I try to stand up, a painful retch ripples through my stomach and diaphragm.

"Ugh."

I burp, the taste of bile on my tongue giving an additional warning that moving isn't a great idea right now. I can't stand and I also don't want to puke on one of the few things of value that I'll be able to take with me when I move out, so I use my feet to propel myself away from the desk, slowly rolling to the window beside it. I park myself directly in front of the fan shoved into the casing, then carefully lean back in the chair and sit still with the nausea. Very still.

How did I get this drunk?

I spent a significant portion of my early twenties pounding vodka in Russian social clubs and never suffered worse than a few blackouts.

The last time I threw up was in high school. I'd gone to a party where I'd unsuccessfully tried to hit on five girls and ended up nursing a bottle of 151 in a corner. Maybe this is how my body responds to rejection.

Wait. Someone was in the document. Someone not Sydney was in the document, typing like they could see me. What was that about?

A deep and melodious howl pierces the night, raising the hairs on my arms. I know this sound—one of my mom's shitty exes was a hunter, and this is the sound of a hound raising the alarm.

Count.

In the months we've lived here, I've heard the occasional bark from him—it's usually Toby that engages in barkapalooza—but nothing like this.

There's a movement across the street, in Mr. Perkins's place, on the first floor. I feel woozy and the flickering light from the television in his living room doesn't help, but there's definitely someone moving around in there.

Shit.

A post on the OurHood app said there's been a spate of break-ins, but I know the cause of that rumor. And no one around here would choose his house of all places, would they?

Maybe he's getting a late-night snack, but I've never seen him up this late. He's usually awake and outside by six—he's one of my constants, sometimes deviating but generally always following the same pattern. Something is extremely off right now, and out of it as I am, my unease solidifies into clear foreboding; something bad is about to happen. When you have been the bad thing, you get pretty good at knowing what the calm before the storm feels like.

I lean forward, peering through the whirring blades of the fan; the motion makes me want to hurl so I reach up to turn the power switch to zero.

Count barks again, and I squint to see what's happening through the slowing blades. Mr. Perkins walks into the living room slowly, then is blocked by the fan blade. He looks left—fan blade. Now his head is turned back sharply over his shoulder—fan blade. When I look at the other front-facing window, I spot two bulky shadows pass the glow of the television. Another revolution of the fan blade and the shadows are gone. I want to say it was my imagination, but Count is barking more insistently now.

I see a light turn on in one of Terry and Josie's windows—she's likely up to post a noise complaint on the OurHood app—but it's taking all of my concentration to focus on what's going on at Mr. Perkins's.

I grip the edge of the window frame and pull myself to a standing position. Black spots appear at the edges of my vision and my body is bathed in sweat, but I have a better view now. I see Mr. Perkins turning around, his eyes going wide as he takes a step back.

Count is barking and barking.

Shit.

I have to go help, but my body is so heavy. Have to call someone at least, but when I turn my head to look for my phone the room ripples and spins and I dry-heave.

Three things happen in quick succession: the TV shuts off in Mr. Perkins's living room, leaving the windows dark; there's a loud crash; and Count stops barking abruptly.

Actually, four things happen: I black out.

Gifford Place OurHood/privateusergroup/Rejuvenation

The Housing Authority has relayed some information: internal files regarding the project have been accessed. Likely nothing, but the matter should be looked into and dealt with, along with the FOIA requests.

CHAPTER 10

Sydney

I JERK AWAKE ON THE FLOOR BY THE BACK DOOR, CURLED UP like a dog that needs to go out. The haze of a bad dream releases its stranglehold on me, but the dirty mop taste in my mouth, residue of rosé and Ambien, persists.

I shouldn't have taken the pills, but alcohol hadn't knocked me out and my mind had been running laps around bad memories, and around good memories that now felt worse than the bad ones. I'd drunkenly grabbed the pills out of desperation; I don't even remember how many I downed.

I sit up, wince at the pain in my neck. All of my attempts to knock out and have a few hours of peace were for nothing because the nightmares were so realistic that I'm even more exhausted.

There'd been demons in the walls, banging and scratching as they burrowed their way into the house to make me pay for my lies. I'd tried to run for help, to go to Mommy . . .

I wait for the anxiety from the dream to release its hold on me now that I'm awake, but nothing unclenches. Probably because reality is just as shitty and—oh *fuck*. It's Thursday.

I push myself up to my feet and jog to my bedroom. My cell

phone isn't on the charger, and I start pulling pillows, duvet, sheets onto the floor until I hear a thud and grab for it.

The phone is dead. It was charging last I remember, so I must have used it during my Ambien stupor, as if things aren't already bad enough.

"Shit, shit, shit."

I snatch up the end of the charging cord and plug it in, that annoying image of a battery with a slim red line sitting on the screen forever, like it's purposely fucking with me. Finally, a white apple appears, and then the security code prompt. Without thinking, I enter my old code—the date of the first day me and Marcus had met—which is, of course, wrong. I changed it three years ago, when I started to suspect he was checking my phone.

"You're being paranoid, Sydney."

I put in the new code, the numbers Mommy always played in the lotto.

The phone unlocks and after it connects to the network, the first thing that comes through is a text from Claude.

Yo, you need to chill. My girl saw your wild texts and now she's mad at ME. You're going through something, I get it, but please delete my number.

Ouch.

I can't bring myself to look at whatever humiliating, pathetic message I sent him, so I just delete the whole text chain. I expect to see a response from Drea letting me know how her night went, but she's either still on her date from last night or is trying to enforce her "you can't use me as a therapist" boundary.

None of that matters, though; there's a voicemail from the lawyers. The call I've been waiting on, and maybe my last hope, and I slept through it. I ball my fist and dig it into my thigh as I return the call.

"Gladstone and Gianetti."

"Hi, this is Sydney Green, I—"

"Hello, Ms. Green. Ms. Gianetti left you a message, but her schedule is packed for the next few weeks."

"I'm sorry I missed her call. Is there really no way—"

"No." The receptionist's tone says this is final. "Unfortunately, it seems that there's not much that can be done at this point with your mother's case. She'll be in contact via email. There's also the matter of outstanding payment, which we understand might be difficult considering the situation."

Surprisingly, I don't feel anything. Somewhere, behind the desperation-fueled attempt at positivity, I've known they wouldn't be able to help. "Okay. I understand."

"You might also look into one of the nonprofits. They'd probably have more resources for you to act independently, too."

"Okay." I listen to her rattle off a phone number, but it's already too late.

The truth that I've been avoiding at all costs starts to sink in: I'm fucked from every angle and no lawyer can help with that.

Pain builds in my chest, and I sink to the floor, eyes squeezed shut and barely able to sip in a breath.

I open the text function to my chain with Drea and tap the audio note feature. "Are you home? It's happening again. My chest."

I hit send and then curl up around the phone.

There's nothing I can do about it but wait. I can't afford another medical bill, and even if I could, they'd likely just tell me I need to reduce my stress, which isn't exactly an option at this point.

Maybe it is a heart attack this time, though, because I'm sweating and shaking and the pain in my chest is intensifying. Hell, I wouldn't be mad if this is the big one. Then I could get some rest and someone else could deal with the mess I'm in.

I lie on the floor for a long time, breathing and daring my punk-ass body to put up or shut up, then wondering what my mother would say if she saw me like this. I know what Marcus would say. *"You want to make a scene and act crazy? Fine. I'll treat you that way."*

That memory beats at my chest, but I call Mommy's number and listen to her voicemail, and the panic attack recedes.

I get up shakily and make my way to the shower, where I squeeze an almost comical amount of exfoliating body scrub onto my washcloth, running it over my body until I feel like maybe I've scoured off a layer. After a face scrub and rinse, I head into my bedroom and work a thick body butter into my skin, taking my time, allowing myself to zone out during this familiar daily ritual.

I'm staring at the wall, mind blank and gaze unfocused, when a tiny black spot begins to scurry.

Any calm my little self-care routine has won back is lost immediately. I charge toward the crawling speck, scooping up the water glass on my bedside table and slamming it onto the wall.

It better not be another goddamn bedbug.

My skin starts to itch like the moisture's been sucked out of it, but as I peer through the thin glass bottom of the cup I realize it's just a baby roach. Not ideal, but picking up a can of Raid is easier than steaming all my belongings.

I'm about to move the glass when a remnant of my nightmare comes back to me . . . was it about something scratching in the walls? I slowly lower my ear to the glass like I used to do when I was a kid because I'd seen it in a movie. I can hear my own heartbeat, my own inhale . . . and—

The doorbell suddenly chimes and I jump, dropping the glass. It somehow doesn't shatter after bouncing four times in slo-mo and then rolling under the bed.

I slap my hand at the wall as something scurries in my peripheral vision, but the roach apparently has way better luck than me and skitters off to freedom. We never had roaches when Mommy was here, but back then Miss Wanda still lived next door. She didn't have a dirty kid, and she bleached down her countertops every night, despite the lies Josie told her friends. I hurriedly pull on my underwear, a shirt, and shorts and race to the door, heart hammering in my chest.

When I get to the front door, there's a tall white man in a blue shirt standing outside of it. He's wearing a blue hat pulled low on his brow and is so close to the door, right up against it, that I can't see the street behind him. He's bulky enough to do that.

"Is Yolanda Green here?" he asks, his gaze skirting over my shoulder and down the hall.

My words get all jumbled in my throat and I clear it, and school my expression to one of polite annoyance.

"I'm her daughter. Can I help you?"

"I'm here to read the meter," he says through the glass. "Can you let me in?"

The electrical meters are in the hall closet, meaning I'll have to let him inside the house to check them. The hairs on my neck rise in warning and I don't ignore my gut, even if it is still running on Ambien fumes.

I reach into my pocket for my phone and realize it's still on the floor next to my bed.

"Miss? I need to check the meter." His voice is kind of amused, like he's daring me to be dumb enough to believe him or paranoid enough not to. He takes a step closer to the door so his chest is pressed almost against it. The name patch on his uniform sends a chill through me: DREW.

He taps the glass as if I'm not staring right at him. "We've been billing you on estimates for months now. If you don't let me in—"

"Sydney?"

The "Con Ed" guy looks back over his shoulder and steps out of the way to reveal Theo waiting at the bottom of the stairs. His hair is wet and his expression is . . . off.

"Thought we were supposed to meet at eight thirty," he says, which I have no recollection of agreeing to. I'm wondering if he even sees the weird man looming in my doorway, then his gaze shifts with intentionality behind it. "Oh, hey man. What's up?"

He does another one of those white-guy moves, placing a hand to his brow and scrunching up his face as he gives the meter man a lingering look that makes him aware that he's been clocked.

"I can come back if you've got an appointment, miss," the guy says. Then he's gone, hustling down the stairs, hopping into the passenger side of a white van that pulls off.

I open the door enough to lean out and watch as the van drives out of sight. "That wasn't a Con Ed van."

"Maybe the clown-van clan is back in business." Theo leans back from his hips, then takes a few steps back. "No license plate, front or back. Should we call the police?"

I shoot him a look. "Yeah, so another scary white man can show up at my door, but one who can definitely kill me with no worries instead of probably kill me with no worries."

"Shit, Sydney." He exhales. I wait for him to push back, but he says, "I get that. Just . . . that's a pretty common con. Pretending to be from a utility service. So many cons are just banking on the fact that people will trust you because of the social contract."

I take a step back into the doorway, ready to close the door on the world and this conversation. "Thanks for running him off," I say.

"Have you spoken to Mr. Perkins this morning?" He scrubs his hands over his beard, and it's in that moment that I realize he's hungover. His eyes are red and he's looking the worst I've ever seen him; beard unkempt and a waxy sheen to his skin. "I got kind of drunk last night, but I swore . . . I can't remember everything, but I think I saw something in his window."

My stomach clenches.

"Something like what?"

"Like maybe something happening to him?" There's worry in his eyes. "I think I was trying to get up to see if he was okay but I passed out. I just remember that Count howled, and maybe I saw a shadow in his window. I wasn't trying to get wasted, but Kim left me and I drank some of her expensive wine out of spite and . . ." He shrugs. "No one answered when I knocked on the door this morning."

"Of course not," I say. "He's usually out doing his morning tour of the neighborhood, he wouldn't be home."

Theo shakes his head. "I've been keeping an eye out between puking sessions. He didn't take Count for a walk this morning that I saw."

I curse and slip my feet into the flip-flops by the doorway, feeling the vein in my temple start to throb. "You said you were drunk, right? Was that all you were doing? Drinking?"

"I ate some shrimp scampi, too," he says, and I'm expecting that to be sarcasm, but when I turn to look at him, his forehead is wrinkled and he seems to be trying to remember where things took a wrong turn in his evening. "I'm never drinking Riesling again."

I head down the stairs, passing him and going through Mr. Perkins's gate—he's more likely to be hanging out in City Hall watching *Good Day New York* than up in the apartment. I knock on the window, wait a beat, and then knock again. After three more attempts, I head up the stairs, ringing the buzzer for the first floor, pressing more insistently as my worry starts to pummel me.

Scary Uber driver. Preston in jail. Fake Con Ed guy the morning after Theo saw something in the window.

I think about Mr. Perkins jerking in his sleep the other evening.

I think about how he's been around for my whole life, and how everything I care about is getting torn away.

I suck in a breath. He has to be okay.

Melissa, the college student whose parents paid a year's rent up front, according to Mr. Perkins, comes down. She has on shorts and a too-large tee, and her short dark hair is artfully disheveled. Her bike helmet is in her hand.

She looks back and forth between me and Theo in surprise, as if she didn't expect us to be standing there.

"Sydney, right?" She looks over my shoulder to Theo, a sudden playfulness in her gaze, then she looks back to me. "What's up?"

"Hi. We were looking for Mr. Perkins. Have you talked to him today? Kind of worried about him because I didn't see him take Count for his walk."

"Oh, he didn't tell you?"

"Tell me what?" I ask, not even trying to blunt my annoyance. I hate when people ask a question instead of just giving the damn information off the bat.

"His daughter took him to the hospital. She came by last night."

"Wait, his daughter? She lives in DC. Why would she be up here in the middle of the night?"

Melissa's eyes go wide. "The woman said she was his daughter. Do you think she lied?"

"Did you hear anything strange last night?" I ask. "After his daughter came?"

"No, but I was at work after that." She shrugs, her doe-eyed fear fading. "There was a show at the bar and we all hung out after. I got back super late. Or super early, rather." She glances at Theo. "You saw me come in, right? You were watching from your window."

Theo nods jerkily and she smirks. "You look like you had a rough night, too. What were you up to?"

"I think we can call the hospital and see what they have to say," Theo says, his gaze returning to me.

"Okay," she says. She pulls the door shut behind her and jogs down the stairs. "Keep me in the loop. You know where to find me," she says to Theo with a wink as she passes him.

She pops AirPods in her ears as she unlocks her bike. I'm staring, my brain trying to catch up with what's going on.

"Where's Count?" I call out as she kicks off, but she doesn't hear me.

"Count!" Theo calls out while leaning over the banister, but there's no bark or even whine in response. He looks over at me. "If Mr. Perkins is at the hospital, I'm pretty sure they wouldn't just let a dog hang out in the waiting room. If Count is in there, he could starve. Die of thirst."

I care about Count, too, and I know white people love them some dogs, but Theo's talking probable cause, not liberating paws. A reason to break and enter. A way for us to not have to rely on the word of some girl who may or may not have been up until the crack of dawn doing coke.

I look around. A breeze blows through the leaves of the trees lining the street, but there isn't anyone else on this end of the block. Theo follows me as I walk slowly into the plant-enclosed area that leads into the garden apartment.

"Don't tell anyone, but his door is always unlocked," I say as I turn the knob and push. "Okay, not always."

"I can pick the lock," Theo says casually. "Wait. No, I can't. That wasn't here on Monday."

I'm trying not to freak out, but when I follow his gaze I notice one of the doorbell camera systems has been installed. Since when? Mr. Perkins is into gadgets, but not enough to install a camera, and especially not now when the neighborhood is supposedly the safest it's been in years.

"The fuck? Okay. Okay." I walk over to the window and peer into it—was that movement back there? Or just Theo's reflection coming up behind me? The heat of him radiates along the left side of my body as he moves in closer to peer inside, too.

"I really thought I saw something," he says quietly. "I hope it was a dream."

His words remind me that I'd dreamed of demons in the walls, trying to scratch through to me. Had the demons howled as well? Had it been a dream at all?

"Sydney!"

I turn to find Ms. Candace watching us from the sidewalk. She pushes her sunglasses up onto her cap of gray curls.

"You two look like criminals casing a joint. Trying to get your picture put up on OurHood? 'The Ebony and Ivory cat burglars.' You just need matching striped shirts."

She cackles at her bad joke.

"Have you seen Mr. Perkins?" I walk over to her. "His tenant said something about him being taken to the hospital? We're worried."

She looks between me and Theo and I can just imagine a little caption that says NEW GOSSIP ACQUIRED popping up over our heads. The Day Club Crew are gonna have a field day. Then her gaze settles on me and I see the connection form in her head. Her smile fades.

"Don't worry yourself. He's fine," she says in that slightly raspy voice of hers. "He texted me saying one of the grandbabies had to get their appendix removed, so he went down to help Debbie and Ron with the kids. Maybe that girl misunderstood?"

"Maybe," I say, then look back through the window; City Hall is empty and quiet. I guess it *was* just a reflection.

"You know she drunk half the time, and high the other half, but her parents paid her rent and she hasn't burned the place down, so it is what it is." She sighs. "John will be back before the block party this Sunday. How's the tour research coming?"

She perks up at the last sentence, her gaze sharpening on us and a suggestive smile tightening her mouth.

"We're figuring it out," I say.

"Good. Me and the Day Club Crew are looking forward to it."

"Day Club Crew?" Theo repeats.

"Ms. Candace takes care of some older people from the neighborhood in her house during the day," I say, trying to keep any emotion out of my voice. "None of them like the term 'elder care.'"

"Of course we don't,'" she says. "We aren't elderly. We're finely aged, like that good top-shelf rum."

She laughs.

"They might have some helpful stuff for the tour," Theo says. "Do we have time to talk to them?"

I want to whirl on him, ask him if he remembers he's my reparations assistant, not the boss of things, but he's right. I cross my arms over my chest instead, nod, wishing I could get off this emotional Slip 'N Slide that has me crying, then pissed, then paranoid.

"Yeah, come on by. We're always happy to see you, you know that." Her gaze lingers on me, a little soft and sad. "But whenever you come, you two have to be out before *General Hospital* starts or Paulette will not be pleased."

I throw my hands up. "I know better than to come between Paulette and Sonny Corinthos."

"See you later," she says, leaving me and Theo alone.

"Sorry to make you worry." He stares at Mr. Perkins's window. "It's weird how a dream can feel so real. I swore—" He shakes his head. "I'll meet you back here in half an hour? We can get breakfast before heading to the church."

"Okay. There's a good Caribbean diner across the street."

I head back to my apartment, wondering what it means that Theo and I are just gonna spend the whole damn day together again in the name of research, and then check my texts. Drea's listened to the audio of my panicked freak-out, according to the little check marks that show the message was received, and hasn't bothered to respond. She's online now, and I stop in the hallway, type, and hit send before I can think better of it.

Btw, I died of a heart attack waiting for you to respond, avenge me. xoxo

The message is sent. Marked as read.

No response.

Sorry for being a smartass, I type out. But stop leaving me on read and respond so I know you're okay, *okay*?

Drea is typing . . . pops up in the display at the top of our conversation and relief floods me.

She's okay.

She doesn't hate me.

When I leave to go meet Theo, she still hasn't hit send.

Gifford Place OurHood post by Josie Ulnar:
This is an accountability post. I want to apologize to everyone for the racket Toby made last night. Terriers are rat catchers at heart and, well, I don't know where it came from, but a rat got into our house in the middle of the night. Toby was barking bloody murder as he chased it down, and I'm sure he woke some of you up. Sorry about that!

Btw, if anyone wants, I have a couple of vouchers for the maid service I use. They do an excellent job and really deep clean your kitchen to prevent infestation of vermin.

(2 additional comments . . . see more)

CHAPTER 11
Theo

I'M EATING SOMETHING CALLED ACKEE AND SALTFISH, A KIND of buttery fruit cooked with salted fish and spices. It's heavier than my normal breakfast, but really good.

Sydney is working on a basic plate of scrambled eggs, roasted potatoes, and rye toast. Maybe it's because her braids are pulled up into a bun atop her head now and I can see her face better, but she looks more tired than when I left her this morning.

Her skin is sallow beneath the brown, and the bags under her eyes would have to be checked on most airlines. There's a red mark on the brown skin of her forearm that she absentmindedly scratches every few moments. She also keeps checking her phone, trying to be subtle but with a desperation that makes it clear she's waiting to hear from someone.

I keep thinking about that white van. It had been in my peripheral vision while I watched for movement at Mr. Perkins's, dread growing as the markers for his usual schedule came and went. The van had been parked for so long that I hadn't thought anyone was inside, and when the door suddenly swung open, it made me jump. Something about the way he scanned up and down the street—*too* casually, like a dog that happens to stretch lazily before trying to snag your food—had caught my attention.

If there's one thing I know well, it's how people act when they're up to something shady.

And then he'd headed straight for Sydney.

I want to ask her if she's tangled up in something that would bring a guy like that to her door, but I'm pretty sure she'd say it's none of my business. And she'd be right.

The other thing I know, apart from criminal shit, is that trying to save women from things that they didn't ask me to is a recipe for disaster. We're just two neighbors having breakfast and working on a project, and the project isn't "Saving Sydney."

"Man, I haven't been to church in forever," I say, trying to pull her out of wherever her head went in the half hour she was in her apartment, which is as close as I'll allow myself to being her white knight.

We didn't go to church much when I was young; we lived in Greenville for a year and my mom dated a deacon at a Baptist church in some attempt at finding religion. Lou used to say Jesus forgives all. He kicked us out when I asked the Sunday school teacher why Jesus would forgive Lou for hitting my mom instead of just making him stop it if he really was so powerful.

"What about you? Are you religious?" I ask when Sydney glances at her phone again.

"I used to be," she says. "It's a lot of suspension of disbelief, though, and the idea of someone watching my every move creeps me out, whether it's Santa or Jesus. I guess I'm agnostic now."

"Hedging your bets."

"It's mostly because my mo—" She stops that sentence like a bird running into a clean glass window. "Because it seems like the devil is real with everything going on in my life, so there has to be a God, too. Divine physics, or something."

I smile and wipe my fingers on my napkin, then pick up the camera beside me on the leather booth seat, taking a shot through the window of the church across the street with the first three letters of the café's name, Godfrey's, in the frame. I flip the screen toward Sydney, and she smiles a bit.

"Clever." She sips the dregs of her coffee. My cup has been empty for a while, but she's one of those people who seems to always forget her coffee is there so it's cold by the time she finishes it. Her index fingernail taps on the white ceramic mug. "Are you still applying for jobs?"

I put my camera down carefully. "Why do you ask?"

She lifts one shoulder. "Because you stay getting in my business, Mr. Twenty Questions, so now I'm gonna get in yours."

"Divine physics?" I ask.

"Tit for tat," she replies. "Also, I'm nosy. What is your deal?"

"My deal is—" I catch the waiter's eye and he comes over to refill my coffee, glancing back and forth between me and Sydney as if wondering what a schmuck like me is doing with her. I take my time adding the heavy cream and sugar to the strong drip brew. "My deal is that I'm currently unemployable."

She stares as I sip and I hold her gaze, figuring out my next move.

She places both elbows on the table, leans forward, and props her head on her hands. "Unemployable?"

I'm buffeted between the worry that I've said too much and the nihilistic urge to say more, like the compulsion to drive off a cliff when there's no guardrail.

Right now, absolutely no one knows me. My mom never did. Kim doesn't. My dad tried to but dragged me out of a disorganized fucked-up life with my mom to jam me into his also-fucked-up-but-more-organized situation.

I lean toward Sydney, deciding to at least sit down on the edge of the proverbial cliff and let my legs dangle.

"I . . . am a liar."

That's all I give her for now.

Her expression remains the same except for her eyes. Some of the brightness goes out of them, and even though she's still leaning forward, she may as well have jumped backward across the restaurant.

"Word? How so?"

I clear my throat. "Kim comes from money. I don't."

She tilts her head. "Ohhh, so this is a wrong-side-of-the-tracks romance? Bad boy lusting after the rich chick? I've seen that Lifetime movie."

I know from vegging out with my mom that Lifetime movies don't usually have happy endings, and I wonder if Sydney knows that, too.

"She pursued me," I correct. "We met at this local dive bar. I was there because it was all I could afford. She was there because she was slumming."

"Okay," she says.

"I fell hard, but then I kept thinking about her having all this money and me having none. And I just wanted to impress her. To feel like I was worthy, you know? She went to an Ivy League school. I have a GED."

I pick up my water glass to take a sip.

"Theo . . ." Sydney smiles warmly at me. "This is not Black mammy confessional. I'm not gonna 'oh honey' you and tell you you're good enough and smart enough. Get to the point."

My bark of surprised laughter makes the swallow of water go down the wrong tube and I cough-laugh until my eyes water. "Right. Yeah. I doctored my résumé."

Her brows rise, and I plow ahead.

"Suddenly, I'd graduated from college—a good school, but not so good that I'd stand out. I doctored my work history, too, paid some guys I used to work with to be my references—for much better jobs—if the company bothered to call."

"Did they?" she asks, and I feel an actual physical pleasure, like taking a huge shit when I've been constipated for days, when I shake my head.

"They didn't call. Didn't ask for transcripts," I say.

"And the guy who hired you was . . ." She raises her brows again.

I raise mine back, not knowing what she means.

"White," she stage-whispers.

"Oh! Yeah. We mostly talked about music during the interview. Some band I'd never heard of, but I just pretended I was blanking on the titles of their songs because I was nervous about the interview. Then we talked sports teams because I saw the pennant hanging in his office and I told him about my guys who can get amazing Yankees tickets."

"Wow." She shakes her head and leans back in the booth. "I've been working in a shitty school office and you—"

"Are unemployed. Because eventually one of the administrative assistants was putting together some list of alumni for the company, something completely innocuous, and realized there was no record of me at the school."

I sip more water while she stares at me.

"Is that why your girlfriend was being such a heifer to everybody? Because you lied on your résumé and stopped bringing home the luxury leggings?" she asks. "I can understand that, though I don't know why she took it out on *me*."

I shake my head. "She doesn't know."

Her eyes go wide. "She doesn't know? About the lying? Getting fired? Both?"

"The lying. I haven't told anyone. Except you."

Sydney leans back and raises both her hands, the expression on her face meme-worthy. "Nope. *Nope*. I'm not trying to be your repository of secrets, which is a nicer term for 'the person you kill because you don't want your girlfriend to find out you're a sociopath.'"

"I'm not a sociopath," I protest, though maybe laughing as I say it doesn't help my case. "You've never lied to get what you need?"

She stares at me for a long time and then shakes her head, picks up her purse, and stands up, glancing quickly at her phone as she slides it into the bag.

"Let's go. This is a lot. I just wanted some scrambled eggs and got Dashboard Confessional instead."

"And she's not my girlfriend anymore," I add, standing to follow her. "She told me it was over and then went to her family's place in the Hamptons with the dude she cheated on me with. I think. You're the only person I've told that to, too. Sorry to add to the repository."

I kind of chuckle even though my throat feels weird and rough. I don't want to be with Kim anymore and I'm relieved more than anything, but saying it out loud makes it more real than drinking myself into a stupor did.

Sydney squints at me. "She dumped you and she didn't even know about the lying? What else did you do?"

"Not lie well enough, I guess?" I shrug. "Should've aimed a bit higher and not gotten caught."

"You are *a mess*," she says, shaking her head. "Unemployed, cheated on, dumped."

Soon to be homeless, I mentally add to the list but don't say aloud. I don't want her to think it's a request for help.

She sighs and says, "I meant what I said—I'm not gonna 'oh honey' you. But you get a free breakfast at least for that sob story. And for scaring away the fake Con Ed man."

She smiles, just one half of her somehow still-glossy mouth lifting up, but she's looking at me and it doesn't feel like she's across the room anymore. It's been a long time since I've felt this. Not attraction or desire, or not *just* those things, but understanding. Camaraderie.

I'm going to have to be more careful. Because there's the truth and there's *the truth*, and Sydney's smile is enough to make me think about telling her the latter.

"All right, boss," I say. "Take me to church."

THE CHURCH HISTORIAN, Kendra Hill, is expecting us—apparently Sydney texted her and asked her if she could make time for us. She's not that much older than us, maybe midforties, though there's a touch of gray in the dark brown hair at her temples that makes me uncertain. She brings us into a small office and takes a seat behind a pale green wooden desk, gesturing at the two chairs in front of it.

"This building doesn't look like a church, really," I say. "I've thought it was a school all this time."

"Well, a church can be a basement, a storefront, a living room. It's about the faith contained in a place, not the receptacle. But yes, it was a school. In the time of Weeksville it was one of the African schools, where Black children could get an education. Later, it was the first integrated school in New York. And eventually it became home to our congregation."

She nods, and then sends a sympathetic look Sydney's way.

"How's your mother, Sydney? Is she hanging in there?"

I glance at Sydney, who presses her lips together like she's swallowing bile but nods.

"That's good. Yolanda was always so tough. We're praying for her." She gives Sydney a comforting look. "She mentioned your tour to me, you know, last time I came to visit her. Was so proud of you getting into history. Now, tell me more about it."

"I'm not a historian or anything," Sydney says, her voice more subdued than I've ever heard it. "I'm just trying to put together a little something about the neighborhood from the perspective of someone who grew up here and also is learning things that we don't get taught at school. I'd love to hear any interesting facts you might have about the neighborhood's past since everything is changing so quickly."

Kendra gives me a pointed look, and Sydney lays a hand on my shoulder. "Theo is my assistant. He's working off his reparations debt."

"How interesting. Were your family slaveowners?" Kendra asks, and my big white feelings threaten to make an appearance, though the question makes sense given Sydney's intro.

I shift in my seat. "I don't know. Mom's side of the family doesn't talk about that kind of thing, but it's possible, I guess. A week of being Sydney's research buddy isn't a high price to pay, just in case."

"Seriously. You should be paying me for this education," Sydney says in that tone where I can't tell if she's joking or she actually dislikes me, but she gives my shoulder a squeeze before releasing it, and my abs clench against the sensation it creates.

"Let's see. You already saw the exhibitions down at the center." Kendra grins as she leans back in her office chair. "I think, given the nature of your tour, you might want to look into the ebb and flow of the neighborhood demographics. I won't say it's cyclical, but more like a tide. Bringing one demographic up to the shore, then pulling back and leaving another in their place, and sometimes mixing them all up."

"What do you mean?" I ask.

"There are the Black residents, of course. In the early twentieth century, the neighborhood had lots of working-class Italians. Then we got the first waves of Caribbean immigrants. Latinos. Africans. Everyone lived together peacefully enough in those times of overlap. My grandmother used to tell me about her best friend growing up, a Jewish girl."

"Where did everyone else go?"

Sydney elbows me, and then Kendra grimaces and reaches into her desk drawer, riffling through papers to pull out a folder. She plops it onto the desk and slides out a map of Brooklyn. It's colorful, the majority of it red and yellow with some blue along the waterfront.

"This is the map that created the Brooklyn we know now. See all that red? Those are the places that banks decided were bad investments. If you lived in those areas, it was impossible to get a loan or services that most people took for granted. And if you can't get a loan and your house starts falling down, what are you supposed to do?"

She snorts.

"This is redlining?" I ask.

"Yes," she says. "So. Bankers decide amongst themselves to not give any money to help enrich alllllll of this red area, which just so happens to be where Black people live. Things start to go bad. Everyone who can move does, but oop!—what's this? All the other areas start enacting housing covenants saying 'Hell no you can't sell this house to no black people.' Because our mere presence could turn any other color on this map *red*."

She curls her lip.

"Is that why things went downhill?" I ask, since Sydney is being oddly subdued. "I did a little research, mostly looking at photos. Lots of places fell into disrepair in the eighties."

"Crack," Kendra says, steepling her fingers. "They couldn't get us money, but they sure could get us those vials."

I don't have to guess who *they* are in this situation.

"But there have always been nice houses, too," Sydney counters. "Always."

"Right. Because we had intracommunity support to make up for what we were denied, and that's something you might want to cover, too. Black real estate agencies operated, making sure people could find places to live. Before, you weren't gonna find an ad for a house in this neighborhood anywhere but in Black newspapers like the *Amsterdam News*. Black lending associations replaced bank loans."

"But didn't banks lose money that way?" I ask. I know I'm probably annoying with my questions, but Sydney hasn't Howdy Doodied me yet.

In all the times I'd moved in New York, I'd only thought about how safe the area was for me, not what my presence meant for people in the neighborhood. Not about what advantages I had that they didn't. I was poor, too, after all, even though I had figured out how not to be, for a little while at least.

"Racism isn't generally very cost-efficient," Kendra says. "But they're making their money back hand over fist now that gentrification is in full swing. Out with the old—including us."

I sense Sydney stiffen beside me even though I'm not touching her.

"Is the church getting evicted?" she asks in that small voice that seems so unlike her.

"Eviction is so uncivilized." Kendra's lips press together. "The landlord just kept increasing the rent according to the new property value, while not doing standard repairs and upkeep. Had us freezing our asses off in here last winter." She shakes her head. "We wouldn't leave, so he sold the place. It's going to be a school again, from what I've heard."

"But there's already a school in this neighborhood," Sydney says. "I mean, I work at the school."

"You work at the public school. This is going to be an *independent* school priced just high enough to do the work of segregation for the people who will send their kids there. In the building that was one of the first schools for Black children in America." Kendra shakes her head. "I doubt it was purposeful, but ain't that something?"

I just sit there, embarrassed and sure that anything I say will result in me making things worse.

Sydney sighs, then stands. "I'm so sorry that's happening. Thanks for taking the time to speak with us."

"Yes! Thank you." I nod a few times and shove my hands into my pockets.

Kendra hands Sydney the file folder. "We'll find a way. We always do. I'm excited to come see this tour of yours, though! If you need help with anything else, just call me, okay?"

When we get outside, Sydney stops at the top of the stairs while I keep walking.

"You can go ahead," she says numbly. She's looking out at the neighborhood, but not really. Her gaze is unfocused, and the dark circles smudged beneath her eyes seem even deeper.

"Did you forget something? I can wait." I shouldn't be worried about her. Especially when I need to figure out where I'm going to be living instead of playing historian.

She shakes her head. "You're off the clock. See you later."

"I can—"

Her gaze lifts to meet mine, and when they connect, I see the woman I caught glimpses of through the window over the last few months, the woman who radiated a despair that made my own problems look like nothing, but would slap on a smile when she stepped outside her front door.

"Theo, do you know how many people have told me they're being forced out of their home, job, church, *whatever*, in just the last few days alone? Wait, don't guess. Don't." Sydney's chest rises slowly, then falls. "The shitty part of all this research is that it's like . . . finding all these instances of people burying land mines in the past, finding them right as they're blowing up under our feet in the here and now. This isn't about you. I just need to be alone."

"I understand. Thanks for breakfast," I say. I want to add something else, something that will make her feel better, but I can't even help myself in that department.

I walk off, Kendra Hill's words echoing in my mind. Sydney's mom has both a house and the garden plot, so she's not in a bad position, but the situation overall is sobering. Even if she stays, the people she knows are leaving one by one.

I never lived in one place for too long as a kid. I've never had lifelong neighbors and friends. Sydney's losing all of that, and in return she gets people like Kim, and Josie, and Terry, who either ignore the people who've lived here forever or think they're plotting against them.

I think back to the process of buying our house, which had seemed so arduous and overwhelming at the time. In retrospect, everything had worked out easily. The realtors had been eager for us to move in, and the bank had preapproved a loan that we didn't even need.

No one had second-guessed whether we belonged or were a good investment. The realtors had talked about how we were part of a wave of new people coming in to enrich the neighborhood, make it better and more valuable, without knowing a damn thing about us.

No, that's not true. The realtors had known one thing, that I was starting to see was more important than I'd realized.

Us.

Them.

Gifford Place OurHood post by Jenn Lithwick:
Hey everyone, I know things have been pretty somber, but are we still having the block party this weekend? I've been calling Mr. Perkins, but he seems to still be out of town.

Candace Tompkins: The block party is still on. Nothing short of the second coming could stop it.

Josie Ulnar: Fantastic! I'll be making the potato salad. I'm using this recipe I've been looking forward to trying. Link: <u>Carly's Raisin-tastic Potato Salad</u>.

Fitzroy Sweeney: Frightening!

Derek James: 🧝

CHAPTER 12

Sydney

THE TIGHTNESS IN MY CHEST DOESN'T LOOSEN AFTER THEO leaves. It doesn't as I walk toward the train station, even though it's hot enough to feel like I'm in a sauna. Isn't that shit supposed to relax you? Instead I just feel like I can't breathe.

I spend three hours of my afternoon in the waiting room of a nonprofit that helps with situations like mine, one I looked up after Ms. Gianetti's secretary had told me she couldn't help. The waiting room is packed with people, mostly Black and brown, most sporting either a numbed-out, hopeless expression or one of annoyance. I spend another two hours waiting at the next nonprofit after the first one tells me they can't help, either. When I finally sit with the poor overworked and harassed advocate, she apologetically tells me I need to come back on Tuesday and to bring my mother with me if possible, or something that shows I have power of attorney.

By the time I get back to Gifford Place, I'm exhausted to the marrow and craving nicotine, alcohol, a few snuggles from the bodega cat—anything to make the shit circling round and round in my head just *stop*. The block feels off—there are no kids playing in the street. Len, Amber, and LaTasha sit on a stoop, but they look hunched in and sad instead of like kids enjoying the last days of summer. A police car slows as it passes on the street, and maybe I've watched too much Animal Planet but it reminds me of a predator scanning a herd, looking for a weak youngster to pick off.

The bodega has its gate down during the evening for the first time ever, maybe, when I stop in front of it. It's stayed open through nor'easters and hurricanes, through blackouts and water main breaks, and of course *now* it's closed. As I stare in annoyed disbelief, I hear a clanking noise coming from the metal cellar door embedded in the sidewalk outside the store. There's been everything from a number hole to a social club down there over the years, but this isn't the sound of people gambling or shooting the shit. There's scraping along with the clanking and then abrupt silence.

I stomp on the metal door twice. "Abdul?"

The noise stops, but I get no response.

I know it's probably nothing, but that unsettled feeling descends on me again. I curl my fists at my side and march toward the next bodega, two blocks over. I usually avoid it because the guy who works there is always trying to holla when I just want to buy some snacks and go. I end up getting a whole pack of Parliament Lights because he plays dumb when I ask him for a loosie and I won't beg him for it.

The full box is expensive as shit. I hope Abdul finishes his renovations quickly.

I smoke a cigarette on the walk back to cut the need, deep, greedy pulls that leave me light-headed. My hands are shaking by the time I get to my stoop, and I wonder if I should maybe go to a doctor to get this lack-of-sleep thing looked into because I'm really starting to feel the effects. My mood has plummeted and all I want to do is sit and cry.

I *just* had my period so I know it can't be PMS.

When I open the mailbox and see another bundle of medical bills, the worst kind of déjà vu, I let out a little desperate laugh. Yeah, I'm not going to the doctor anytime soon, unless it's against my will.

Again.

I pull out my phone as I walk through the hallway toward my apartment door, pausing to swipe away the missed calls from bill collectors to see if Drea has texted.

Nothing.

She sometimes does this, disappears into a new bae, eating, drinking, and breathing nothing but them. With a holiday weekend and a surplus of personal days, she could be gone for who knows how long, though I'm surprised that she would boo up right before the West Indian Day parade. This is generally her free agent period so she can whine on whoever.

And at her most infatuated, she still responds to me, even if just with tongue + water drops emojis, or a thumbs-up.

And she never lets a fight drag on. If I piss her off, she tells me. If I start shit, she finishes it, and we get back to normal.

But the Drea is typing . . . message still mocks me from the top of our chat. I bet she started to write something while annoyed and thought better of it, but imagining what it could be, and how angry she must be at me not to even look at the chat and notice, shoots my stress through the roof.

"You're too clingy."

"I can't stand being around you anymore."

"God, you're pathetic."

No. Those are things Marcus would say. Not Drea. Drea loves me. For real loves me.

I shouldn't push anymore, but I feel frazzled by just about everything, and guilty for putting so much onto her, and worried because a million things could have happened on her date with a stranger.

I call her cell, and when it goes to voicemail, I try to sound normal and not like a stalker friend. "Hey, big head. Let me know you're okay, okay?"

After I disconnect the call, I dial her work number, and it also goes to voicemail, but I hang up before the beep.

I call Mr. Perkins again and leave another voicemail for him, too. He was always so bad about leaving his phone on silent. One reason why "City Hall" became City Hall was that people knew you had to just go over and see him, since he never answered his phone. I don't like not hearing from him, but I'm sure Ms. Candace has spoken to him.

When I unlock the door to my apartment and push it open, I'm met with resistance.

I push again and it opens a little and then closes.

Something is pushing back.

Fear slides down my spine and swirls around in my belly, but when I push one more time, I realize that the resistance is coming from the mat on the other side of the door—sometimes the corner rolls back. I let out a shaky breath, tired of being scared of every damn thing. I wiggle the door back and forth, which pushes the mat away and reveals the mustard yellow of a manila envelope.

Drea had told me that she'd slipped the VerenTech info under my door, and I had totally forgotten. She'd gone out of her way for me, like she always did, and I couldn't even be bothered to remember until days later.

I'm almost relieved to realize I fucked up—maybe this is why she's avoiding me. This is fixable.

After closing the door, I toss the folder onto the kitchen table with my other research, shuck off my grimy clothes, and head directly into the shower. Lathering up my washcloth and scrubbing until my skin tingles is cheap therapy, and by the time I slip on shorts and a tank top, I'm still exhausted but feel slightly less like I'm in a tar pit of depression.

Night is falling outside and I open the back door to let in a breeze; the neighborhood is too quiet for a summer night, and I jump when a lone cicada suddenly bursts into song somewhere nearby.

Mommy's Coney Island ashtray, from way back before she quit smoking, rests next to the place mat. I brought it inside a few weeks ago, breaking the "no smoking inside" rule, because every time I tried to relax out back, Toby would go off like I was coming for his Purina. I sometimes imagined him clutching his dog bowl the same way his owner clutched her purse when I was behind her on the walk home from work one day just after they moved here.

Whatever. Toby and his owner can kiss my ass. I have more important things to focus on.

The envelope is thin, especially compared to the stacks of papers already on the table. When I open it and pull the papers out I realize this isn't what I would've gotten if I'd gone downtown to make the request. Each one of the ten pages has FOR INTERNAL USE ONLY stamped in red in the top right corner. I grab the lighter from the tabletop and a cigarette, light it, and scan the first page.

> The Company (VerenTech) acknowledges that this Memorandum is a public record subject to disclosure but do hereby require that we be notified of any and all FOIA requests, both during the city selection process and in the event that this city is chosen, to allow the Company to seek a protective order or other appropriate remedy.

Legalese is not my jam, but I'm pretty sure that this is VerenTech asking the City of New York to snitch if anyone asks about what they're doing. I have no idea if this is normal or not, but asking for a list of people who requested information that should be public in order to seek "a protective order or other appropriate remedy" against them is ominous as hell.

I had requested information. I'd been denied but . . .

I take another drag from the cigarette.

The second page, after the "snitches get stitches" clause, is full of terminology I fully have no fucking idea what to make of.

The third page seems to be from some kind of census report on the neighborhood surrounding the old medical center. My neighborhood. Number of inhabitants, racial breakdown of the inhabitants, median income, how many people make use of SSI, WIC, Medicaid. These numbers are bumped up by the housing projects, but it's somewhat alarming to see the totals highlighted in red below a certain income level.

There's a block of text in a memo area under the numbers.

> Area is centrally located. It's at the convergence of several subway lines, making it ideal for commuting into Manhattan. There is also commuter train service to Long Island and Penn Station. Tree-lined streets abound and there are many parks, small and large, though most are currently used as hangouts for delinquents or drug dealers. It is also within reasonable walking distance from Prospect Park, meaning the goal of closing gap between the Park Slope operations and the Northwest sector can be reached within the next few years.
>
> JFK is not far, for those who travel often, and access to and from Long Island and its beaches is convenient for those with property there. These resources are cur-

> rently underutilized. While many of the brownstones and apartment buildings have not been kept up, a surprising number will require minimal work to meet our standards. We anticipate a full rej-

I turn the paper over but there's nothing on the back and the next page is from a different report. A quick flip through shows that all of the pages were printed slightly too big, cutting off portions of the text.

I didn't know that VerenTech had a Park Slope campus. That doesn't make sense, given how everyone made such a big deal of the project about to get started in my neighborhood.

The fourth page is clearly from another report, given its numbering, and lists "incentives" from the city that VerenTech is currently considering, and I inhale wrong and start to choke. The tax subsidies alone amount to over a billion dollars. A billion motherfucking dollars.

This is a lot of money at play, before anything else is even on the table. It's more than a little rage-inducing when thinking about the redline map Kendra had given us, and how little investment the neighborhood has been deemed worthy of.

The next page is just columns of numbers that mean nothing to me, but the last three pages are easily understandable.

VERENTECH HEADQUARTERS CAMPUS, 5-YEAR PROJECTION reads the first page, and it's a mock-up of an immense shining tower right in the middle of the neighborhood, like the mother ship for those alien cranes hovering everywhere. At its base is the renovated medical center that will serve as the research and development building. The buildings around it are the familiar ones that have always lined these streets.

I flip to the ten-year projection; in this illustration, the campus has spread. A few more tall buildings—this time condominiums, with storefronts along the bottom. For this to work out, a few other buildings will have to be torn down. There's a condominium where the YMCA should be, too.

My mom told me something about the YMCA maybe moving to a bigger space, which would make sense if an office building accommodating thousands and thousands of new workers was moving into the immediate area, but it's still unsettling to see such a major change neatly laid out.

The fifteen-year projection shows a neighborhood that's completely unrecognizable to me at first glance, even though it's my street. Condominiums, large faux brownstones and smaller glass-fronted cubes, have replaced several of the familiar houses.

I stare at the image for a long time before I notice that there are people along the bottom edge of the paper, slightly cut off by the bad print job. All of the little illustrated heads I see?

Belong to white people.

Something slams upstairs, right above my head. A door in Drea's apartment? I didn't hear her come in the front, but maybe she crept up because she's still mad at me.

Sulking and evasion aren't Drea's usual style. I pick up my phone and check our text chat even though I know damn well she hasn't responded: Drea is typing . . .

Enough is enough.

I shove my feet into my house slippers and head out into the hallway. I pass the coat closet under the stairs, pushing the door that's always slightly ajar shut, and walk to the bottom of the steps.

"Drea?" I call up the stairs, and the frightened-sounding reverberation of my own voice jump-starts my pulse. There's no reason to be scared. This is the house I grew up in. Any spirits that linger here have either had a lifetime to make their move or wish me no harm.

What if it's not a spirit?

The question slithers icily down the nape of my neck.

I head up the stairs, just to prove I can. Mommy would have been ashamed at how I'm acting this week, shook by every little thing. One time when I was about eight, I woke her up to tell her a monster was living under my bed. She told me to get the .22 and shoot it, then take my behind to sleep.

I laugh a little at that memory, fortify myself with it.

When I get up to the second landing, there's silence behind Drea's door. Usually when she's home, there's music or humming, or just the thrum of her energy—the same thing that first drew me into the light of her friendship.

"Dre?" I knock. Silence.

I turn the knob.

It opens.

The apartment is sticky with humidity and smells of sage, coconut, and shea butter. Everything in the living room fits Drea's personal color palette—yellow, teal, and orange, bathing you in brightness as soon as you step through the door.

The late-afternoon light from the sun setting behind the buildings across the street spears into the apartment, pinning down

Drea's belongings around the apartment: the altar with a half-burnt sage bundle and various crystals; the heart-shaped couch pillow I cross-stitched her name into during our home economics class; her college diploma, framed with a photo of me, her, and Mommy at her graduation.

A door slams down the hallway again and I jump, then breathe a sigh of relief. One of the best parts of her apartment layout is she gets the bomb cross-breeze, but if she doesn't put a doorstop under her bedroom door, it'll slam and open, slam and open.

I head back to her bedroom, pushing the door open and sliding the wooden triangle under it with my foot. The color scheme in here is different—all white and purple. I head over to her window; her polka-dot curtains flap in my face from the breeze but then go still after I shut the window.

She must have been home at some point today if her window is open . . .

My body tenses. This is where her air conditioner should be. Her brand-new air conditioner. There's no reason for there to be a cross-breeze because this window shouldn't be open.

My head starts to spin a little and I realize I'm not breathing. My brain is too busy trying to piece everything together, and has forgotten basic functions.

I have to get out of here. The air conditioner is gone, Drea didn't tell me she was moving it, and anyone could've come in from the fire escape. They could be in here right now.

I start to dash out of the room, but a dark stain on Drea's white duvet catches my eye and I skid to a halt.

Dried blood is dark like that.

I walk slowly toward the bed, heart in my throat and the fear threatening to blot out any sense I have left. Then the stain *moves.*

Tiny flecks of it crawl around the edges, and this time it's not my mind playing tricks on me.

It's not blood. It's a clump of bedbugs.

A ripple of repulsion passes over my skin, leaving itchiness in its wake.

I run for a giant plastic bag from under the kitchen sink, force myself to ball the duvet up around the mass of bugs, and shove it into the bag, then run it outside after double-bagging it four times over.

I don't think as I'm doing it, or feel. I'm on autopilot, just like last time . . .

I don't know how much time passes after that. I search every crevice of her bed, her floorboards, her closet, but find no other evidence of the bugs.

I start to shove her clothes into bags to be heat-treated, but it's too much.

I'm overwhelmed and she might not appreciate me all up in her stuff, especially since she already thinks I'm unhealthily obsessed with the bedbugs. I didn't take a picture. By the time she comes home, I'm going to look like a maniac who threw away her favorite duvet out of spite.

She's already suggesting therapy and I need to calm down. I don't think she would hurt me purposely, like Marcus did, but the bite of restraints against my wrists isn't something I want to feel again.

I place her clothes back into their cubbyholes and try to get the closet back to the neat state it was in before I tore through it looking for bedbugs. When I have it back in order, I pick up a few slips of paper that drifted out from the bottom-left cubby.

A receipt from the old Foodtown that's currently being renovated so it can be reopened as a Whole Foods–type supermarket. A phone number and smiley face scrawled on a ripped scrap of paper with a blue ballpoint pen. An ATM deposit slip for fifty thousand dollars.

Fifty thousand dollars.

Drea tells me about all her side hustles, and especially if they pay even remotely well.

Fifty thousand dollars. What would pay that well and in a lump sum?

But this was from around the time I was in the deepest shit with Marcus. Maybe I'd forgotten, or she hadn't wanted to rub it in while I was suffering. Yeah, that makes sense.

There's a scan of the check itself on the receipt, which is dated from before I'd returned home. The name of the company it was issued by is hard to read at first, or maybe I just don't want to see it, but it's all too familiar to me.

I stare at it for a long moment, trying to reconcile it with what I know of the company. Drea would never . . .

She would never.

She'll explain when she gets back. Of course there's an explanation.

I march mindlessly back to the apartment downstairs and barricade myself in my bedroom with a bottle of wine and my cell phone. I wrap my hands in socks to keep from hurting myself as I scratch at imagined bugs crawling over my skin, and I jump at imaginary flecks of black just out of my line of sight. I can't distract myself with TV because I need to hear if there are any more noises in the building, but I take a sip every time the possibility of what that check means pops into my mind.

By the time the sun rises, the bottle is empty, I haven't slept a wink, and Drea still hasn't come home.

Gifford Place OurHood post by Kaneisha Bell:
I just want to put out there that a strange white man showed up at my door and asked to come in and do a "valuation" of my house. This was the first I'd heard of any of this, so I didn't let him in. I called the police, and they said they'd send someone out to get a statement, but no one ever came. Everyone keep an eye out.

Candace Tompkins: @Fitzroy Sweeney @Gracie Todd

Asia Martin: That is scary as fuck. Do you think he was trying to do a home invasion?

Josie Ulnar: No, no, we had our home valuated last week and it's fine. They just come in and take a look around. It's so they can figure out the property tax. You have to let them in.

Asia Martin: We don't *have* to do shit, actually.

CHAPTER 13

Theo

"NORTH AMERICA. BRAZIL. THE DUTCH WEST INDIA COMPANY was founded explicitly to wage economic warfare. It's in their charter. I thought the Dutch were a neutral people, but maybe I was thinking of the Swiss."

Sydney grunts a response. Her behavior is worrying me. I've been talking for ten minutes straight and she hasn't smiled, hasn't made fun of me, hasn't responded to the Dutch West India Company facts I'm spouting to impress her.

She stares into space as she waters the sunflowers along the edge of the community garden, the dark circles under her eyes so startling that my stomach twisted at first glance, mistaking them for black eyes. I'm starting to wonder if she's slept at all this week—it's hard not to notice that she's more fidgety and fatigued every time I see her.

I'm also wondering why her problems, which she hasn't asked for help with, are making me so antsy.

I keep talking.

"But the craziest thing I found was that a lot of these guys made their money from slaves—uh, enslaved people."

"Duh. I thought you were supposed to be good at research,"

she says. I can tell she's trying for a jab, but it lands more like a weak poke.

I press on, trying to revive the Sydney who's so passionate about history.

"Well, that's not the crazy thing. After slavery ended, all these guys needed new jobs, so they just moved into the banking sector, even founding some of them. Like you know Veritas Bank? Started by a Brooklyn-Dutch former slave master. You told me before that the banks were all tied up in slavery, when you talked about that crash, but it's like all these guys never gave up much power, they just . . ." I struggle to find the right way to say this, the right words to convey how royally fucked this is. "They just put on a different suit. Things didn't change that much. They were still controlling all the money, and in a way they were still controlling the people they didn't own anymore, because they controlled who got money, where money was invested. And one of the Veritas directors even lived in this neighborhood! His last name was Vriesendaal, like the old sanitarium."

"Wow," she says, but there's no excitement in her voice. None of the passion from when she showed me her ideas, or even when she interrupted during the brownstone tour. "Good work. I can use that."

I keep talking. You can usually talk people out of bad moods, just like you can talk them into other things. Keep the words flowing at a steady pace. Lull them into a kind of distracted comfort, or push them into annoyance. Either way, their reaction is under your control.

"And what kind of name is Usselincx, the name of the guy who founded the company? It sounds like the super-obvious villain in a movie. 'Mwahaha, my name is Usselincx and I came here to steal land and get trounced by the British, and I'm all out of—'"

"Theo." She cuts a glance at me through squinted eyes. "You're wandering very close to the borders of Howdy Doody Land, and also tap-dancing *just* next to my last nerve. Step lightly."

I shouldn't be happy to have drawn this reaction from her, but that's the first time she's looked remotely up-and-at-'em today. I do my best approximation of a soft shuffle next to a patch of lettuce and she playfully swerves the spray of water in my direction, though she makes sure not to get me wet.

I feel slightly ridiculous for having just literally tap-danced for a woman I supposedly don't care about, but her expression is a little less taut, and there's a bit of light in her eyes.

She turns off the hose and wipes her hands over her shorts—longer cutoffs than she's worn the past few days, accentuating her hips and thighs without revealing them. I take a deep breath and pull my thoughts in the opposite direction.

"Ready to meet the Day Club Crew and pump them for history?" she asks.

"Let's go."

WHEN WE GET to Candace's house, I hate that I'm shocked at how nice it is, mostly because the outside is so markedly in a state of disrepair. I wouldn't have picked this as one of the nicest places on the block, and I excel at that. Kim had always been annoyed by this house, saying it was being wasted. She would have thought differently if she'd stopped being a jerk long enough to be invited inside.

The inner door is glass embedded in dark wood, allowing you to see into the bright open-plan living room/dining room/kitchen area that takes up the floor.

The walls are an elegant eggshell and the furniture all looks expensive and classy. A long window along the kitchen wall floods the entire floor with sunlight from the backyard. It looks like a picture from the Boomtown app, except there are Black people in the frame.

At the dining room table sit three elderly women and an even older man, judging by the number of wrinkles on his face. He moves his mouth in the familiar way of someone with uncomfortable dentures working them with his tongue. One of the women is thin and wearing a scarf on her head, another has her hair in a straight gray bob, and the third has one half of hers undone—the other half has been put into a boxer braid, a style Kim was crazy about after seeing it in some fashion magazine.

Candace goes to stand behind the woman and begins braiding the other half of her hair with quick efficient twists and pulls of her fingers and wrists.

"Who's this man?" the woman with the scarf asks. There's the slight singsong of Caribbean accent in her voice, but the wariness is unmissable. "Another come try to steal we homes?"

I don't know how to respond so I look to Sydney.

"Hi, Miss Ruth," she says, taking a seat at the table. "This is Theodore. He owns the house where the Paynes used to live."

My name isn't Theodore, but I nod in the woman's direction anyway as I take a seat. "Nice to meet you, Miss Ruth."

"Ah, it was the Payne house he took? I like him, then. I was so glad when that family left, let me tell you. I couldn't *stand* Doris Payne, always thinking she better than everyone, trying to talk down her nose to me." Miss Ruth's accent grows harder to understand as she gets agitated, but I try to follow. "She look funny at my husband, asking him to come fix her kitchen sink and all that! I smack she black she white, and she never talk to him again."

She nods decisively and the other women make noises of commiseration. I have no idea what she just said but I nod, too.

The old man works his dentures, then says, "Doris was a good woman in my book."

"Of course you would say so, Fitzroy," the woman with the gray bob says in an accent that could be British.

Sydney chuckles, an encouraging sign of life.

Candace shakes her head. "Theo, that's Gracie and this is Paulette. Paulette don't talk much."

The woman getting her hair braided stays silent but keeps a wary gaze locked on me, even as Candace finishes her hair and pats her shoulder before taking her own seat.

"How are you doing, Sydney?" Gracie asks politely as she reaches for the teapot in the middle of the table and fills two cups before handing them to me and Sydney. "Haven't talked to you much the last few months."

"I've been busy," Sydney says. "You know how it is."

"Well, no, I don't know, since I'm an old crone who spends my days watching stories with these miscreants, but I understand."

That gets another laugh around the table, but Gracie's blithe behavior doesn't completely distract from the curious worry in her eyes.

I take a sip of the strong tea and try to keep my expression neutral as the bitter liquid hits my tongue, but something must give away my urge to do a spit-take because Gracie's gaze meets mine with amusement dancing in her eyes. "Have you never had bush tea before, young man?"

"No," I manage, eyes watering. "It's . . . strong."

"Good for the health," Fitzroy says. "That's why we old-timers are still here and kicking."

"Don't worry, it's not poison," Gracie adds, then tilts her head. "Not for *us*. But come to think of it, it *is* a recipe passed down from generation to generation, and back on the Bajan plantations it was called 'buckra's do-fa-do.' Many slavers came to an unfortunate end after having a cup."

Fitzroy snort-laughs. "Not enough of them, though!"

I wait for Gracie to laugh, too, and tell me she's joking, but she just takes a sip of her tea and stares at me over the rim. I hold my cup awkwardly, knowing this is some kind of test but unsure whether it's to see if I'm dumb enough to believe there's a poison that works only on white people or dumb enough not to.

There's a taut silence and then I think *fuck it* and take a sip.

Candace starts laughing, her eyes wide. "You think Gracie won't poison you? Boy, this woman has gone through five husbands and I *know* some of them deaths wasn't natural."

"I have no idea what you're talking about," Gracie says demurely. "I just wanted to see if the young man could take a ribbing."

She winks at me, and though she's maybe sixty-five, I fully understand why men kept marrying her even if she was possibly a murderer.

"Sydney!" Miss Ruth calls her name suddenly, like Sydney hasn't been sitting across the table from her the whole time. "I heard you left that man of yours, the one with a forehead like that Black *Star Trek* alien. I say, 'Good riddance.' Good for you. Never liked the way he acted when he came around here." She dusts her hands in an exaggerated motion, then claps.

Sydney's chest heaves up and down before she opens her mouth to speak.

"Uh, thanks, Miss Ruth. I just had some questions about the neighborhood for the history tour," she says. "Can we talk about that, please?"

Miss Ruth doesn't look happy about being denied gossip about Sydney's ex. I'm bummed about it, too.

"You can't ask your mother?" Fitzroy asks.

"Yolanda is not well, remember?" Gracie chides, and Fitzroy startles. Her glower dissolves into a pitying smile when she turns to Sydney. "Fitzroy is more like Forgets-roy these days. Ignore him. We all do."

Sydney nods tightly, then blinks a few times and says, "It's fine. I do have stories from my mother, but do any of you have fun facts about the neighborhood or people who lived here that I can use for my tour?"

"I have stories, but not ones you can use," Miss Ruth says, and they all laugh.

Fitzroy scratches at his bald head.

"I came here before your mother, I believe. In seventy-two," Fitzroy says. "I bought my home from a Jamaican man who worked at one of the Black real estate agencies. I think, now, all the white agencies come and push them out, too. And then they sell to the white people. But a few years ago, it was mostly us selling, and mostly us buying. At least on Gifford Place."

Between this and Kendra Hill's conversation, I'm realizing that I'd never thought much about Black communities, or Black people, really.

I had, of course, but in the same way I think about the U.S. Postal Service. It exists, and functions, mostly, but I don't know the nuts and bolts of how things get delivered. When I think of a Black community, the first thing that comes to mind—even if I don't want it to—is crime. Drugs. Gangs. Welfare. That's all the news has talked about since I was a kid. Not old people drinking tea. Not complex self-sustaining financial systems that had to be created because racism means being left out to dry.

"You have to own property. You have to," Gracie says. "My father always told us that. That's why they don't like to sell to us, you know? Making up stories about property value dropping like they aren't the ones who decide the value." She makes a derisive noise. "Truth is, if you own, you have power. That's why they always try to strip it away."

"Listen to all this capitalist talk," Miss Ruth says with a head toss. "What we need is revolution."

"Ruth, you own five houses. Don't even start," Candace says severely. "Your head would be the first on the block on *this* block."

Ruth shrugs. "I play on the game board I'm given, Candace. At least if I sell four of the houses, maybe I'll be able to pay the property taxes on the fifth. They can pry my house from my cold, dead fingers."

"Ah, that reminds me of a story, Sydney." Fitzroy nods. "When the blackout happened, way back when. I had to stand in front of my house with my cricket bat. Said, 'Booooy, you wanna try it you can try it' to every knucklehead who tried to take what I had worked for. Not a window was shattered, not a plant pot was overturned." He laughs deeply and then coughs, and Candace walks over, picks up his cup, and holds it to his mouth so he sips.

"The blackout a few years back?" I ask.

"No, there was one in seventy-seven," Sydney says. "There was looting and all kinds of wild stuff."

"Looting." Gracie snorts delicately.

"Yeah," Sydney continues. "My mom told me the TV we had when I was a kid was one she 'found on the street' in front of an electronics store during the blackout."

All of the older people around the table chuckle.

"Well, I don't know how she got that TV, but I do know that someone stepped to your mama while she sat on the porch smoking and watching the madness," Fitzroy says. "That man ended up dancing away from the end of her revolver. I thought I was doing something with my cricket bat, and she was over there ready to shoot."

Candace laughs. "Oh, you know Yolanda's folks were those Virginians."

"She never told me that," Sydney says, bittersweet laughter in her voice. "But I can imagine it. She told me she wasn't raised to take mess but she knew how to clean it up."

"I can't believe I don't know anything about this blackout,"

I say, itching to pull out my phone but not wanting to be rude. "What caused it?"

"It was on purpose," a quiet voice says, and when I look across the table, Paulette is staring at me. Her dark eyes are hard, and her voice doesn't have a Caribbean lilt, but sounds more like an imitation of a New York accent from an old movie. "They wanted us to destroy everything, so they could come in and *fix* it. Turned off the lights. Started trouble in the dark. They got a foot back in the door then, a toe, but it wasn't enough damage. After that the drugs came, all of a sudden, and the violence, and the cops. Breaking everything down, so they could come in and build it up for themselves."

Candace sighs into the heavy silence after that statement. "When I said Paulette don't talk much, I meant when she does, it's illuminati mess from watching too many YouTube videos."

Paulette's gaze hasn't swerved from mine. "He knows. He's one of them, always sneaking around at night, always watching. Here to break and build, break and build." Her voice is rising steadily, gaining strength. "Race riots, they call them, but who started them? Why would *we*? Who profited? He's one of them!"

Her last words bounce off the high ceiling and reverberate in the room. Her breathing is heavy and she's looking at me as if she sees through the smile, the goofiness, right down to the poor trash grifter core of me.

Candace leans across the table and takes Paulette's hand. "Paulie?"

Paulette looks at Candace for a long minute, gaze unfocused, but slowly she comes back to herself, then smiles. "Hey, Candy."

"There we go, honey." Candace gives her hand a squeeze.

"We should get going," Sydney says, and I feel terrible because I'm the reason we should. My mere presence was enough to give this woman a panic attack, which is annoying, because I haven't done anything to her. And I can't say that or defend myself because, well, Howdy fucking Doody.

I stand up. "Thanks for the tea."

"Break and build," Paulette mutters accusatorily, but doesn't look my way again.

"Thank you, everyone," Sydney says.

"Don't be a stranger. You should come by more, even if your mother isn't around," Ruth says. "We're here for you."

Sydney nods, then goes around the table giving hugs.

I wave, still awkward, and Gracie raises her teacup to me. "If you don't die from the tea, you can come by again, too."

Gifford Place OurHood/privateusergroup/Rejuvenation

Emergency board meeting in the next 48 hours. Turn your notifications on for exact time—attendance is mandatory, long weekend or no.

CHAPTER 14

Sydney

"SHE WAS KIDDING, RIGHT?" THEO ASKS AS SOON AS OUR feet hit the slate sidewalk in front of Ms. Candace's. "About the poison?"

His heavy brows are all bunched up and there's a slight flush on those sharp cheekbones of his.

"I don't know," I say, because I'm feeling kind of evil and he's conveniently there. "I guess we'll find out soon enough if you—"

Nausea hits me before I can finish the joke, and not from poison tea. It's the stomach-roiling ache of buried pain that resurfaces unexpected at the worst times, natural as a whale breaching the surface, not giving a single fuck whether boats are caught in its wake.

Tears fill my eyes and I walk a bit faster so Theo can't see my face.

"She was joking. You'll be fine." I fan my face. "It's hot as hell. I hate sweating."

I lift the bottom of my shirt and wipe my face, hoping Theo is too distracted by either my weirdness or my exposed skin to notice the breathy sob that escapes as I wipe my "sweat" away.

I drop my shirt and adjust it at my hips, scrunching my nose a few times instead of sniffling out loud. A few yards away, leaves and branches peek through the community garden's fence, waving in the breeze.

"Are you—" Theo starts, then stops. "Let's go get something cold to drink from the corner store."

"Okay."

I wish he would take my hand and lead me there, even though it's only a couple of buildings down, how Mommy would hold my hand when I crossed the street, even though I was old enough to watch for cars myself.

But of course he wouldn't do that. He's just my neighbor.

He holds the door open for me but when I step inside, I'm disoriented. Everything is clean and bright instead of the comfortingly run-down state the store had been in before. It looks like someone from some quick-makeover reality show pulled an all-nighter—the walls are white, the light fixtures are nicer, the shelves have been replaced, and apparently so has the stock. There's a fresh-fruit-and-veggie section where the freezer full of ice cream had been. The shelves are clean enough to pass a white glove test, and there's nary a Goya product in sight. The word *organic* is *everywhere,* and the hot-food prep area is gone. Instead, there's a fridge with premade sandwiches, wraps, sushi, and quinoa salad.

It even smells different, the greasy odor of the grill replaced by a new scent that's more like the lack of one.

"Abdul, this is wild," I say. "Did you get a loan or something?"

But when my gaze searches around for the new placement of

the cash register, Abdul isn't there waiting to call me *habibi* and slip me a Parliament. The guy behind the counter is slightly paler, with sandy brown hair and sharp brown eyes.

"Abdul had some issues with his papers," he says, then flashes me a smile. "I'm Tony, the new owner. Nice to meet you. I'm looking forward to becoming a valued part of the Gifford Place community."

"What? You mean he's . . . gone?"

"But not forgotten, clearly," Tony says with a wink.

I turn on my heels and head to the wine fridge, my head feeling fuzzy. Abdul is gone. Grill man is gone. Just like that.

I automatically reach for the wine I've been buying for months, but my hand closes around a tiny bottle of kombucha health drink. I stare at it, my sluggish brain trying to catch up with this latest change, but I feel a gaze drilling into my back. When I glance to my left, Tony is leaning all the way over the counter watching me.

"Need help with anything?" he asks. "If you're looking for the forties, we don't sell malt liquor anymore."

I slam the fridge door a bit too hard and walk up to pay.

"You like kombucha?" Theo asks. "It tastes like vinegar."

I ignore him and place the bottle on the counter. My skin is crawling. There's no lotto machine, no people standing around fantasizing about what they'll do with their Mega Millions when they win. No bins of cheap candy. No character.

No Abdul.

The panic starts to thrum in my chest again.

"That isn't covered by WIC," Tony says *nicely* as he scans my drink. I'm starting to understand that this is the same way Josie says *nice* things on OurHood posts. It's a thin veneer that if scratched away would reveal some shit I'm definitely not in a state to handle right now.

"Not that there's anything wrong with WIC or forties, but is there any reason you're making assumptions about my drinking habits or financial status?"

He shrugs. Smirks. Rings up the drink, which costs five damn dollars. "Just being helpful. And making sure people understand what kind of establishment this is now."

When I pull out a twenty to pay, he makes a big show of taking out the counterfeit money tester and running the marker over it, holding it up to the light and scrutinizing it. I almost walk out but I need my money back.

He finally hands me my change, except it's a five-dollar bill instead of a ten and a five.

"I gave you a twenty," I say. "You stared at it long enough, you should know that."

My politeness reserves are gone, depleted by trying to restrain my nerves, which are stretched to the breaking point.

Tony looks befuddled. "Did you? I don't think so."

"I. Did."

"She did," Theo says from beside me. "Come on, man. Give her the money."

"Or . . . what?" Tony asks with a smile, leaning on the counter like some old drawing of a kindly neighborhood grocer.

"What?" Theo asks, the sudden bass in his voice surprising me.

"If I say she gave me a ten, who could prove otherwise?"

Tony's voice and expression haven't changed at all, and there's something dangerous about him now precisely because of that.

"Let's just go," I say, plucking at Theo's shirt.

"No." When I look at Theo he is *tight*. "Give her the money. Just be cool and give her the money, man."

Tony looks down at us in amusement.

"Someone needs to make a purchase in order for the drawer to open again," Tony lies calmly.

Theo pulls out two crumpled dollar bills and throws them on the counter, then picks up a severely overpriced peanut butter cup. "I'll take this."

"Sure thing." Tony takes the money, flattens each bill out, then rings up the purchase. He seems to debate a second before handing my ten dollars to Theo. "Sorry about the confusion. It's hard putting things in order when you're getting settled in."

He doesn't even look at me again. I turn and storm out of the store and hear Theo following close behind. He catches up in a few steps. "You forgot your carbonated vinegar and your money."

I whirl on him and snatch both from his hands.

"What the fuck?"

"Whoa. I think you mean 'Thanks for getting my money back.'"

"No! I said we should leave, and you went full white dude who doesn't want to be told no!" I feel so dumb, yelling at him with tears in my eyes when he just helped me.

Ungrateful. Needy.

"So, we should have just let him steal your money? What was I supposed to do?"

I squeeze my eyes closed and my mouth shut and try to force back the rage that wants to explode out of every orifice because he's right. When the feeling subsides, I say, "Yes. I was going to let him just steal my money. Because I did the mental math on how much time and energy I'd waste dealing with his bullshit, and that's before factoring in what happens if the police show up. I'm tired, okay? I—"

I stop myself. I can't tell him. I'd pegged him right when he walked into Mr. Perkins's place. He was a strange white man, not my friend. I'm not sure I even have friends anymore.

Drea is typing . . . flashes in my head and I fight the urge to scream again.

"Look. Thank you. But I need to go home now." The words feel like dust in my mouth.

"Sydney." He looks like he wants to apologize, but I shake my head.

"You're relieved of duty, research intern."

"Wait, what? Like, for today or forever?"

I ignore him and he's smart enough not to follow me.

When I get to the house I ignore the new batch of bills that've arrived, the new pile of cards promising quick cash if you just pull up your roots and leave everything you know. I put the kombucha in the fridge, grab a cigarette from the pack on the table, and pry open the door that leads to the backyard.

The heat-swollen wood resists until I tug so hard that I stumble back, cracking one of my nails in the process. Toby starts barking through the wooden fence, startling me, and for some reason that's what causes the tears to start in earnest this time. I plop down on the back step, glad that most of the yard is paved over because the part that isn't has thigh-high weeds that I'll have to deal with sooner or later.

The dozens and dozens of plant clippings I've been ignoring out here have mostly managed to survive, at least. Some things do that without always needing help. It's pathetic as hell to be outdone by a cherry tomato bush.

A tear drips off the end of my nose, soaking through the thin paper of the cigarette as I light it.

"Dammit!" I drop the lighter onto the ground as the flame licks out and burns my thumb; the dog starts barking even more wildly.

Our conversation with Kendra, the check in Drea's room, Paulette's fear of Theo, Tony's shit at the brand-new bodega, Drea disappearing . . . it all swirls around in my head, threatening to overwhelm me.

I start to wonder if maybe I shouldn't just give up on the tour. The neighborhood is changing too fast; maybe everything will be gone before I can even make the first demo. Maybe none of this matters because Mommy, the only one who actually believed I could do this, isn't here to see it.

I exhale a cloud of smoke and shake my head, then wipe the tears from my eyes. I need to do this, even if only once, for the block party. Just to show that we were here, and we're still here, and that fact matters, even if I throw out all the notes I made and the tour ends up being me bullshitting anecdotes about the people who made this neighborhood what it is.

Toby suddenly yips in pain, and I glance toward the fence. Toby is a menace, but I don't want him getting hurt, either.

"Arwin! Leave that dog alone, will you?" Josie's voice grates through the wooden slats of the fence.

"I'm just playing, Mom. *You* leave *me* alone!"

Lord, if I'd ever spoken to my mother this way she would've death-glared a hole into my soul.

Josie says, "Sorry, honey. But I'm trying to relax on my day off. And gardening is my way of relaxing."

"That stuff smells!" Arwin complains. They are talking *entirely* too loud for two people right next to each other, driving my blood pressure up another point or two.

"It's fertilizer. Do you know what that is?"

"No."

"It's shit, sweetie."

Something about the way she says the curse word with such deliberation and relish, to her child, makes my shoulder blades tense up.

Arwin just giggles and yells, "Shit! Shit!"

Josie laughs, too. "Sometimes you have soil that isn't good for growing things in anymore. It needs time to become fertile again. So you cover it with the shit, and then you wait. You let the shit do the work, then you come in and plant your crops. My grandfather taught me that. His grandfather taught him that."

My phone vibrates in my hand and I'm so on edge that I almost drop it. I stiffen in the moment right before a name pops up on the screen, but it's Len, not Drea.

Shit. I was supposed to go meet him in the garden.

"Hey," I say, trying to sound like something other than a

stressed-out wreck. "I'm sorry I'm late. I'm gonna head over right now. Can you wait a couple more minutes?"

"No." His voice sounds like it did when he was a little boy, and then he clears his throat. "I was sitting on one of the benches waiting for you, with the kids, and the cops showed up."

"What?" I stub out the cigarette, and I'm already through the back door and jogging past the kitchen table when he responds.

"Yeah. Um. They—they kicked all of us out? Everyone who was just chillin' or gardening. Said it was on order of the owner, and I was confused because I thought your moms owned it. I tried to ask them what was happening, but they started pushing me—"

He stops and takes a shaky breath, and in that moment I hear the aggressive tone of a police officer in the background ordering people to disperse. I've heard that voice and that order on too many videos followed by hashtags on social media.

"I'm coming, okay? Just listen to the officers and walk away from the garden."

"Okay."

"Stay on the phone with me, Len. Don't hang up until I get there."

My hands shake as I lock the door, and then I run hard down the street, the soles of my sneakers pounding the pavement and my heart a wild, fearful thing trying to escape my chest.

No. No. No. No.

My disbelief keeps pace with my feet. This can't be happening. Not after everything else.

When I get to Mommy's garden, I find two officers standing in front of the chain-link fence. Just behind them, a wiry white man with graying hair is removing a new padlock from its plastic casing. The padlock Mommy used for years, more a deterrent than actual security, is on the ground, broken.

Inside, a crew of three or four other white guys in construction-worker uniforms of jeans and T-shirts are walking around examining everything. Taking notes. I see the decorations the kids had been making for the block party on the ground under their boots.

I'm too shocked to feel anything.

This is it.

This is the end of everything.

In my peripheral vision, I see Len standing with Ms. Candace. A few middle school kids on their bikes stand with feet on the ground and hands gripping their handlebars. Some of the older people who often come relax in the garden, or tend their own plots, keep watch, too.

I walk up to the officers, a strange sensation in my head like when the pressure drops on a plane and your ears stop up. Or like when the husband you thought you were giving a second chance gifts you an ebook titled *Divorce for Dummies*.

"Excuse me, officers. May I ask what's happening here?" I manage to ask in my most polite, least threatening voice, even though strangers are invading Mommy's garden.

My stomach twists.

"We're here because the rightful owner of this land has reclaimed it from illegal usage," one of the officers says. He's wearing the same reflective aviator lenses Drew the Uber driver sported and sweat is beading up on the pink skin of his face—the garden is in direct sunlight at this time of day.

"The rightful owner?" I repeat. "This lot had no owner that could be traced. My mother checked several times. It had become a dumping ground and the city gave my mother a deed because she cleaned it up, made it better. The city said—"

"The city is not the owner," the man with the lock says, slipping the key into his pocket as he saunters up. He has the face of a guy who would stand behind you on the subway and accidentally brush against your ass every other time the train took a sharp turn. "I'm the owner. I tracked down the relatives of the woman who originally owned this lot, and I bought it from them."

"No. That doesn't make sense."

"It makes perfect sense," the man says. "You people just decided you could do whatever you wanted, without the guarantee of the law. I have the guarantee of the law."

"I have a deed," I say, the pressure in my head increasing. I'm not smart enough to be scared in this moment as he smiles smugly at me, his gaze flicking to the police officers.

This isn't a ten-dollar bill.

It's my mother's garden.

Rage, pure rage, pulls my shoulders back and forces me to take a step closer and look down at this man. "Show me the proof of what you said."

"I don't have to show you anything," he replies, amused.

I turn to the officers, not expecting help but having no other recourse. I *cannot* let this garden be taken. It's the cornerstone of everything I have left.

"Please. This has been our community garden for years. There are trees. Do you know how long it takes a tree to grow? Please tell him he can't do this."

"Just show her the deed," one of the cops says, though he doesn't seem moved. "If you don't, we're gonna have a bunch of these people getting angry and I don't feel like doing any paperwork before Labor Day weekend."

The guy smiles and hands me a paper that was folded up in his back pocket. It's a smudgy photocopy that supposedly shows proof of land purchase for five thousand dollars by 24 Gifford Place Real Estate Management, from . . .

"I can't even read these names," I say, the copy crinkling in my hand. "Who approved this?"

"The Brooklyn housing authority."

My gaze fixes on the amount paid and any composure I had evaporates.

"Only five thousand? Do you think I'm fucking stupid? I could whip up something better in Photoshop." My voice is rising but I can't help it. He's just here trying to take everything. Everything. *No.* "I could find out where *you* live, make a fake deed and say it's mine, if that's how this works. You wanna wake up and find me in your damn living room with my feet on the couch? This is bullshit."

The man's smug patience suddenly snaps, and he lunges toward my face until his nose is almost up against mine. "Look, bitch, I don't want any problems from you. The lot is *ours.* If you wanna fuck with us, if you wanna try to hold things up, you're gonna regret it. I will *make* you fucking regret it."

"Bitch?" My face is hot, and I reflexively pull my braids back into a ponytail with the hair tie on my wrist in one smooth motion. "Who are you calling a bitch?"

"What are you gonna do, *bitch*? Hit me?" He lifts his face toward mine so his nasty breath blows in my face. His eyes are flashing with an anger disproportionate to the fact that *he's* the one who started this shit. "Try it. Try it. I'll have your ass locked up so fast your fucking head will spin."

"Officer, sir, are you going to let this man threaten her like that, sir?" Len asks, distress in his voice. The officer looks in his direction and takes a step toward him.

"Officer!" I call out, and his attention shifts back to me. "Officer, please. At least let us get our things. This is some kind of misunderstanding, but until it's resolved, let us please just get our equipment and whatever we have—"

"No," the man says from behind them. "No entry to the property."

"Sorry, ma'am," the officer says, shrugging with a slight grin. "I have to adhere to the property owner's wishes."

The second officer turns to the crowd and starts shouting. "Everybody disperse! You, put that phone away! Nothing to see here! Nothing to see here!"

"But—"

Behind him, two of the men inside start pulling up plants. The others start piling up gloves and buckets and gardening tools, overturning the wooden benches Mr. Perkins and some of the other neighbors made at the beginning of the summer to replace the old rotten ones.

"Why?" I croak out. "Why are you doing this?"

"Ma'am, are we going to have a problem?" The second officer rests his hand on his holster and my stomach turns.

Yes! I want to scream. I want to scream until my throat is raw and bleeding. Instead, I stand there silent and shivering even though it's so hot that my shirt is soaked through with sweat. I've failed my mother again. I imagine her face when we toured the retirement home, how she'd looked at me and said, *"You know you're going to have to take over the garden for me if I come here, right? You better watch some YouTube videos so you don't kill my plants."*

"Come on, Sydney."

The voice seems far away, but someone takes my arm and pulls me back. The grip is strong and reminds me of my mother, trying to keep me from danger.

"But Mommy's—"

"Sydney, let's go!" Ms. Candace squeezes my arm harder and pulls me away, and Len comes up from behind; I realize he's covering my flank, and that's enough to get me moving.

I look back one more time. The officers and the man who stole my mother's garden are laughing. They're laughing and I can't do a damn thing about it.

I reflexively take out my phone, pull up my log, and dial the last person I'd called: Mommy. I just need to hear her voice, to apologize.

The phone stops ringing and I wait for her voicemail to pick up, but there's only silence. Then . . . an exhale.

The dread in my body constricts to a sharp pain in my chest.

"Hello?" I whisper.

No response, but someone is there—I know with the surety of a child who refuses to let their feet hang off the edge of the bed.

"Hello?" Tears well in my eyes.

They hang up on me.

Ms. Candace rubs my back when I grasp the rim of a trash can in front of Etta Mason's house and throw up.

"Etta will understand," she says over and over again. "Anyone would understand."

Gifford Place OurHood post by Candace Tompkins:
I think we should all discuss the loss of the community garden. There's no way that man is the rightful owner. We need to know what happened and how.

Asia Martin: Who has the money to prove him otherwise?

Jenn Lithwick: Oh no! I heard what happened! How awful. Is Sydney okay?

Jen Peterson: Can someone really lie about that? I mean, the police were with him? They would know if his claim was real, right? Maybe I'm being naive but the alternative is . . .

Asia Martin: . . . business as usual, Jen. That's all it is.

Jen Peterson: I'm sorry, Asia. I just can't believe something like this could happen in Brooklyn.

Jenn Lithwick: Honey . . .

CHAPTER 15

Theo

AFTER THE RIESLING INCIDENT, I'M STAYING WELL AWAY FROM booze, which is a pretty abrupt change of pace for my body. I'd wanted a beer pretty badly after the weird spat with Sydney outside the corner store, and even more after going to see a room for rent a few train stops away. As expected, it was someone's curtained-off living room, but it will be fine as a temporary base while I figure out what the next step will be.

Instead of cracking open a cold one, I go to the gym, needing to work out the feelings bobbing around recklessly now that I'm not drowning them with booze or distracting myself with Sydney.

Some people get to a zen place while working out, but my thoughts race as I swing my arms on the elliptical. Life had been stalled for months, it seemed, but things have kicked back into gear with a vengeance—my world is entirely different than it was a week ago. I made a friend, found a purpose—however temporary—then lost my girlfriend, my new friend, and my purpose. Oh, and also my house.

Now I've made the dubious decision to room with a seventy-year-old Polish ex-con who's way too interested in my cooking skills and wanted to know if I could get the viruses off his computer.

William, the weird guy from the real estate place, suddenly steps in front of the elliptical. He doesn't say anything, just looks up at me expectantly like we were already in midconversation and he'd just made a dirty joke.

"I'll be done in five minutes," I say.

"It's cool. I'm more of a weight room guy." He purses his lips, then frowns. "You never called me."

"Called?"

"About the job offer. It's not like they take on just anyone at BVT, and I thought you had what it takes. You look like . . ." He considers me with a kind of detached amusement, like I'm a ukulele or something. ". . . Like a guy who doesn't have scruples, when it comes to making money."

I don't let my rhythm show it, but his words jar me. I slow a bit, unsure of what turn this situation is about to take.

"What makes you say that?"

He shrugs. "I'm not judging you. We could use guys like that because things are starting to get intense. Did you hear about the community garden on Gifford?"

The question is gleeful and a little gossipy.

My stomach drops as an image of Sydney on her hands and knees, miserably tending her plot, pops into my head.

"Hear what?"

"Some developer ganked it," he says. "Slid right in with a new deed and was like, 'Yeah, this is my shit now. In your face, bitch!'"

I consider just knocking my fist right into his mouth to shut him up.

No. I've backslid a lot in the last few months, but I don't do *that* anymore.

"For a second it looked like things might go sideways. The cops talked sense into everyone so things panned out, but that's the part where we need more guys like you." His hyperfriendly expression shifts just subtly enough around his mouth and eyes to become hateful. "I wish I could've been there. I've put up with months of attitude from that—"

"I thought the community garden already belongs to somebody," I say. "Wouldn't a developer just make an offer to whoever owns it?"

William shakes his head. "I guess they *could* do that. There was a provisional deed given by the city because the lot had been vacant for years and was an eyesore. Blah, blah, blah. You can pay the person who owns it. But if you want to get it for cheap, all you have to do is *find* the original landowner or their next of kin, and buy it from them. They don't even have to stick around. They can pop up, take a quick five K for prime Brooklyn real estate, and then return to wherever it is they've been lurking for years."

I'm no longer moving on the elliptical, just glaring down at the smug asshole standing in front of me and also kicking myself. "You saying this is a scam?"

"People might call it that, but no one can prove anything. Or maybe they don't want to prove anything." He shrugs. "You know how it goes."

I stare at him.

"Oh, you don't? Okay, I'll play along."

I hate this feeling, of someone dangling a threat in front of me and not just getting to the part where I can either hit them before they hit me, or run. "Did you want something?"

"I know you need money. And a place to stay."

I should be surprised, but it seems Kim told multiple people that I was a bum and she was going to leave me. Why not the realtor?

"I can't make you do anything, but you need to really think about your future here. Don't let your pride, or your penis, get in the way of getting paid, bro. Call me."

He holds up an imaginary cell phone beside his ear, then changes it to a thumbs-up pushed in my direction, and then walks off toward the weight-lifting room.

I stand there, sweating and trying to connect two pieces of information that I really hope are not connected. Anyone could have taken an interest in the garden, right?

I clamber off the elliptical, shower quickly, and jog back out into the gross humidity.

When I get to the community garden, it looks like one of the old pictures of Brooklyn I'd seen, back when the empty lots were used as garbage dumps. All the plants have been ripped up. The benches and flower boxes and planter pots are in a pile against the wall of the adjacent building. Bits of chewed-up-looking leaves spot the ground with green, and absolute dread fills me.

I think about Sydney's voice cracking when she talked about not being able to maintain the garden. How over the last few days, she's wilted like the plants she tried so fruitlessly to keep alive. How earlier today she sent me away because I was a bumbling idiot who didn't understand how things worked around here.

She must be wrecked right now.

I suck in a deep breath and head to her front door. As I get to the bottom step, something sharp grazes the back of my ankle and tugs at my shoe. I turn to find Terry viciously tugging at his dog's leash.

"Toby, you little bastard!" He tugs hard again. His face is screwed up with anger, like the dog being a little monster is someone else's fault and not his.

"Hey, Terry," I say out of reflexive politeness even though his dog just sank its teeth into the foam of my New Balances. He looks up at me, his gaze jumping back and forth between me and Sydney's door. He grins.

"I knew it."

This is a weird way of saying *Sorry my untrained dog bit you.*

"I told Josie that you needed to just get this out of your system and then you'd be able to think straight. Even if you and Kim don't work out, it'd be a shame if our numbers went down. We have an apartment for rent, you know."

"Okay." I scratch my head and start turning to head up the stairs.

Two Black guys walk slowly across the street and Toby surges forward, barking like he wants to take a chunk out of them. Terry loosens the leash instead of pulling it back, and the men decide to walk in the street. Terry nods his chin toward Sydney's door again.

"Look, just go get it out of your system. Don't worry, we've all had *that* phase. Hell, Josie and I still travel down to the Caribbean every year to scratch that itch, though now that we live here . . . well, you clearly understand the convenience."

"What?" I have no idea what he's talking about.

He inclines his head toward the house. "Is she any good? I mean, that mouth looks like it could suck the shellac off a—"

I drop my duffel bag to the ground, though the strap is still loosely between my fingers. "Watch what you say next, man."

Another thing I'd worked on while trying to fit in with Kim's life was my temper, but my limits are being tested hard today.

"Hey, hey, I was just being neighborly, no need to get touchy. Have fun!"

He trots up the stairs with his dog.

After taking a minute to get my anger whack-a-moled back into its proper place, I ring the doorbell to Sydney's apartment a couple of times.

No answer. Maybe I should just leave. But I've seen her crying alone in her apartment as life in the neighborhood went on around her too many times. She'd never invited Drea down, or gone to Mr. Perkins or Ms. Candace. Sydney always tries to soldier through alone—maybe she needs someone to come barging in, to know that someone cares enough to try, even if it is the annoying neighbor from across the street.

I ring the doorbell one more time, telling myself that if she doesn't come out, I'll go home. The better to peep into her window and make sure she's okay.

There's the sound of a dead bolt unlocking down the hall and then a sliver of light expands into a diffused glow, and Sydney steps into the hall. Her braids are in a sloppy ponytail on the side of her head and she's wearing old basketball shorts and a white tank top.

She's walking slowly, hesitantly, and I can see the surprise in her face when she makes out it's me.

Surprise, but not disappointment.

She opens the door halfway and says, "Hi," with a voice that sounds like a bruise.

"I just heard what happened," I say. "To the garden. Are you okay?"

She pushes past me a little to look back and forth down the street, and she's warm and smells like some kind of vanilla-laced pastry and cigarettes. Sweet and bitter. The scent lingers as she pulls back. "Come in."

"Huh?"

"Come *in*," she says with an edge of annoyance that reassures me.

She closes the door after me and locks both locks, then pads past me and moves through the hallway toward her apartment. I follow, the scent of cigarette smoke growing stronger the closer I get to the door.

When I get inside the apartment, she repeats her closing and locking routine, jerkily tugging at the doorknob afterward as if checking the sturdiness of the locks.

"You're alone?"

"Yes. Drea isn't answering my calls. Mr. Perkins isn't answering either, even though the block party is only a couple days away. Ms. Candace tried to come in, but I—I couldn't talk to her." She plods to the kitchen table and picks up the cigarette that sits balanced on the edge of a white ceramic ashtray with *Coney Island* written in tiny starfish along the side.

Sydney smokes like the femme fatale pacing the hapless detective's office in a noir film. She stares into the distance with unfocused pain in her eyes, lifting the cigarette to her mouth in a smooth arc and closing her lips around it, something that doesn't seem practiced or contrived given her current state.

I'm reminded that even though they stink and cause cancer, a cigarette is sexy as hell in the right hands.

"Did you see the garden?" she asks on the exhale, then rolls her bottom lip with her teeth.

"Yeah."

"How bad is it?"

"It's bad." I try to break this as gently as I can while not giving her even a smidgen of hope. "They ripped up all the plots and piled up all the wood and other stuff. The garden is gone."

She sits down at the kitchen table—more like her legs give out and she slumps into the chair that was already pulled out. Tears well up in her eyes and her hand is shaking when she raises the cigarette this time.

"Sydney?"

She inhales and tears slip over her cheeks, suddenly, as if she's been just holding them back this whole time. She doesn't sob or make any sound, just sucks at that cigarette, then reaches for a napkin from the holder in the middle of the table and wipes roughly at her face as she sniffles.

"Fuck, I'm tired."

"You've mentioned that." I pull out a chair next to her at the table. "Tell me what's going on, Sydney. Or if you don't want to, just tell me what you need right now."

She looks at me, her eyes still glossy and her expression something like stoic.

"Get the scotch out of that cabinet. Top shelf." She doesn't say *please* and I feel like that's part of what she needs right now, too, so I just stand up and do it. I grab two glasses without her asking, then place them down and pour.

"Why did you really get fired? For real?" Her mouth trembles, but her hand is steady when she raises the cigarette again. "I know you weren't telling me the whole truth. I'm used to accepting half-truths from men. But right now, with all of this mess going on, I need to know."

I purse my lips and exhale hard through my nose, take the gulp of booze she didn't.

Then I tell her the truth.

"They caught me trying to steal," I say. "Because I got greedy. It wasn't enough that I'd grifted a position people bust their asses for years to get. It didn't matter that I was making more semi-honest money than anyone in my family had ever made through any means, dishonest or otherwise. Once I had a little, I thought, 'I can get more. And I'm gonna take it.' Typical, if I've learned anything from you the last few days."

"Completely typical. Except you were stupid enough to get caught." She giggles and I wonder if she wasn't already drinking before I got here.

"So you should know that my name isn't Theodore, like you told Candace," I say. "Well, it is. In Russian. Fyodor. Named after my dad, who was tangled up with stuff considerably more dangerous than white-collar crime. I went to live with him after I got into some trouble and had to drop out of high school, lay low. I worked construction with him, but also got tangled up with the stuff he was tangled up with. I guess this thing with Kim was my way of going straight."

Sydney looks at me with wide eyes, the ash building up on the end of her cigarette. "Mafia?"

"Something like that, but a million times less interesting than the movies. I got out before I moved to New York, so I don't know, maybe this is where all the cool mafia stuff happens." People glamorize it, but it'd been just another job with no insurance and a low life expectancy when it came down to it. "Anyway, here I was at this fancy office. And I wasn't stupid or anything. I fit in fine, and I started small. There was a group in my department who always wanted cocaine. And I told them I could get it for them. I'd take their money, buy a little of the good stuff, a little of the not-so-good stuff, and a little of the probably bad stuff. I made a profit, the cokeheads were just happy to have some coke, and all was well and good."

"Wow. And here I was thinking you were just a regular degular dude, but Fyodor was trappin' at the office." She snort-laughs a cloud of smoke.

"Yup. And eventually, I realized that I had access to all these people's bank account information. And maybe I could make some transfers."

"Theo!" She slaps the table, eyes wide in disbelief. "You didn't."

"I did. Kim wanted this house and kept saying it was fine if she had to pay for everything, which made me feel like I *had* to contribute because, I don't know, toxic masculinity? In retrospect

I should have just let her be my sugar mama instead of committing multiple elaborate and unsustainable crimes to get out of a life of committing small sustainable crimes. Hindsight is twenty-twenty, I guess."

Sydney laughs, sharply, abruptly, and I'm surprised to find that I can join her.

"All this to impress some woman who cheated on your ass anyway. I feel that." She takes a gulp this time when she raises her glass.

"Yes and no. Part of it was that all that money was sitting there and I knew, intimately, how little work most of these people did to earn it. Kim's family are the most miserly people ever, and the accounts were held by so many people just like them. Everything was about helping them cheat to get more money, to not pay employees who were owed money, to avoid taxes, and to hoard it because they didn't ever want to spend what they had."

I grit my teeth and look at her, expecting to see judgment, but her expression hasn't changed much.

"You got caught," she says.

"I triggered some internal system before any transfer went through. *Then* they started looking into my background. Fired me without prosecuting because they didn't want to make the company look bad, but my name was blacklisted within the company, with our partners, within the industry's whisper network."

"And Kim?"

"Didn't know. Was understanding at first, when she thought I got downsized, but couldn't understand why I couldn't just get another great job. She thought I was lazy but apparently never realized I was just a bad liar and a criminal. The former is worse than the latter in her world."

Sydney drains the last of her drink and thumps at her chest. "My turn."

I'd expected more of a reaction, but she seems unfazed by my confession. She grabs the bottle, pours some more scotch for herself, and then tops me off.

"I was married, like I told you. Mommy never liked Marcus. Told me he had the fingernails of a cheater and a forehead like a billboard. I didn't listen, of course. He was from a nice family and said all the right things. When we had to move to Seattle for his first job out of grad school, Mommy hated him even more but wished the best for me."

"Did he hit you?" I ask, because I need to prepare myself for that particular kind of rage.

"No. He never hit me. Just . . . I never could do anything right once we got there. I couldn't find a job because the market sucked." She raises her glass to me and I raise mine in return. "And his job was so stressful, some kind of start-up that he never wanted to talk about because 'You wouldn't understand.' It started with dinner. Suddenly my food was too spicy or too salty or not healthy enough. Then I wasn't cleaning the house well enough. Then I wasn't well-informed enough and he didn't want to bring me around his colleagues in case I embarrassed him . . ."

She laughs bitterly. "And then, 'Hey, you've gained some weight.' 'No, I would never cheat, stop being paranoid.' And then, 'Maybe I did cheat but you're crazy, we should have you committed.'"

"Jesus, Sydney. You didn't deserve that. You know that, right?"

She gives me a jerky nod.

"Seriously. You're beautiful, you're interesting, and even if he didn't think so there was no reason for him to treat you badly."

She exhales deeply.

"Thanks. It all feels so silly now compared to everything else. While that was going on, Mommy started having some health problems. She couldn't work as much. Started falling behind in the water bill payments, the taxes, and she didn't want to bother me with any of it. I told her everything was fine, and she told me everything was fine, and guess what?"

"Nothing was fine," I volunteer.

She nods. "One day she gets a call saying that she's in danger of losing the house because she's racked up back taxes. This person is calling from a program to *help* people get their debt in control and make sure they don't lose their homes. She doesn't want to bother me because she knows I'm not doing well, so she doesn't even mention it. She doesn't tell me anything! She just agrees to their terms and conditions because she wants to make sure she doesn't lose the house, my inheritance. Who does that?"

A tear starts to slip down her cheek and she brushes it away hard. "Then whaddaya know, a year later her debt has ballooned. The company that was supposed to have prevented this doesn't know how this happened but they can *help*. They're willing to pay off her debt for her. All she has to do is sign the house over to them and the debt will go away. She can stay in the house until . . . until she dies. It'll be just like the debt never happened. They'll even give her some money. At that point, she knew things with Marcus were bad. She knew if she could get some money for me, maybe I would leave him. The house wouldn't get passed down in the family like she'd dreamed, but she wouldn't have to worry about me paying off her debt because someone else had taken it. And I'd still have someplace to come back to. Sounds legit, right?"

Her eyes are so filled with hurt, a hurt I understand completely—the pain of grabbing a proverbial hot doorknob, pulling the door open, and not being able to let go as your mother's bad decisions flambé you in their backdraft.

"I'm sorry." I don't know what to do, so I gently pry away the cigarette that's burned down to the filter and put it in the ashtray before holding her hand.

"I came back after the divorce and she didn't tell me anything then, either." Her voice is hoarse, breaking every word so I have to lean in to understand her. "She didn't tell me anything until she got sick, and then she only told me because she realized how they'd fooled her, stolen all her hard work from her so that it added up to less than nothing. She got mad then, and told me, 'Don't you let them take my house. Our house. No matter what happens to me.'"

Sydney's eyes are unblinking and empty as her gaze meets mine.

"She's in the garden. Mommy is in the garden."

CHAPTER 16

Sydney

I START SHAKING NOW THAT I'VE SAID IT OUT LOUD—I FEEL like I might shiver myself right out of my seat.

I can't believe I've told him. I wasn't supposed to tell anybody. Why him?

Mostly because he was there, but maybe because he looks so concerned. Maybe because I'm fucking lonely, and he told me that I'm beautiful and held my hand.

No.

It's because this secret has been turning me to ash from the inside out and I've hit the *I'm not feeling so good, Mr. Stark* threshold. If I hadn't told him, I would have been lost.

Theo is still holding my hand, and I expect his grip to slacken but it gets tighter. "Hey. Whoa. What do you mean she's in the garden?"

"Um." My throat tightens painfully and I try to breathe through it so I can speak the words that have tied this house I love so much around my neck like an albatross. "She got really sick and—and she didn't want to be a bother anymore. The money she'd gotten from the people who stole the house was gone so fast with all the medical bills. Her health insurance was shit. My savings went like that." I snap, or try to but my hands are shaking too much. "We were watching her favorite movie in her bed. *Con Air. Con Air*! God, Mommy has such bad taste in movies. If I would have known—"

I suck in a breath, caught off guard as I think about the last night with her. How I'd snuggled up next to her too-thin body and kept cracking jokes about how bad the movie was—how she hadn't told me to stop interrupting, like she usually did.

"That's an underrated classic," Theo says calmly, like this is a first date and we're making small talk. "I grew out a mullet after watching it."

I sniffle and swallow the tears and the snot and the pain. "She told me she loved me when the credits rolled. She told me that if she died before we were able to get the house back legally, I couldn't let anyone know because she wouldn't be able to rest knowing she'd failed me, and any kids I had, and any kids they had. Generational wealth all lost because of one mistake.

"I found her bottle of painkillers empty the next morning. And she was . . . she was . . . There couldn't be a death certificate, right? Then they'd know. I buried her in the garden that night."

It hurts thinking about her face so still, her body so . . . empty. About wrapping her up in her favorite blanket.

I jam my fingertips against my forearm and rub—I remember how cold and slack she was beneath my fingers. I can't stop *feeling* that memory.

Theo breaks the silence. "You moved her by yourself?"

"Yeah." He doesn't need to know about Drea. After that night, we never mentioned it again. And I told her if anyone ever asked,

I would never, ever take her down with me, would deny it even if she tried to confess. But it's been so heavy on my soul. And Drea's, so I thought. But there's that check. That check with the name of the company that tricked my mother in the "issued by" area: Good Neighbors LLC.

The lawyer told me that sometimes companies like this give money to a person who helps them convince their marks to sign the house away. But Drea couldn't have . . . she'd never . . .

Theo stands up and his sneakers squeak on the tile behind me. Maybe he's going to call the police.

I hear the fridge door open and the *snikt* of a bottlecap being twisted off. He places a bottle of water in front of me, sits back down, pulling his chair slightly closer to me. His right arm is along the back of my chair, and his gaze is locked on my face.

"Drink the water." He waits until I pick up the bottle and take a sip, urges me to take another, then says, "So your mom . . . died. And you buried her in the community garden?"

I nod, waiting for him to tell me the thing that keeps me up at night: what an awful, evil daughter I am. How I failed her. Buried her like a dog, and didn't even give her soul the chance to have her memory honored and celebrated. I'm not religious, but I wonder all the time if I've somehow damned her along with myself.

"Where in the garden?" Theo asks.

The words fall out of my mouth. "Behind the shed. There's a strip of sunflowers. She's under them."

I can't bring myself to look at him in the long silence that follows, but glance at him from the corner of my eye when I hear him shift in his seat.

"Well, I think that's nicer than being in a cemetery somewhere with a bunch of strangers. You buried her someplace she loved." He sighs deeply and smooths both hands down his beard, but then nods. "It's illegal as fuck, but I'm not exactly one to judge that. I can't imagine how hard this has been for you, going there every day, not able to tell anyone. How unfair it was that you were pushed to make that decision." His gaze rests on me, and there's no judgment among the various emotions in his eyes. "I'm sorry, Sydney."

It's the last sorry that breaks me. He's said it a few times, but this one finally sinks in. I've gotten so used to apologizing for being too weak to carry my own burdens—I don't know if anyone's ever apologized to me for how heavy they are, even if they couldn't do anything to lighten the load.

I put the water bottle down and drop my head to the tabletop, one swift motion to hide the fissure of pain his words open in me. A silent sob chokes me up, but the bands of fear and panic that have been squeezing me for months fall away.

I can breathe. I take in a deep shuddering breath, and when I exhale it's like a dam breaking.

He rubs my back and lets me cry; the tears pool on the table and cool against my heated face, but I don't stop.

At some point he slips his arm through mine and half carries me to the couch as I sob and sob and sob, but for the first time in a long time, it feels something like relief. I keen into his chest, and he just cradles me.

I don't even care if he reports me to the police after this, really. Right now, it feels good to be held without judgment, without feeling weak or evil or like I let Mommy down, even if just for a few minutes.

I don't know how much time has gone by when the sobs taper off, but he's still holding me, still rubbing his hand over my back.

"The people who scammed her out of the house don't know," he says. His voice is rough and low.

"No. They keep calling to check in and I keep making excuses. But I'm starting to feel crazy, like they're watching me. Like they're gonna find out and then come and take everything. And the garden, today . . ." A wave of full-body terror seizes me as I remember the breathing on the other end of the phone.

No. They would have just arrested me, though that seems inevitable.

"If they start digging for a foundation. They'll find her. It'll all be over. The house will be taken. I'll be in jail."

The well of panic I've just cried out starts to fill again.

"Okay. Okay. Don't worry about that for now. It usually takes a while for a place to get building permits and all that jazz." He's still speaking as if this is a perfectly normal situation, and it helps to calm me. Maybe it isn't normal, but it is what it is.

"I don't think these people are exactly bound by the rules," I say. "The deed they had was approved, but it was fake. I know it was. The supposed new owner of the plot got so mad when I questioned him, like how people blow up when they're trying to hide something and want to scare you from the truth. And there's nothing I can do."

We sit in silence. Theo's heart is beating fast even though he seems outwardly calm, and I remember him grinning at me and telling me his own secret.

Theo is a liar. A grifter, with possible ties to the mob. He's a man I've known for just a few days.

I've entrusted him with the one thing that can destroy what's left of my life and possibly take out Drea, too.

"Please don't tell anyone," I say, not nearly as upset as I should be because my body is limp like a wet washcloth. I'll probably be angrier with myself tomorrow. But I've felt so heavy for so long, and now I'm light, like I could float away from all these problems for just a little bit.

"Go to sleep, Sydney." Theo brushes his hand over my braids, then exerts pressure, holding me against him. It's this stillness that makes me realize I'm shaking.

"But—"

"Just go to sleep," he says gently.

I do.

WHEN I WAKE up a few hours later, I'm stretched out on the couch and the throw blanket from Target that usually rests on one of the arms is tucked around me. I sit up, head throbbing and face swollen, and find another bottle of water, some Advil, and a cold compress from the freezer sitting on the coffee table. They've been there for a while, judging from the condensation.

I consider that maybe this was a farewell gift before he went and called the police—though, maybe they would have been here by now? Unless they're at the garden . . .

But he isn't exactly the kind of person who would want to invite the attention of the police, either.

I palm the two pills and take a sip of the water to wash them down, then pick up the cold compress and stare at it for a minute. This is some thoughtful shit.

I lay it over my swollen eyes, but when a memory flashes in my mind from that horrible night in the garden, I pull it off, throw it back onto the coffee table, and go to the kitchen to look for another cigarette.

There're other things I should be doing. Going to the police myself, to explain what happened? Running off to Belize, which has no extradition treaty but does have those cute manatees? I could create a new life as a never-married manatee tour guide whose mother is absolutely fine but won't come to visit, and no one would ever know about my past.

I giggle at the thought. The giggles are a little wild even though my thoughts are surprisingly calm given the situation I'm in.

That's what happens when life keeps throwing shit at you—the last months, hell, even this last week, have been enough to push someone over the edge. But I'm still here. And now that I can think clearly, I'm starting to suspect that some majorly fucked-up shit is going on, besides the fact that I had to dig my own mother's grave.

I'll think it through after another cigarette.

I'm fidgeting with the packet's flip top when there's a hard knock at the apartment door.

I feel a spurt of anger that I won't even get to enjoy this last drag in peace before going to jail, where I'll have to pay who knows what price if I really need a hit of nicotine.

I won't even get to go to the block party.

"Sydney?"

I fling the door open to find a strange white man standing there in jeans and a T-shirt. No. It's Theo, his hair darker because it's wet and his beard shaved to reveal the harsh angles of his jaw, which do a lot toward containing and putting into perspective all those other prominent features on his face. I thought the beard was great, but I like this smooth-faced stranger at my door, bearing gifts.

He holds up a plastic bag, slowly. "I, uh, went for a walk. Got some guava tarts from the Caribbean bakery because it was the only place open this early. Do you like those?"

I'm about to answer when I notice his nails. There's a solid crescent of dirt under each of them. That dirt wasn't there yesterday evening.

"Theo."

I pull him inside by the front of his shirt and slam the door behind him.

"So you *do* like guava tarts? Good."

I grab one of his big hands with both of mine. There are blisters that will soon form into calluses on the palm pads below each finger. There is the dirt. When I sniff him closely, there is the smell of sunflowers.

"Theo. Did you—?"

He shrugs, runs his other hand through his hair. "You know who's the last person to get stopped for doing some weird shit like digging in an empty Brooklyn lot in the middle of the night? I mean, a cop car did stop and—"

"What?" My heart thumps so hard in my chest that it hurts.

"—I told them I was burying my . . . dog. I'm sorry, it was the first thing that came to mind that would work. Then the cop got all misty-eyed about his German shepherd."

"Where is she?" I ask, my heart in my throat.

He looks at me for a beat longer than it should take to reply. "There was nothing there. *No one* there. Under the sunflowers."

No.

"They took her?" I ask, gripping his hand harder, but he shakes his head.

"They messed things up, but there was no digging before I got there. I didn't find her."

My entire body flinches from this as multiple thoughts hit me at once: someone moved Mommy, Drea is gone, Theo will think I'm crazy, people hurt you when they think you're crazy.

Maybe he wouldn't be wrong, thinking that.

"I buried her there," I say quietly. His hand squeezes mine and I look up at him.

"I believe you."

"Don't just say that to—"

"If you say you buried her, you buried her. We'll find out where she is." He squeezes my hand again, the pressure steady and comforting. "Everything is going to be okay."

On some level I know it's wrong, macabre—*fucked up*—when I bring his hand to my mouth and kiss the back of it.

Mommy is gone.

Drea has seemingly abandoned me—maybe she's the one in Belize with her $50K. She'd looked up countries we couldn't be extradited from, after all.

Theo is here, in front of me, looking at me with kind eyes that have no trace of doubt in them, his hands rubbed raw from an attempted exhumation.

No one has ever tried to save me.

My fear and pain and fatigue burn away in the generous light of his attempt, leaving a roar of the emptiness inside of me, and the feeling that only one thing can fill it right now.

I pull him by the hand to the bedroom, glancing back over my shoulder to look at him.

"Sydney?" He pauses at the threshold of my bedroom door, despite my attempt to tug him after me. "Are you sure?"

"Yes."

"You've been through a lot and—"

"You just said you believed me." My voice is trembling because my body is. "I'm telling you that I want you, need you, right now. Do you believe that?"

He nods and steps into the room with me, and everything else falls away.

There's no fear of all the awful things that've happened before this moment, or all the bad things that might happen after. Just the relief of his gaze, so fucking intense as he looks down at me. The expectation of his touch, his heat, his scent, his presence . . .

I expect him to be gentle, but he drops the bag on the floor and his hands move toward my shoulders like he's been holding himself back from it for days. His fingertips press into my shoulder blades as he pulls me toward him.

Theo's gaze roams all over my face before he meets my eyes, reads my confirmation there, and kisses me.

I'm not the only one who needs this right now. Our kiss is like two drowning people searching for a life preserver, finding each other instead, and deciding that roaring waves aren't so bad if you can fuck in the lulls between them.

His mouth moves as desperately as mine, his tongue searches as frantically; a groan slips between my lips but I can't pinpoint its origin—him or me.

He backs me up to the wall of the bedroom, one hand sliding from my shoulder to my neck and resting there—not squeezing, but simply restraining. Holding me, keeping me from falling apart. Heat sears through my body at his touch, at the fact that he understands it isn't roughness that would hurt me right now, but coddling. His eyes are too kind for his touch to be gentle—I wouldn't be able to stand that. So he holds me as his mouth crushes into mine and his hips grind against me, his arm wedged between us.

He glances into my eyes a few minutes later, face flushed and eyes stormy. His fingertips stroke under my jawbone as he asks, "Do you need more?"

When I nod, he lowers his hands to my hips and his mouth to my neck, sucking at my skin, rubbing his lips across my collarbone. My nipples are hard points through the fabric of my camisole and he teases them through the fabric with his teeth as I drive my hands into his hair. He uses his chin to drag the top of my shirt down, and his light stubble teases my sensitive skin before he sucks a nipple between his lips.

For the first time in months, my mind is gloriously clear, all of my troubles and pain hacked away by the pleasure of Theo's tongue swirling over my nipples, first right, then left, of his hands pressing my hips against the wall so that when they lift involuntarily my ass is forced to remain against the wall.

"Theo." I shove at his shoulders and his hands are off me instantly, his tongue a second later. He looks up at me, brows raised, and when I push him again, he tumbles back onto my bed with a grin, hands already reaching up to catch me to him as I scramble on top of him.

I fumble in the bedside table drawer for a condom and lube, and Theo takes advantage of my raised hips and shoves down his pants and boxers.

He follows my lead as I roll us over, but stops moving as I reach between our thighs to pump his veiny shaft, to slide the condom on and warm the lube using my fingertips.

He's looking at me all gentle again, so I lift my head and kiss him hard as I hold his gaze, tease his bottom lip with the threat of a hard bite. I feel his grin between my lips, and then he thrusts into me.

He doesn't push into me roughly, but I still gasp at the slow, teasing stretch of him. He's thick, hot, and hard inside of me, his weight crushing me to the bed. He doesn't move for a second, as if adjusting to being encompassed by my tight heat.

"Sydney." He lowers his head and kisses me, and when I slide my hands into his hair and tug, when I nip his bottom lip again, he pulls out and drives into me hard.

After that it all moves too quickly, this almost violent desire caused by the care in a crescent of dirt. I'm half off the bed at one point, my head banging against the floor, then on my hands and knees. I flip him onto his back, riding his dick desperately because I need this release, need . . .

He brushes away tears I didn't realize were rolling down my cheeks with one thumb and strums my clit with the other, and I buckle against him as the orgasm hits me like a cleansing wave.

CHAPTER 17

Theo

NOT THINKING TOO DEEPLY BEFORE I ACT HAS LED ME DOWN some pretty bizarre paths in life.

Committing crimes with my dad. Lying to get hired at some hot-shit company. Buying a house with someone I'm not married to while having no real knowledge of how owning property works. Trying to siphon money from rich people, and getting caught.

Searching for my neighbor's mom's body so I can move it to a safe location.

I'd thought about the first time I handled a dead body as I shoveled up humid mounds of dirt looking for Yolanda Green. My own mom had been watching back then, blood-spattered and angry at *me*, like I hadn't just saved her from being the one on the receiving end of a shotgun blast.

Mom and I don't talk about that.

Ever.

We don't talk about how I was seventeen and had to leave town abruptly at the beginning of senior year. That's when I moved in with my dad and learned some things from him that would have come in handy with burying that first body, or maybe would've put a stop to the situation before it got that far.

I don't know where Sydney's mother is, but I believe that Sydney put her in the ground. I could be wrong, but I've been wrong about worse things.

What I'm not sure about is what happened after I got to her apartment. She wanted me, I wanted her, but maybe it was just one of those weird emotional pressure-valve-release things and she was happy for it to end there.

We both passed out after that first round of sex, waking up hours later to the sound of afternoon noise on the block. She got up and had a cigarette, brushed her teeth, and then we did it again, more slowly this time but just as intense. Then we slept some more, until she pulled me into the shower with her after we lay sweating on her bed for a while. In her clawfoot bathtub, she stood naked and soapy beneath my hands, dodging the shower spray because she didn't want to get her braids wet as she kissed me.

It seemed like some surreal dream outside of everything that's happened over the last few days, but now we're back in reality. My body aches from grave-robbing and weird sexual positions and she's sitting across the table from me, mouth full of guava tart and wide eyes darting back and forth, everywhere but my direction, as she chews.

The air conditioner whines in the background and I fumble around for something to say. I don't know the banging-after-attempting-to-hide-a-body-for-you etiquette.

"This is awkward as hell," she finally says, then takes another bite of her tart and pulls her feet up onto her chair so her knees press against the table and block her chest from view. She's wearing a thin-strapped white tank top and black capri sweats that are both loose and formfitting.

I nod in agreement. "Definitely at the top of the weird-first-dates list for me."

She chuckles, crumbs dusting her smile as her gaze finally lands on my face.

"Mine too. I guess." She sighs. "I think . . . I need to talk about the weird week I've been having. If not finding my—anything in the garden hasn't led you to believe I'm crazy, then maybe you're the only person I can talk about this with. I've actually managed to sleep for more than a couple of hours, and my brain is somewhat functional, though I wish it wasn't."

"Try me."

"You saw the Con Ed dude who tried to get into my house," she says quietly. Her eyes widen. "Didn't you? That happened, right?"

"Yes. I saw him, I saw the van, and the entire situation was shady. Look, just tell me what you think is going on. I'll believe you, okay?"

A sliver of this is bullshitting; I don't know her that well and any number of mental illnesses could be at play. I don't think that's the case, but even if it is, *she* believes whatever she's about to tell me, and we can take it from there.

She twists her mouth. "And if . . . if what I say is crazy, will you tell me that? And not just call the cops on me?"

I nod. "I won't call the police."

She takes a deep breath. "There's been other stuff, besides that. Two days before the Con Ed guy, I got into an Uber, and the driver locked the doors and drove me to a semi-deserted street. He started saying wild shit about being an ex-cop and civilizing the neighborhood and—I don't remember everything. It was terrifying."

My stomach tightens with the sudden fear of what can happen to a woman trapped in the back of a stranger's car. "Why didn't you tell me?"

"I didn't know you," she says. "This week has been like three years long, but this was before you even came here to have coffee."

She could have disappeared before I'd even had the chance to get to know her.

"Plus, there's no record of the driver in my account." Her hands shake a little now and she puts the half-eaten tart down. "Everything started to happen so fast that I couldn't keep up. That same day, Preston got arrested on some bullshit. And then Mr. Perkins was gone. Drea hasn't responded to my texts and calls. I heard noise upstairs in her apartment a couple of nights ago, and when I went up there, there were bedbugs on her bed. A lot of them."

Her increasingly speedy words crash to a halt as she shudders.

"They took the bodega. And then the garden. Everything is . . ." She presses her palms to the outside corners of her eyes and pulls back, stretching the skin while blinking rapidly. She's trying to prevent another deluge of tears.

"What do you think this all means?" I ask, sounding calmer than I feel. I'm getting that feeling of something bad heading our way.

"I don't know," she says. "It feels like someone is messing with me. Not just me. With all of us. But that doesn't make sense, does it?"

I'm trying to piece together the random things that don't seem random to her and figure out how to respond when a familiar howling bark comes from outside the house.

"Count," Sydney says, the tart dropping onto her plate as her body sags with relief. "Thank god."

She hops up and jogs out of the apartment toward the front door, and I follow at a slower pace; if I'd jogged after her, I would have rammed right into her when she stops short at the top of the outer stairs.

The moving truck comes into view as I step out behind her. There's a dark-haired middle-aged woman and her blond-fading-to-gray husband standing out front as movers cart their belongings inside. He's wearing khaki shorts and a button-up shirt and she has on a breezy, expensive dress. Neither of them would look out of place at a gathering at Kim's parents' house.

They have a dog on a leash, an old hound who looks up at Sydney and tries to run to her, only to get tugged back.

Sydney slips into flip-flops and starts walking slowly down the stairs. "Count?"

The dog strains toward her again and the woman tugs the leash hard enough that he whines sharply.

"Down, boy," the man says. "Be a good boy."

"Are you our new neighbor?" the woman asks with that slightly condescending smile Kim's mom always used to give me.

"I'm Mr. Perkins's neighbor," Sydney replies. "He's coming home today."

The couple look at each other, seemingly baffled, before looking back at Sydney. "We own this house," the woman says. "Our daughter Melissa moved here first, since she was starting school, and then we decided we wanted an adventure in the city, too."

"Brooklyn is the number one most happening place to live now, even more exclusive than Manhattan," the husband adds, his voice a parody of a country club Chad that isn't a parody. "All of our friends are just flocking here, and we didn't want to be the last ones!"

They laugh, and I just watch them, my whole body feeling heavy as my brain tries to fight what my gut is screaming at me: This isn't right. This definitely isn't right. They're just moving into someone's house. Mr. Perkins's house. The man I possibly saw something happen to, and who I was told was visiting his family.

"No," Sydney says. "Mr. Perkins is coming back for the block party. And that's his dog."

The man looks taken aback. "We got this dog at the shelter. Someone had abandoned it—you know *some* people don't like dogs. Reminds them of when they could be chased down and returned to slavery. That's what I heard."

"It really is a shame," his wife says, frowning. "The dogs didn't do anything to deserve that kind of hatred."

"Whoa," I cut in, but Country Club Chad talks right over me.

"As for Mr. Perkins, trust me, he was paid more than enough to be able to move somewhere else. Wherever he wanted. I don't see what the problem is."

"He wouldn't move without telling me or anyone else," Sydney says angrily. "And where would he go? This is his neighborhood. We're his neighbors! He wouldn't just leave us."

The woman steps closer to her husband, as if she's scared of being attacked.

"This isn't a very hospitable welcome," the husband says in the same tone he used to chastise Count. "And if you want to continue, you should know I'm close friends with the chief of police."

"Sydney, come on," I say, doing my own Country Club Chad parody. "Let's go to my place."

She resists my tug at her arm, then whirls up the steps to her house and down the hall.

"Oh wait. You're Kim's latest? Weren't you at the house last summer?" the husband asks while Sydney's gone. "She always picks up the most interesting playthings. I guess you do, too."

"You know Kim?"

His brow wrinkles. "Of course—"

"Charlie! Go make sure the movers don't break that. It's been in my family for years and he just dropped it without a second thought!"

Charlie gives me a strange look, the look you give someone when you greet them like a friend and then realize they're just a similar-looking stranger.

He and his wife head over to the moving truck, tugging Count along with them, and Sydney storms back down the stairs with my duffel bag over her shoulder, various papers shoved haphazardly inside. She glances at Charlie and his wife as they stand next to a giant carved-wood African statue that the movers are about to take up the stairs.

I guide Sydney into my house—Kim's house—and into the first-floor apartment. Which isn't a cauldron that hasn't been cleaned for a month, like mine. Sydney and I push aside the expensive curtains and glare at the people who claim they bought a house that wasn't for sale.

Terry and Josie wander over with Arwin and Toby, greeting the newcomers with a combination of air kisses and firm handshakes.

Sydney pushes past me and drops onto the couch. "Am I going crazy? Please tell me the truth, because I already thought I was, but *this* feels like I'm going crazy for real."

I flex my hands, breathing slowly, trying to collect my thoughts. Mr. Perkins was so kind and welcoming to me, and constant, and now he's just gone.

"I was at the meeting," I say. "He had no plans to move, and he wouldn't leave his dog if he did. If you're crazy, I'm crazy, too."

She covers her face with her hands for a few minutes and I don't push her; a moment of quiet wouldn't hurt either of us right now.

Eventually, she sighs shakily through her fingers and her head pops up.

"I'm thinking about the tour," she says, which is maybe the last thing I expect her to say.

"The tour? You still want to do it tomorrow?" I can't keep the edge of *you're kidding me* out of my voice.

"We looked up a lot of history. We talked to a lot of people. And some of those things are ringing bells for me now."

She looks at me for a long moment, as if waiting for me to guess, but I have no clue what she's talking about.

"I researched the past and present of Gifford Place. Of Brooklyn. I wanted to throw my middle finger up at Zephyr, at VerenTech, at . . . at you."

I get what she means, but it still chafes. "At gentrification."

She nods. "But I hadn't found the *thing* that ties it together. The hook, like brownstones, or famous architects, or whatever. And if I'm right, this hook is fucking old and sharp. There are patterns in all of these situations that were just going to be stops on the tour, spiraling out from the beginning." She pauses, licks her lips. "None of this is happening by chance. How could it?"

"What do you mean?" I ask. I told her I would believe her, but I'd already dealt with Kim's paranoia—

Kim's words slam into me.

"There are just so few of us."

"We need to know whether there's anything to worry about. Safety-wise."

They had a private group on OurHood . . . What for?

Charlie knows Kim. Knows me.

Sydney kicks the coffee table that I've always hated away from the couch, pulls my duffel between her legs, and starts picking through the mess of papers. When she speaks, her words spill out in a rush.

"Okay. Boom. Remember when you came to Mr. Perkins's before the meeting and I was reading about Underhill? Well, no, you wouldn't remember that, but this is what I was reading." She pulls out an old yellowed pamphlet. "It's this British dude jerking off about how great killing Native Americans is so you can take their land *and* about how America is great because it's so uninhabited. The cognitive dissonance of that, right? He wouldn't be out there killing Native Americans if no one was on the land. He was a mercenary for the colonizers, basically, and the Dutch hired him to kill the Natives around here. He helped pave the way for New York City as it is now."

"Okay." I take the pamphlet and stare at it, going along with her but worried for the first time that her beliefs are going to fall into the "all in her head" category. "So, this was in the 1600s?"

"Yes," she says. "Now think about the info from the heritage center. The laws preventing Black people from passing down property they owned to their children were put in place in the 1700s. Weeksville was founded in the 1800s because you had to own land to vote, which is why they made it so hard for Black people to own land." She's nodding as she talks. "The people in Weeksville build a whole community, and then boom, suddenly the government just *has* to plow right through with Eastern Parkway, like no one lived there? Just like they did with the indigenous people. Just like they've done with so many communities when you do even the most basic Google search for this. Central Park was built on a Black community. I am leaving a whole lot out right now, but it's like this cycle repeating over and over again."

"Hey. Maybe we need to just think on this a bit," I say.

"You don't see the pattern? I thought you said we were both crazy. Damn it, Theo." She plucks a packet of papers out, flips a few pages, and then shakes it at me. "These are internal documents from the VerenTech Pharma proposal. Compare this description of the neighborhood and Underhill's little manifesto."

Her eyes are wide, begging me to make the connection, so I glance back and forth between the two pieces of evidence she's given me.

"Okay, are you saying you think some dude from the 1600s is involved in the VerenTech Pharmaceuticals headquarters?"

She closes her eyes and pinches the bridge of her nose before speaking.

"No! I'm saying that this VerenTech memo *feels* like the same thing. How they talk about all the resources in the neighborhood that are underutilized, even though we're *right fucking here*? And now Abdul is gone and some racist motherfucker owns the bodega. Mr. Perkins—the Mayor of Gifford Place—supposedly just up and moved, without telling a single soul?"

"Where did you even get this from?" I ask, flipping through the pages.

Her hand slaps to her mouth then.

"Oh no. Fuck." She pulls out her phone, swipes around, and her face falls. "Drea. I got it from Drea. She's been typing for like three fucking days!"

I look at her, hunched over her phone, eyes wide, body taut with terror. I should get far away from here, right now. This is above my pay grade. I was going along with her, but right now she's possibly having a psychotic break. Something is going on here, though, even if Sydney's behavior is freaking me out.

I think of William Bilford mimicking the *kaboosh* of a nuclear bomb.

"Remember what you said about how you got caught at your company?" Sydney's voice is suddenly dull. "That you triggered some internal system, or something?"

She gently pulls the VerenTech pages from my hand, flips to the first document, and reads it. "'The Company (VerenTech) acknowledges that this Memorandum is a public record subject to disclosure but do hereby require that we be notified of any and all FOIA requests, both during the city selection process and in the event that a city is chosen, to allow the Company to seek a protective order or other appropriate remedy.'"

"Other appropriate remedy," I repeat, taking the papers back from her. That seems like something designed to scare people on its own, but along with everything else it's kind of ominous. "You know, there is a chance that Drea ran off. She's an adult."

"She wouldn't," Sydney says, a sudden fierceness in her tone. "It's possible she made a mistake, but we've been friends for half of our lives. She's never let me down and she sure as hell wouldn't run from me."

The look in her eye is how my mom looked at me when she'd let her asshole boyfriend move back in after telling me he was gone for good—indignation, hope, and desperation.

"Okay." I nod and flip through the projection pages that show the future plans for the neighborhood. "Sometimes a company tries to push their luck. Get in ahead of the competition. Or ahead of anyone who might want to stop them. Same as a gang or any other criminal enterprise."

I look at the clean, reimagined future of the neighborhood; this is what was sold to me and Kim by the realtors. They'd talked of revitalization and changing demographics and I'd nodded along because of course that had nothing to do with me, but I'd still get to reap the benefits. And when there are benefits to be reaped, there's always someone ready to do some illegal shit to get even more of them.

I know that all too well.

Sydney sits on the floor beside the duffel bag and wraps her arms around her knees, staring at the couch as she thinks.

"I'm worried about Kavaughn, too. Len said he went down south, but it's not like him to just dip like that."

Kavaughn, the guy I replaced as her researcher, the reason I inserted myself into this mess to begin with.

She grabs her phone again and makes a call, putting it on speaker this time. We both stare at the picture of the thick-necked man on the screen.

"Jesus Christ." I pick up the phone as an automated message announces that the number is no longer in service.

Sydney looks up at me. "What is it?"

I wave the phone from side to side as his picture fades away. "This is the guy that came at me in front of the medical center that I tried to tell you about. He was on something. I assumed he was just your average methhead—"

"Meth isn't the drug of choice here, Theo. And especially not for Kavaughn."

"Okay, whatever. He was high. But at the meeting, Len said Kavaughn went to visit his grandmother, right? And if he was high and roaming around grabbing people, wouldn't someone in the neighborhood know he was back? I can't have been the only person to have seen him."

"Kavaughn doesn't mess with drugs," she says, shaking her head. "He is absolutely a 'drugs are a tool of the oppressor' type dude. He doesn't even drink coffee. Are you sure it was him?"

I close my eyes and bang my fist lightly against my forehead as

I remember when he bumped into me. I'd assumed he was trying to attack me, but in retrospect . . . I saw that fear in his eyes.

"Please. Money."

Was that really what he'd been saying?

"Mommy is in the garden. Mommy." That's what Sydney said. I'm not used to adults calling their mothers that, but . . .

My stomach lurches.

"Did he live with his mother?" I ask.

"With his grandmother, but she raised him, so she was basically his mom."

His garbled words repeat in my head, but this time I don't imagine he's begging for money for his next fix. I imagine he's asking for what most disoriented people ask for when they're terrified. The sounds are so similar.

"Mommy? Bring Mommy. Help. Please! Please!"

I'd reacted to what I was taught to think when a large Black man ran up to me acting strangely.

Drugs.

Crime.

Danger.

And when the cops asked me where he'd gone, I ratted him out. A couple days later, I'd glibly pulled on a Black Lives Matter T-shirt and got pissy when I was called on it.

"Was it him?" she asks again.

I want to lie to her, to ignore my disgust with myself and the fear growing into a palpable presence in my torso.

"It was him. For sure." I look at her. "I'd stopped because I thought I saw something moving through the window in the old hospital. And when he attacked me . . . it was right after I asked him if he wanted to go to the hospital."

She stares at me, that distance in her gaze again, and I don't volunteer that I snitched on him to the cops.

"Okay, let's just . . . process for a minute," she says.

I pull out my own phone and sit beside her. At my last job, I learned that most companies have their fingers in many pies, no matter what their business. Hell, even before that, working with my dad in low-level shit had taught me how a front operates. How dirty money gets clean.

"Most of this stuff happened after the VerenTech announcement," I say.

She nods.

I hear William's *kaboosh* again.

I Google "VerenTech + Brooklyn + Real Estate." The first few pages are a mix of articles from this week celebrating the borough's winning the VerenTech contracts and older ones warning of the harm the company might bring. Nothing stands out, but I scroll until something snags my eye:

> VerenTech, which is primarily known for its pharmaceutical endeavors but is also the primary shareholder in Bevruch Ten Properties (BVT Realty) . . .

That's the agency Kim and I used. I flash Sydney my screen.

"They're the ones putting up all those condos," she says, her voice surprisingly subdued.

As Sydney gazes over my shoulder, I Google "VerenTech + Bevruch Ten Properties."

This time only a handful of results show up. One is a link to an r/shadybusiness forum page about the VerenTech campus search.

Brooklyn can have them. Everyone forgets about the town they bought in Connecticut in the early 00s. Promised tons of wealth, but they used eminent domain to kick people out of their houses and then never built their location there. Local businesses all closed down because they had no customers. Politicians and investors all lost big. It turned into a ghost town.

There's a link in response that I hesitate to click on but do.

A diagram of all the businesses connected to VerenTech pops up in a new tab. Smaller or larger circles reflect how much money each subsidiary produces for the company overall. VerenTech (pharmaceuticals) is large, but only slightly smaller is the circle representing Civil Communities Inc. (private prison company).

"These motherfuckers," Sydney growls.

Several smaller circles cluster around that, offshoots of that company. The third-largest circle is BVT Realty, and the fourth is . . .

"Veritas Bank. Isn't that the one you told me about?" Sydney asks. "The one the former slaveowner started?"

"Yeah. And when I looked them up, a lot of the headlines were people calling them out for offering subprime loans to minorities in the lead-up to the 2008 housing bubble bursting."

"Gaining how many houses when the foreclosures started rolling out," Sydney says bitterly. She expands the circle around BVT Realty so that a pixelated name in a smaller circle takes up most of the screen: Good Neighbors LLC.

"Those are the people who stole Mommy's house. Drea—" She takes a deep breath. "Drea once told me that BVT got special treatment, which is why they're building here more than anyone else. She also said someone had pulled lots of strings for the VerenTech deal."

"I'm no Robin Hood, but one of the reasons I felt okay stealing from my job was because so much of the money coming in was graft, pure and simple," I say. "They laundered more cleanly than the job I had before, but people who have money use that money to make more of it, and they don't care who they hurt while doing that. VerenTech has more money than most of us can imagine."

"They chose Brooklyn, out of all the places vying for their new campus," Sydney says. "The most expensive place, but the one that would make them the most money once they got us all out of here. If they've been collecting houses since the earlier housing crises . . ."

"Yeah. It's possible that this has been years in the making."

Sydney meets my gaze, and I confirm what she said a minute ago, because something like this bears repeating to make it real.

"Something shady is going on here, and it's connected to them."

CHAPTER 18

Sydney

I WRAP MY ARMS AROUND MY KNEES.

"You know, sometimes my mother used to send me these illuminati videos she got from her friends—she barely knew how to text but could forward those—and I would shake my head like she was being foolish. But this whole situation makes those videos seem quaint."

I squeeze my eyes shut as the connections keep forming in my head, lighting up as they do.

The police presence has exploded over the last few years, with cops stationed en masse at subway entrances and stepped-up foot patrols that were supposed to increase safety, but haven't for the people who lived here. Preston and the many other people in the neighborhood who've been arrested over the last couple of years have likely been taken to VerenTech's jails and prisons. All the new condos going up in any available slice of land are owned by BVT. Veritas Bank, the biggest lender to the new businesses opening—and the owner of so many of the defaulted loans of the past—is part of VerenTech.

And all the people who moved away and never checked in with old neighborhood friends. Where were they?

"We can't tell anyone this, can we? This is lock-you-up-and-sedate-you shit." I shake my head, trying to stop the conspiracy theory domino rally. "Even if it's true."

"Especially if it's true," Theo says.

I never want to see the inside of an institution again. I was only at the one in Seattle for three soul-breaking days, trying to explain that I was fine, that Marcus had lied, that I wouldn't hurt myself or him.

Just the thought of being ignored while I screamed the truth, again, makes me want to vomit. It took months to assure myself I wasn't actually crazy after Marcus's final act of humiliation, and all of this is making me start to doubt again.

"What am I supposed to do?" I get up and pace. "I'm not walking into a police station and announcing there's an organized movement to kill Black people and steal our land. Even though it's been happening in this country for generations and it shouldn't be hard to believe. Can we even call this a conspiracy theory? I mean . . . that's why the police exist in the first place. Of course they won't help!"

The last of my good nerves fray, so that I'm hanging on by a thread. Theo stands and steps in front of me, blocking my restless stride and forcing me to look up at him.

"We'll figure this out, okay?" He runs his knuckles over my jawline, gently, and I take a deep breath.

"How?" I want to believe him. So bad. But at this point I don't see any way this ends well.

"Sydney." Theo is grinning as he calls my attention back to

him, though his eyes are somber. "I need you to channel the confidence of a mediocre white man. I'll give you mine. We'll figure it out because we don't have any other choice."

"Right. Right." I take a deep breath, steady myself a bit. "Do you have chamomile tea or something? I prefer scotch, but I need something that won't affect my thinking."

"Let me see," he says, then heads down the hallway to the kitchen. I hear the hiss and catch of a stove being lit, and jump out of my seat ready to fight when it's followed by a curse and a metallic crash.

"I'm okay!" he calls out.

I drop back onto the couch pillows and take a deep breath. There's no chance in hell that I can actually relax, but I try to collect my thoughts, which have scattered like fish in the koi pond at Prospect Park running from an off-leash dog.

My gaze darts back and forth around the living room, really absorbing the differences between my house and this one. The paint is new, and looks like the thousand-thread-count sheets of paint. There are little glass terrariums everywhere—when I stopped in one of the new boutiques that's opened up, the smallest one with a tiny succulent was fifty bucks.

An eight-by-ten of Michelle Obama sits on the mantelpiece, and a giant painting of an old white dude hangs above it, the kind you see in the lobbies of banks and government buildings. It's one of those paintings where the beady eyes follow you anywhere you move in a room.

It jump-starts my nervousness and I get up, creep over to the window, and peek through the curtains, the icy breeze of the air conditioner blowing over my face and calming me a bit. The moving truck is still parked there but appears to be empty, and no one is outside Mr. Perkins's place.

When I lean closer to the window so I can see a little farther down the street, my thumb rests against the air conditioner and comes away sticky.

I bend down, blink against the cold air hitting my eyes, and then freeze in my crouched position.

There's a tacky spot in the shape of a heart on the front of the air conditioner. And when I check the make and model . . . it's the same as Drea's.

I remember her purple-tipped fingers pressing the sticker onto the air conditioner after I'd helped her install it.

"Now it'll spread the love. Get it? Get it?"

My brain refuses to process the importance of the heart-shaped glue mark, or the fact that the air conditioner that's gone from Drea's room is now here at Theo's house. Fyodor, who worked for the Russian mob at some point. Who tried to grift a major corporation. Who offered to pick the lock to get into Mr. Perkins's house.

Who clearly would do anything for money.

Theo, who helpfully pointed out that all of this shit had started up when the VerenTech deal went through, who found the perfect pieces of evidence to support my conspiracy theories, but who'd left out the fact that *he'd* elbowed his way into my research and my life at the exact same time.

Dammit.

I'd watched Theo through his window sometimes—had he been watching me? These real estate companies would do seemingly anything to get their hands on people's properties. If I thought a company would murder, it wasn't that far of a stretch to believe they could hire a moderately attractive man to spend a few days seducing a lonely, broken woman before finishing the job.

Nausea roils my stomach at the thought, but it's as possible as anything else in this trash fire of a world.

Something lights up to my left, drawing my attention from the internal scream I'm swallowing, and I glance over to see an iPad on the lower level of the perfectly distressed couch-side table. I don't even pretend not to be interested—that was what I did with Marcus at first, averting my eyes when a message popped up on his screen. It's supposedly bad to snoop, but Theo's own admission plays in my head.

"I . . . am a liar."

I lean over the arm of the couch and tilt the iPad so I can see the messages coming in under a conversation labeled *Honeycheeks*.

They're getting settled into the Perkins place. I still think we're moving too quickly. People are going to notice.

Sydney is too unreliable to pose a real threat, but I'm taking care of her today. I was going to earlier, but they just had to bring that damned dog with them. Charlie said they wanted the house AND the dog, but I thought his wife would wait until after we were done to trot it out.

You know how she is with dogs. 🙄

I hate rushing things too, but I'm not in charge here. Besides, my father is pretty sure even if they all notice, it won't matter. Other corps have razed entire towns. In the past, they've dropped bombs, polluted water. No one cares, lmao.

True. I could record myself shooting one of them in the face and get off scot-free, lmfao. No one will pay any attention to this. 😈

I hate that she's in my house. Gross. ☹️

Sorry. I had to make a decision after she ran into the street. She'll be handled ASAP.

Good. She was so mean to me!

👧🔪😏

😘 Hurry up. Your little cowgirl wants to ride and if you finish fast enough we can fit it in before the meeting. 🏇

I'll try, tonight's revitalization is going to be pretty intense—we have to get everything contained so it lines up with the parade. Everyone already associates it with violence so it'll provide even more cover.

You'll have to wait a few hours for this 🦴. Keep yourself entertained—and send pictures.

A picture comes through almost immediately: Ponytail Lululemon, Theo's supposed ex-girlfriend, half-naked in a nasty-looking public bathroom mirror with her hip jutting out to give the illusion of ass where there is none.

The clanking of cups in the kitchen signals that I've read enough. I tiptoe toward the living room door. Luckily, the house adheres to the rules of New Brooklyn; the flooring is new and doesn't squeak like at my place, and there's one of those big-ass mirrors in the hallway so I can see what that traitorous motherfucker is doing in the kitchen.

Theo has a box of tea in one hand and his phone in the other, tapping with his thumb.

I've panicked a lot over the last few weeks, and the last few hours. I've relived past betrayals and uncovered one and now two more. Mommy and many of my neighbors are gone, directly or indirectly thanks to this company, and if the word *rejuvenation* means what I think it means, more of us will be gone soon.

Right now, if I cry one more tear, or give in to panic, I might as well just let Theo kill me right here and leave my neighbors and friends for dead.

My last fuck disintegrates uneventfully, but in its wake it leaves the knowledge of what I have to do. Of what Mommy would want me to do.

"Don't let them take my house."

I head back to the duffel and grab it—it's his, but it contains what little evidence I have and also: Fuck him. If I can inconvenience him a little bit, good.

A sharp white edge of paper sticks out of the side pocket and I push it in more deeply, then quickly tug it out to peek at it. It's a business card. Motherfucking Bill Bil, for BVT Realty.

The same company Theo just acted surprised to learn was part of VerenTech.

Okay.

I'm not being paranoid. The one person I thought was on my side is not. Again. I refuse to feel upset—this is what I get for depending on everyone else to help me. This is what I get for not being strong enough to do things on my own.

That ends now.

I grab the duffel and quietly jog to the door.

"You want honey?" Theo calls out.

I don't know if he repeats himself because my response is the quiet click of the door closing after me.

Gifford Place OurHood/privateusergroup/Rejuvenation

Review of the door-cam footage, store surveillance, and the in-app microphone override make it clear that we can't wait any longer. We can find another explanation, but if we don't move now, the entire project is in jeopardy. Geolocation shows Green is moving toward the house marked next for clearance.

CHAPTER 19

Sydney

I JOG ACROSS THE STREET IN THE DARKENING EVENING LIGHT, hiding between parked cars to watch a black sedan with tinted windows that slows, then keeps driving. Was it Drew? What would happen if I ended up in the back seat of his car again? I doubt he'd let me out this time, and a key between my fingers probably won't cut it.

Toby barks from somewhere behind me, and I turn and look up. On either side of my house, Mommy's house, the brownstones are inhabited by strangers who are no longer just new neighbors, but likely people who want to do me harm.

A siren whines to life a few blocks away and I flinch. The roar of a jet engine overhead makes me wonder if they might have drones watching us.

Everything seems like it might be a means to hurt me. Every. Goddamn. Thing.

Laughter tinkles through the window of Josie and Terry's house, and that's the rage straw on the camel's back for me.

I came back to Brooklyn to find home, and these bastards have taken even the comfort of the familiar from me. Taken my mother's dignity, and my best friend's loyalty, and my community. I can never get those things back, and they think they'll get away with it because no one cares.

They don't count my pain, our pain, in their idea of care.

They're gonna learn today.

I jog up the stairs to my front door, the key slipping out of the lock two times before I manage to turn it.

Once the door is shut and locked behind me, I stand for a moment and take several deep breaths, filling my nose with the familiar scent of potpourri, wood polish, and dust that always made coming home feel real. Even though it's the opposite of what I would normally do, I slip on the pair of old Timbs I usually wear while gardening and never wear into the house. I don't know what's going on, and you can't stomp someone with Old Navy flip-flops.

I jog up to Mommy's apartment, and when I open the door, I'm hit with the stale, stifling hot air of an un-air-conditioned top floor. Sweat beads on my brow as I close the door and engage the multiple locks. The duffel bag rests against my hip as I scan the apartment, and a sudden vibration makes me jump about a foot in the air before I realize it's my phone.

Fucking Theo.

My jaw clenches and I beeline for Mommy's bedroom, the one place in the house I haven't been since that night. The room is simple, light blue with a dark wood bedroom set and a rarely used vanity, the kind with lightbulbs around the mirror. It made me feel so glamorous as a kid when I'd sit in front of it, cataloguing the features that were so similar to those of the woman I thought was the prettiest in the world, and sneaking dabs of her lipstick and blush.

It's dark in the room, even though the blinds aren't closed—it's already evening, somehow, as if time has stopped making sense along with everything else I thought I knew.

Her bedroom window sits in the faux-parapet, the high tower, where I can look down on those who might come to get me. Where I once watched my friends pretend to battle to save me.

No one's fighting for that job now.

I stand in the doorway, staring down at Mommy's bed, my teeth pressed together so hard that I feel like they might crumble. The bed is bare except for its mattress cover because we used her favorite blanket to wrap her up.

Drea had helped, had given me the recommendation for the lawyers, had promised to help me fight to keep the house. She said she didn't know why Mommy had agreed to sign over the house, and Mommy had never mentioned Drea pressuring her—but pressure wasn't always blatant.

Drea'd betrayed us, gotten paid, pretended to care, and then left me to fight this alone.

Has she pretended to be my friend all this time? Has she hated me all these years when I'd thought of her as a sister? Did she tell them where the body was, and that's why Mommy is missing?

Wait. Theo is the one who told me her body wasn't there. That might be a lie too. Everything could be a lie.

I purposefully unclench my jaw and take a deep breath. No time for memories, or for questions.

I'm in Mommy's room for a reason.

I head for her closet, pull down one of the familiar blue cookie tins as the persistent vibration of my phone purrs in the duffel on the window seat. No, this tin is too light. Must be her sewing things. I place it back on the shelf—Mommy did not tolerate me digging through her belongings and I learned as a child to put things back exactly as they were.

I find what I'm looking for in the fourth cookie tin I pick up, the heaviest one, the one with things rolling around like marbles inside.

I place it on the bed, sweat rolling down my temples and pooling beneath my titties from the top-floor heat of this room, and fight with the slightly rusted lid, eventually winning the battle. The lid pulls free and there it is. Mommy's little silver revolver. It's not shiny anymore, how I remember it, and it's old enough that people would clown me if I posted a pic of it on social media, but I'm not pulling it out for social media clout.

My grandfather had given the gun to her when she'd come up north, but she'd known how to use it since she could walk. That's what she told me, at least. Her parents taught her how to hunt for food, and how to protect herself when the white boys from town got bored and came cruising through their neighborhood looking to do evil, or if the Brown boys she'd grown up with suddenly didn't understand the word *no*.

I pick it up, the heft of it a familiar comfort that grounds me in the swirling tornado of my thoughts and fears. Mommy taught me how to use it early, and then taught me never to touch it unless there was an emergency.

I think she'd agree this counts, given what I know of her definition of *emergency*.

Fitzroy told us the story of Mommy making a man dance at the end of this gun during the blackout. He probably didn't know she'd run my daddy off the same way. I only found out the truth toward the end of things. We'd been watching *Goodfellas* in her bed, and during the scene where Karen shoves a gun into Henry's mouth as he's sleeping after she finds out he's cheating, Mommy laughed so hard she'd lost her breath. I forced her to take a few sips of water and asked what was so funny.

"Just . . . memories. That's how your daddy woke up after the first and *last* time he hit me," she said, her gaze soft and unfocused and the slightest smile on her face.

"I wish I'd told you that earlier. How to treat men who want to make you small, crush you under their heel." She looked into my eyes, her gaze loving but hard. "I put my gun in your daddy's mouth and I made him apologize. And then I told him, 'If you *ever* hit me again, you better kill me, because next time I won't hesitate to pull this trigger.' He left not long after that. Before he knew about you."

I grasp the bullets from the box in the tin with clumsy fingers and load them into the chamber, thinking of all the people who think they can hurt everybody else with no consequence. Most times they're right. They live long, successful lives while using other people's necks as ladder rungs.

I don't have a plan just yet, but this is not going to be one of those times, if I can help it. I'm not going to let VerenTech, Josie and Terry, Ponytail Lululemon, or anyone else continue to take what's mine.

Something flashes into my eyes through the window as I push the chamber back into place with the heel of my hand. Theo is in his window across the street, eyes wide and waving around a mirror with a flashlight pointed at it, some kind of Boy Scout trick to get my attention. I give him the finger, jamming it up into the air hard and then pressing it to the glass as my rage at his betrayal flares up in me.

I expected him to have dropped the act already, but his hair is on end and his face is flushed as he tosses the mirror and picks up his phone, waving his other arm and pointing at me, waving and then pointing at the phone. I can see that confused brow knit of his from all the way over here.

I shake my head, pissed off that he has the nerve to look legitimately distressed, but I don't take my eyes off him even as I stick the Ziploc baggie of bullets into my pocket.

He bangs his windowpane and because his window is open, I hear him when he yells something in frustration.

"Please!"

And because I'm not my mother's daughter, just her diluted progeny, I second-guess myself. One doubt is all it takes. I pick up the phone when it vibrates again.

"Sydney, what the—" He reins himself in, and through the window I see him drop his hand onto his hip in an almost comical way. "You need to get out of your house now. He's downstairs. Can you go down a fire escape? He's in the house."

His panic hits me like a wave through the phone, so real, or maybe, like the phone call that trapped my mother, just some fast talking designed to lure me into a trap. Theo knows how to do that—talk and talk and make you feel safe.

"Who is *he*? Why should I believe you after your little conversation with Kim? I saw you texting her while you were in the kitchen! I read the messages."

I watch him, expecting him to show some sign that the jig is up, but his exasperated expression doesn't change. "I remembered where I'd first heard the name VerenTech and was looking up something. What messages?"

"The ones that popped up on the iPad in the living room, *honeycheeks.* Next to Drea's air conditioner. The one missing from her room."

"That's Kim's iPad. And her new air conditioner." He shakes his head. "And 'honeycheeks' has never been in my vocabulary. The closest I've gotten is 'Howdy Doody.'"

I want to believe him so badly it hurts. The possibility that everyone has betrayed me is too much to deal with.

Theo suddenly dives mostly out of view, then the top of his head from his eyes up returns. "He's on the second floor now, in Drea's apartment. The fake Con Ed guy. He was in the cab of the moving truck and I saw him get out and go into your house. Please." His voice breaks. "I know we're in this insane situation and nothing makes sense, but I wasn't talking to Kim. I have no idea what Kim has to do with any of this. I like you and I wouldn't try to hurt you. The only thing I did is—"

"What? What did you *do*?"

"I've been stealing from the rich people in the surrounding neighborhoods," he says in a rush. "Not like Robin Hood, the money was for me. The uptick in car break-ins and house burglaries people have been talking about was me. And one of the guys I use to fence the stuff asked me if I had any leads on real estate. I told him there was an empty lot."

"What?" My grip on the gun tightens.

"He asked me if I knew any places going for cheap in my neighborhood, to keep an eye out because he'd heard the Veren-Tech deal was going to go through. I told him there was an empty lot being used as a garden because I assumed he'd *ask to buy* like a regular person. I don't know if he had anything to do with this stuff, I swear. I swear, Syd."

His gaze connects with mine, then he stands and runs out of the room. I hear the pounding of his footsteps and his heavy breathing through the phone. "He's heading for the third floor. Hide somewhere, now. Now, Sydney! I'm coming for you."

He hangs up.

I still don't know if I can trust him, but I decide that at the very least, I will hide. I'm feeling mad petty, but I'm not gonna die just to spite Theo by ignoring his warning.

I close and lock my mother's bedroom door. The fake Con Ed dude was big. He likely has something letting him bust through the locks on the outer apartment doors—maybe he even has the key.

What he doesn't have, what none of these motherfuckers trying to take over my neighborhood have, is the knowledge of someone who grew up here. Someone who doesn't see these houses as just a place to show off to their rich friends or post pictures of on Boomtown.

Wood cracks with a loud split in the living room—the outer apartment door, which confirms that Theo was telling at least a bit of truth: someone is trying to get me. I slide into the closet, close the door behind me, and turn the key that sits in the lock inside of it. The lock isn't heavy duty, and was installed to keep visiting kids and nosy houseguests out of Mommy's things when locked from the outside. Locking it from the inside was another "in case of emergency" bonus—the poor woman's panic room.

I tuck the gun into the waistband of my pants, and do the thing I received my only ever spanking for; not because I'd done anything bad but because I'd scared the shit out of my mother by disappearing for hours.

I push through Mommy's dresses and trousers, still hung neatly and carrying the scent of her, and unlatch the door in the wall at the back of the closet. It leads to the servants' staircase, a feature built into many of these brownstones. For once, the excess of the rich people who lived here in the past comes in handy.

Thanks, Frederick Langston.

I step into darkness and close the secret door behind me.

The air is surprisingly cool, and what feels oddly like a breeze blows up toward me even though our steps don't lead down to a cellar like many people's do. After the initial jolt of fear at what might be lurking, I turn on my phone's flashlight and start making my way down.

I try to walk quietly—these stairs are a hundred years old at least, and the last time they were maintained was when Mr. Perkins made a bunch of repairs after I got stuck in here that one time. Twenty-five years ago?

After the first few steps don't break beneath my weight and an army of rats doesn't swarm up the passageway toward me, I gain a bit of confidence.

I start to move faster, the darkness crowding down the stairs and up behind me, where the weak phone light doesn't reach.

A spiderweb clings to my arm and I shudder, but when I hear crashing upstairs, in the bedroom, I could give a good goddamn about a spider or a creaking stair. I'm jogging now. One more short flight of steps and I'm into the coat closet on the first floor and out of this—

The sole of my boot comes down on something not soft, but not hard like a wooden step and not flat like one, either. I look down at the glow coming from the phone that's suddenly illuminated under my shoe. At the familiar brown hand holding it tightly.

All I can see is this hand, the LED screen shining against the matte purple acrylics at its fingertips. The screen, now cracked, shows dozens of calls and messages, mostly from me. The battery power is a sliver too thin to be seen, but reads 1%.

"Drea," I whisper, and even though I resolved not to cry and not to panic, that was before this horror lurking around the bend in the staircase. My sinuses burn and tears well up. "Fuck, Drea. Why?"

I can't bring myself to look at her face yet, and though some part of me knows I need to move past her or die, my ass drops down to the steps and I tug the phone from her hands, wincing when she seems to hold on to it. We played like that sometimes, me tugging to see what wild text she'd just received, but this isn't a game.

It's rigor mortis.

I put in her unlock code and our text chat opens on the screen. I finally see the last thing she'd been typing. The unsent message that has been haunting me for days.

Luv u. Im sorrrrrrtttyyyyyyyyyyyyyyyy.

The phone shuts off, and I sit unmoving and unbreathing as the darkness blankets on us both.

CHAPTER 20

Theo

I HAVE A CERAMIC KNIFE FROM CRATE AND BARREL IN ONE hand and a ridiculously tiny crowbar shoved in my back pocket as I jog across the street—Kim's vast array of power tools are suddenly put away somewhere instead of lying all over the place and tripping me up. Maybe she thought I would sell them, or more nefariously, maybe she didn't want me to have anything to defend myself with.

Kim, the woman I thought I could pin my future to.

Kim, who had texted something that made Sydney flee in terror.

Kim, whose father's name had come up as a VerenTech Pharma shareholder as well as a lawyer for BVT Realty as I'd waited for the water to boil, as Sydney had freaked out and run away.

The iPad is in my other hand, but I haven't read the messages because I have to go fight a man who's likely a trained killer with the assistance of a kitchen knife.

Not being able to call the police when you need help really sucks, I'm learning.

I stalk to the house, aware that eyes are on me, tracking me from windows I used to peep into from my own and from the cameras that have popped up on several of the houses. A shadow is silhouetted by the warm lamplight in Melissa's apartment. The curtains flutter in Josie and Terry's living room, and Toby barks.

When I get to Sydney's top step, I push the door open—the wood is splintered around the lock as if someone has forced their way in with a much bigger crowbar than the one I'm packing. I peer into the dark hallway, but can't see much since dusk has mostly fallen and the place is filled with shadows. My eyes start to adjust, and that's how I see the wall swing open. That's how I see a darker shadow slip out.

Sydney.

The iPad pings suddenly, the screen going bright and illuminating me as I instinctively turn it to read the message that's come in. Sydney's head whips my way as my eyes skim over the messages, the latest of which is Did you get rid of the skank?

An earlier response from whoever Sydney assumed was me has a knife emoji aimed at a Black woman.

I am holding a knife. Sydney is a Black woman.

Correction: Sydney is an armed Black woman.

"This looks really bad," I say, holding up the knife and the iPad as she points a gun at me. "I really wish I'd read this beforehand. I would have carried the shovel over instead."

Her gaze is empty, her expression blank, but her whole body is shaking. "Drop it."

I put the knife down.

"Okay, let's get out of here," I say. "You have the gun, you have the power, we can figure this out once we're outside."

Tears spill from her eyes and her expression crumples and then smooths as she battles to keep her composure.

"Did you know about Drea all this time?" She sucks in a breath, and turns the gun from side to side but with the muzzle always pointed at me. "While I worried and checked my phone? While I was pissed off at her for taking their money? Did you know she died like a rat in the wall?"

Her voice fades into a broken, wounded wail, and I understand that something horrifying has happened in the few moments since I talked to her on the phone.

A second shadow moves against the wall near the top of the stairs—someone walking slowly along the second floor landing.

"We need to get out of here," I press. "Remember? The man who—"

"Did. You. Know?" Her eyes are wild, and I don't think she even remembers that someone is trying to kill her, or if she does, she's stopped caring.

"I didn't," I say gently. "I'm sorry, but—"

I reflexively chuck the iPad as hard as I can as the shadow takes solid, bulky form at the top of the staircase. I'm sure it doesn't hurt much as it smacks into the man, but it does the job of knocking him off balance—a bullet bites into the wall to the right of Sydney's head.

He's got a gun. With a silencer.

"Mother*fucker*," she growls, turning and popping three shots off at him. She *isn't* using a silencer, and the sound echoes loudly in the hallway.

The intruder twists and tries to dodge, but the motion paired with at least one bullet hitting him sends him sliding down the steps. I snatch up the knife and run to meet him as he reaches the bottom.

He tumbles ass over feet when he hits the bottom landing, and I jump onto him before he can get his bearings. I straddle his chest with enough force to crush his solar plexus between the steps and my body weight, knocking the wind out of him. His muscles tense beneath me as he pulls against something; his gun hand is between the poles of the banister and in my peripheral vision I see Sydney trying to tug it from his grip.

Shit. One wrong move and he might—

No. She smashes a booted foot into his elbow and I hear him hiss, followed by the sound of something heavy hitting the ground.

I bring a fist down on his nose and then his windpipe with one hand before plunging the knife into his side with the other. It goes in smoothly, gives barely any resistance as I twist, and I finally understand why Kim paid so much for this thing.

He cries out, and tries to throw me off, but I press down with all my weight, jabbing the knife with one hand and punching him in the side of the head with the other, again and again, until he stops resisting and goes limp beneath me.

The light switches on and I blink back over my shoulder at Sydney. My left hand is wet and stained red, and I use the bottom of the guy's black T-shirt to wipe it off. The iron-rich scent of blood, like a butcher shop, and shit fills my nose and I try not to gag.

The face of the man who tried to kill Sydney is bloody and swollen, but I can see that he looks a little like me: tall, burly, light brown hair. Kim has a type. He shakes a little, and writhes as I take his cell phone and hold his thumb to the home button. When it unlocks, I get up, not looking at him again.

After quickly changing the password so I don't have to worry about it automatically locking me out, I pick up his gun, walk over to Sydney, and open his texts.

I knew things were over, but seeing a nude of your recent ex sandwiched between requests to kill the woman you currently have . . . something with is just a bit of a mindfuck.

Did you get rid of the skank?

I reply with 👩🏾🔫, and then in a second reply, 👻.

And my loser ex? pops up.

Ouch.

I send a 🧔 and a 🔫, this time following it up with a ☠️, then screenshot the conversation.

Sydney's hand grips my arm. "He was honeycheeks?"

"I think," I say. My heart is racing and I feel kind of like I'm gonna puke, but it passes. "Kim is supposed to be in the Hamptons. That picture isn't her parents' place, though. I don't know why she's involved in this. I don't know what she has to do with hired killers. Fuck!"

The anger I felt when the man took a shot at Sydney isn't going away, isn't fading as I come down from the high of the fight. He lets out a rattling breath and I want to walk over and kick him in the head, stomp him . . .

No.

"What happened to Drea?" I ask Sydney, remembering her defiant hope in her friend and the emptiness in her eyes when she stepped out in front of me.

Sydney's eyes fill with tears, and I slide my free arm, with the gun in my hand, over her shoulder and pull her into my side. She points toward the door through which she seemingly magically appeared in the hallway.

"Even if she did betray us, I never wanted this. Ever. I couldn't tell what they did to her. I think she tried to escape through the old servants' staircase. I don't know why, even though I was—"

She raises a fist to her mouth and I feel the dry heaves rack her body.

I can't tell her everything will be all right anymore. I hold her more tightly, my thoughts going a mile a minute as I try to figure out how we get out of this. There are at least two bodies in this house, one of which we're responsible for and the other of which could easily be pinned on us.

Her best friend is dead. There's a man bleeding out on the floor—a man my ex sent to kill her.

An OurHood chat notification pops up on the screen. I tap into the account and see that the notification is coming not from the main Gifford Place hub, but from a conversation under the heading PRIVATE GROUPS. There are two groups, Marketplace and Rejuvenation Planning, but only the second is highlighted.

Gifford Place OurHood/privateusergroup/Rejuvenation

Kim DeVries: Dad, I told you I would handle it. They're dead. So is her friend who got the photocopies. So is the guy who snuck them to her. This loose end is tied off.

Mikel DeVries: Are you sure? The last thing we need is this popping up in the news. Everyone else will be handled but she was the only one who stuck her nose where it didn't belong. Make sure her house, emails, social media, and close friends are cleared too.

Kim DeVries: It will be taken care of.

Josie Ulnar: Do you know how many stories are reported each day that should have people burning this country down? Dozens. A few people get mad on social media. Every once in a while, some poor sap goes to prison for a few years to satiate the plebes. To be frank, if we pull off tonight's rejuvenation with minor complications, it doesn't matter who finds out.

Josie Ulnar: As I tell Arwin, we are the sticks and stones, and we are the words. No one can hurt *us*, especially not social media stories, which have the life cycle of a fruit fly. Let's just get this done.

Terry Ulnar: Yes. We have contacts in most major newsrooms, and there is always a more titillating spin on the story. With the parade and parties this weekend, there will doubtless be a shooting or molestation for them to focus on. If not, we'll make one happen.

Kim DeVries: Besides, what can they do, call the police? lmao Let's just get ready for the meeting tonight. After the rejuvenation, the next phase is going to move fast and we have to get our press releases, contracts, and containment services lined up.

Sydney is reading over my shoulder and I'm pretty sure both of us are too shaken up to really process everything that's happening.

"What is a rejuvenation?" Sydney asks. "They keep mentioning it."

I scroll through the group conversation but see nothing else that makes sense to me.

"Can't find anything," I say. I click to the other private group and see a post asking if there are any houses available with central air-conditioning. It seems to just be a real estate listings page. "There are posts in the other private group, but we need to get out of here. They might figure out this guy didn't finish the job soon."

She nods, then continues to nod as if running through things in her head. "They're gonna do something big tonight, something worse than what they're already doing. That's all we need to know."

I check the gun to reacquaint myself with the feel of one and make sure there are no tricks to it. It's a simple Glock, older model with a silencer screwed on. Sydney checks her revolver, too, loading bullets into the chamber to replace the ones currently lodged in her hallway and in the body of the man on the floor.

"Sydney? Sydney?" Someone is calling her from outside.

"Let's go," I say.

When we step through the front door, there are people gathered in the street and more arriving, the glow of the streetlights silhouetting them.

Of course they're out there.

This is a neighborhood where people care about each other, and three gunshots went off in Sydney's house.

Ms. Candace is front and center, hands resting on the head of her cane. "Sydney, what was that noise? Is that blood all over you? What in the—"

Her words drop off as the streetlights and every other light on the block blink out, leaving us in darkness.

CHAPTER 21

Sydney

WE'VE HAD BLACKOUTS AND BROWNOUTS IN THE NEIGHBORhood since I've moved back—when the grid gets hot, we get shut down so the richer neighbors can stay cool. The fact that the electrical company feels comfortable admitting that seems sinister given everything else going on.

I can think of a million possibilities tying this coincidence to all of the fucked-up things that happened this week.

Maybe the other power outages had been conditioning. We're used to this happening now. We're not supposed to worry that the rest of Brooklyn is bright in the distance, not knowing or caring what goes on in the dark at Gifford Place.

This knowledge combines with the darkness and the humidity, pushing me down into the asphalt. My heart was already beating out of my chest and now I get goose bumps despite the heat because this blackout *feels* different.

Drea is dead. She's never coming back.

Rejuvenation.

A man just tried to kill me in my own home.

Clear out.

My breathing starts to come fast and shallow, the pain in my chest a seed of anxiety ready to sprout and bind me, choke the breath from me.

No.

I have to keep it together.

An image of Drea's last words, in text, pops into my head. I force it away. If I think too much I will die. That's the bottom line here.

I take a deep breath. And another.

Breathe.

"Well, shit," Ms. Candace says from somewhere next to me. "This ain't good."

A hand closes around my arm, and even though I'm ready to bash anything that touches me, Theo's low voice follows immediately. He squeezes my arm twice and then his hand slides down to grip mine.

"This reminds me of . . . one time, one of my mom's boyfriends took me on a night hunt," he says. "He got a kick out of chasing panicked creatures through the dark. This feels like that. Except I'm not one of the hunters this time."

"Let's walk Candace back to her place," I say as, one by one, cell phones glow into the darkness around us, like giant blue lightning bugs floating up and down the street.

"Damn, I wanted to watch the game tonight but the network is down, too," a man I don't know by voice says, sighing dramatically as he waves his phone around. "Can't even use my phone as a hotspot. Fuck outta here with this shit, man. Look. Look. Medical center been closed down for years, and they got electric?"

He waves his phone down the street.

His friend, standing beside him, laughs. "You think they got a TV that play ESPN in there?"

Their joking only adds to the sense of unreality, because when I look down the street, there *are* lights on in the old hospital.

"They're having a meeting," Theo says quietly. "And the lights are on in the hospital VerenTech just bought. I don't think that's a coincidence. I swore I saw something in there the other night."

"What was that noise that came from your house, Sydney?" Candace asks again, nudging at my other arm.

"Firecrackers. I think you need to go be with Paulette, Ms. Candace. She's probably scared since she doesn't like . . . Oh fuck." Paulette's ramblings about the '77 blackout come back to me.

Earlier I was telling Theo how these things happen in cycles, white people clambering into a hood, be it the original Algonquin hood or closer in history, like Weeksville. If I'm right, what Paulette said makes this darkness even more frightening.

Break and build.

This is the breaking point.

I look down the street in the direction opposite the hospital in time to see more cell phone lights blink on in the distance—no, not cell phone lights. It's the faraway mirror images of the cell phones near us on reflective surfaces.

"It's the cops," I say aloud, grasping toward where I last heard Ms. Candace. After snatching humid air a few times, I catch hold of her wrist.

On the other end of the block is a phalanx of cops—I assume. I can't really make out much except for the reflection of light sources in their plastic riot shields and dark, bulky silhouettes.

I very briefly assume they're here for me and Theo or the man bleeding out in my hallway, but no. They wouldn't need this many cops, or shields, for that.

Break and build.

Night hunt.

Rejuvenation.

"Disperse!" a voice shouts through a bullhorn as the march of footsteps sounds through the street. "Disperse! Anyone continuing to riot will be arrested and puts themselves at the risk of lethal force."

"Continuing to riot," the man who had joked about the hospital repeats. "The fuck? Ain't nobody rioting."

"Everybody get inside," Theo shouts, jogging and pulling me along toward Candace's house. "Get inside your houses and don't let anyone in."

"I'm not going inside *shit*," another man says. "We didn't do nothing and—"

There's a flash of light and a whistle where the cops stand, and then a canister is tumbling toward us, end over end, shooting smoke. It lands by the man who was talking and he reflexively kicks it, sending it back toward the growing cluster of police.

"Assault against a police officer is a felony offense," the cop with the bullhorn says, and there's laughter in his voice.

They charge.

It's a short run to Candace's, but she's old. We start to fall behind as she limps, but one of the guys next to us scoops her up without a word and sprints to her stoop, then keeps going without waiting for a thank-you.

A knot forms in my throat as he melts into the darkness. This is what Gifford Place has always been to me—someone helping you without a second thought and keeping it moving.

This is what the people behind this *rejuvenation* are trying to destroy.

Jenn and Jen's door opens and they pop their heads out.

"What's happening?" Jen asks, her eyes wide.

"Go back in and don't come out," Theo says harshly.

Jen looks hurt. "I just want to help. Should we call the police?"

"Baby, go inside," Ms. Candace says in her firm but friendly tone as she opens her own door. "Shit is about to get real, and I don't wanna see you hurt, okay?"

Jenn comes up behind Jen, pulls her in, and slams the door shut.

Candace looks down at me and Theo. "And you two. Get in here, now. You need to tell me what's going on."

Her voice is a little less gentle with us.

"We have to go to the medical center," I say, thinking about those lights that shouldn't be on. "We'll come check on you after. Get inside, hide, don't let them find you."

Candace puts her hand on her hip, her patience gone. "Girl, if you don't stop playing and get your ass inside this house!"

That tone would have worked on me any other time, but Candace doesn't understand. Doesn't know that some of our friends are dead or in danger.

I think of Drea's face, when I'd finally looked at it. She didn't look peaceful like Mommy had. Foam had dried at the edges of her mouth and her eyes had stared toward the door, as if she'd been expecting me to open it and find her.

I hadn't.

I'd walked past her, how many times?

I'd heard scratching in the walls. Maybe it had been her. Maybe—

"Sydney!"

Theo yells right in my face and I realize that I was starting to give in to the panic.

"Let's go."

Theo holds my arm as we run, and he guides me across the street as another smoke bomb streaks by us. The hospital looms ahead of us, the brighter lights of the lower floor illuminating the base of it and making it look even more imposing.

"Where are we going?" I ask.

"When I saw Kavaughn, he appeared out of nowhere but it was *here.* If he got out, then there's an entrance or exit we can use to get inside."

I watch him as he looks back and forth, his jaw rigid and his shirt splattered with the blood of a man he killed for me.

"Why are you doing this?" I ask. "This isn't your neighborhood."

And I'm not anything to you.

"Maybe not," he huffs. "But you know us strange white dudes have a hero complex. Of course I'm gonna swoop in and save the day."

"If you don't get killed," I remind him.

"I'm hoping to avoid that outcome."

I don't want anyone else to die, but I really hope Theo in particular avoids that outcome, too. I don't know if either of us will, given the war zone sounds coming from my neighborhood.

We skirt around the chain-link fence and he moves to touch it but then pulls back. "Either running in these jeans built up some static electricity or this is now electrified. It wasn't the other day."

Shit.

The cops are starting to reach our end of the block. There are knots of people tussling in the streets.

Think, Sydney.

"Remember I told you those urban legends about people getting pulled underground?" I ask. "Now that we're in the middle of this, years and years of rumors that people have been kidnapped and dragged into this hospital start to make more sense."

"When I did the research, I did see a brief entry about supposed underground tunnels to the hospital," Theo says. "It was debunked, but the rumor said they were built during the war when the hospital was a factory. If those are still in use . . ."

"We were always told the mole people would get you if walked on subway grates or metal cellar doors . . ." I look over at the bodega. "Come with me."

I grab Theo's hand and dash across the street to the bodega, to the metal cellar door outside it. And people kept mentioning feeling rumbling underground, and I've felt the shaking in the middle of the night myself. "I heard something in here the day before Tony arrived. Maybe there's a way in through here."

I try to lift the door, but it doesn't budge.

"Hold on," Theo says, then pulls what seems to be a baby crowbar out of his back pocket.

I raise my brows at him. "You just carry that around with you?"

He slides it between the two metal doors and starts working it back and forth like a berserker until finally whatever locking mechanism is holding the door closed from inside pops. He makes a big show of lifting first one cellar door open, and then the other.

I stand in front of the stairs that lead down into the darkness, and he stands beside me.

"You were saying?"

A riot gear–clad cop suddenly appears from around the corner, running at us full-tilt—I only register his presence as he's on top of us. Without thinking, I push Theo out of the way and take a few quick steps after him. The cop barrels through where we'd been standing and steps right into the space where the metal doors should be.

His arms swing wildly as he tries to steady himself, so close to me that I feel the breeze created by their windmilling, smell the scent of cheap Rite Aid cologne and sweat.

As fast as this is happening, my reflexes register that I can reach out to him. Steady him.

I don't.

He tumbles forward and his chin catches the edge of the metal-lined inset cellar door before his hand does; his neck snaps with a quick, sickening *crack*.

I stand there in shock for a second, and then press my lips together. Years of watching over-the-top comedies have trained me to laugh at the sheer slapstick of the situation—the arms waving, the shock on his face because of his miscalculation. One hysterical yelp escapes from between my lips before I cover my mouth with both hands; hot tears run from my eyes and form rivulets where my palms meet my cheeks.

This shit is real. Really real. I don't feel bad for the motherfucker, and I know he'd've been laughing if it were me, but this is *real*, and there's nothing funny about it.

Drea's face frozen in agony flashes into my head and I force the image away.

A light shines down the steps into the darkness of the cellar—Theo's reached past me with his phone. We need to make sure the cop is dead and not down there waiting with gun drawn. The light reveals that the dude's head is twisted all the way to the side at the bottom of the cement steps.

Something moves near his waist, and for a second I think he's still reaching for his gun, but it's Frito, who's apparently escaped Tony's remodeling. She sits on the cop's ass and meows up at us.

I check for the revolver—it's still tucked snugly between the elastic waistband of my sweats and the cushion of my belly. I pull it out, the heat of the metal comforting; Mommy had held this gun in her hand, maintained it. It's part of her, like the house and the garden. Like Gifford Place. Like me.

Theo still has the gun he took from Con Dead back in my hallway.

My neighborhood is under siege. There's a very good chance neither of us will make it out of this situation alive, given how much money and power are at stake.

I force myself to start walking down the steps into the darkness of the cellar, because there's no turning back.

"Let's go."

CHAPTER 22

Theo

I WATCH SYDNEY DISAPPEAR INTO THE CELLAR BUT DON'T move.

What am I doing?

My eyes sting as a cloud of tear gas is carried past me on the breeze. Flashlights shine wildly in the night, highlighting raised batons coming down on innocent people. I've been tangled up in some shady stuff, but I am in way over my head.

Going down into that cellar, where a cop is lying dead, is a very different decision from running across the street to Sydney's house when I'd seen a man hunting her.

This conspiracy may very well be real, but like Sydney just said, this isn't my neighborhood. I already put money down on a shitty room. I could put this gun down and leave. I'd be safe; any of the cops surging down the street who saw me would assume I was with them.

And if I walk away from this and pretend it never happened, I might as well be.

I follow Sydney into the cellar.

"Close the doors after you," she says when I'm halfway down.

"We don't want one of us to fall down here like this asshole did."

I pause at her words, then nod and pull the metal doors shut. The lock is busted but hopefully no one follows us in.

Sydney's phone flashlight is still on, and the dim glow illuminates her searching the body.

When I get to the bottom step, she looks up with a ferocious smile, teeth clenched and eyes wide. I'm sure if I placed my hand at her throat, her pulse would be pounding like mad. I've seen the same look before, and have probably given it, after pulling off a job that could have ended with me in a body bag.

She hands me a Taser, taking the cop's gun for herself, and I snort as I see the compact Glock.

I hold up the one I took from her assailant for comparison. "Matching set. Standard police issue."

"Of course that guy was a cop. Of course. This is all just—" She inhales deeply, then tugs the cop's Maglite from his belt and stands from her crouch. Bright, crisp light suddenly fills the rest of the cellar and thank god, there's nothing here but stacks of flattened cardboard boxes and some cat food.

"Shouldn't there be inventory?" Sydney asks. She stalks around the space, shining lights into every corner. Her efficient stride knocks over a box of Meow Mix and the contents spill on the floor, to Frito's content. Sydney passes the light over the bare cement walls and we both search for a few minutes, neither of us commenting on the muted noise of screams outside and, eventually, a gunshot that makes us both jump.

"Maybe I was wrong," she says, leaning down to stroke Frito, who's winding around her feet. She stays bent, flashlight tucked beneath her arm and pointed behind her, and that's when I see it—the thin strip of shadow in the cement wall.

I step around her with the crowbar. The flat edge of it *just* fits into the slit, but I don't have to do much more than one lever. This door swings back into the cellar smoothly. Quietly.

"I can't believe I made fun of you for having that," she whispers as it opens, and then we both tense.

A breeze blows my hair back as I step in front of her with my gun raised. A hallway is revealed as the door touches back against the cellar wall, completely open. No, not a hallway.

"I guess the rumors about the tunnels were right," Sydney says in a barely audible voice. "It's creepy knowing this was underneath us all this time."

It's not the unfinished tunnel that had come to mind when the teens at the planning meeting had talked about mole people. It's professionally done cinder block painted beige with a garish yellow strip running along the top. Halogen tubes are spaced evenly along the walls, and it's surprisingly wide, the ceilings high enough for a truck to pass through.

It looks like—

"It's part of the hospital," Sydney says as she cautiously peeks out, and turns her head from right to left. "This has to be it."

When I peek out after her, I get the full effect of what she means. It has the same old, sterile, and unwelcoming atmosphere of most public hospitals.

The tunnel stretches down to the left but on the right there's a set of beige double doors, with aluminum plates along the bottoms, about ten feet away.

She grips her gun and starts walking right.

“Should we come up with a plan?” I ask.

“Like what? Shoot all the white people except you?” She glances at me, then back toward the approaching double door. “That’s the only information we really have.”

“True. Awkward. I guess we’ll play it by ear.”

Our footsteps echo in the hallway and I keep turning around to make sure the sound isn’t someone sneaking up on us, but the hall is empty. There’s no motion except for the flicker of one of the halogen bulbs that needs to be changed.

When we get to the door, Sydney asks, “Ready?” in a voice that shakes with fear. Her hands are trembling, too, and she quickly tucks the Glock into the back of her waistband and pulls the .22 revolver out from the front, flipping the safety.

Her hands steady, but she shifts her weight from foot to foot, probably feeling the same anxiety that’s crawling over my own skin.

“Ready,” I say.

My breath is coming fast as I push the door open and she stalks through ahead of me. We’re greeted anticlimactically with another set of double doors, and our breathing fills the small space as we psych ourselves up to walk into danger again.

Just as Sydney takes a step forward toward the door, someone pulls it open slowly from the other side, and the sound of benign chatter precedes whoever it is.

“Shit, they need to fix these doors already; the other one is jammed. Anyway, yeah, they said I could have the Perkins place, then they went and gave it to that shithead Charlie," a familiar voice says. William Bilford's voice. "Like fuck that, I've been doing all the legwork for months and I *told them* I wanted those fireplaces. At the Jones place, I'll have to get the fireplaces rebricked and get rid of all the cement over the backyard."

The front end of a rolling gurney pushes through the doors into the vestibule, followed by an unfamiliar woman's voice. "At least you got to call dibs, I just have to wait, even though I've put up with—"

A brunette with her dark curls pulled back, wearing a blouse and slacks, stares at me, leaving her sentence unfinished.

"Who's this? Is he one of the researchers?" She squints, trying to place my face.

"Did you change your mind?" William asks me, clearly amused. "Once shit started going down? I told you to get in early."

"Ms. Gianetti?"

It's only when Sydney speaks that they even seem to notice her presence. The woman startles.

"Ms. Green." The woman looks dismayed. "What are you—?"

"I guess this is why you couldn't help my mother get her house back?" Sydney's voice is low and vicious, angrier than I've ever heard her.

"No, it's not like that," the woman says, her eyes darting between me and William. "I tried my best, but there was nothing to be done."

"Of course there was nothing to be done!" Sydney points the

gun at her. "Tell me the truth. You helped cheat a sick older woman out of the home she'd poured her life into."

"She isn't that old," Gianetti says. "And nothing we did was illegal. You can try finding another lawyer, but the responsibility to read the fine print and think through the sale falls onto the homeowner."

"How could you do this to people?"

I've seen Sydney freak out, but right now her voice is flat. I want to reach out to her, but these people hurt her, not me. And she's so out of it that she's not watching their movements.

The woman doesn't answer her and Sydney pushes. "How do you do some shit like this and think you can just get away with it? Don't you care that you're hurting people? Don't you care that you're ruining lives, taking from people when you already have enough for yourself?"

Gianetti suddenly looks annoyed when she should be frightened. "I'm tired of you people. You're saying all this now when you weren't even responsible enough to make your appointment on Thursday! Just like your mother, crying after the fact and expecting special treatment. If your mother wanted to keep her house she should have paid her taxes and not been so ignorant she fell for—"

The woman's words are cut off again, but not by surprise or by a question—this time it's by the bullet currently lodged in the area of her brain located behind her palate.

The blast of the gunshot reverberates in the vestibule and the woman keels forward onto the gurney, eyes wide.

"Christ, Sydney," I yell, jumping back, but she ignores me, her focus laser sharp on William.

"Bill Bil." She turns her gun toward him. Her voice is loud, like her ears are still ringing. "Got anything to say about my mother?"

"Didn't know her, but she was a very fine woman, I'm sure." His expression is smooth like an oil slick even though bits of his colleague's brains have splattered on him.

"Good. Then you can answer some of the many questions we have." Sydney's gaze drops down to Gianetti and then moves back up to William. "What is this gurney for? Why are you talking about having dibs on Mr. Perkins's house?"

He shrugs, glances back over his shoulder. From where I'm standing, I can follow his line of sight to the red emergency alarm lever on the wall a little more than an arm's length away from him.

"I think there's been some kind of misunderstanding." William takes a step back and Sydney closes the space between them.

"If there was a misunderstanding, you'd be a little more concerned by the fact I just blew a hole in homegirl's head. *Talk*."

"I'm just doing my job, right? They told me I could choose from one of the houses on the street if everything went well." His hand reaches behind him and I take aim for his shoulder.

"Stop moving," I say.

His hand stills.

"How did you think you would get that house? Magic?" she presses. "How can you lay claim to something that belongs to somebody else?"

"I didn't know they were hurting people," William continues, tears springing up in his eyes. "They said they were paying people for the houses."

"Then what's the gurney for?" Sydney asks.

"Oh. This? Um." His eyes dart back and forth between us. "Well . . ."

The gurney suddenly surges toward Sydney—I've been watching his hands, not his feet, and he's kicked it toward her. It hits her in the thighs before rebounding off her, and she stumbles back into the door. William leans back, his fingers grasping toward the alarm.

My gun is already aimed. The element of surprise is all we have and if he alerts people to our presence we're dead. I squeeze off one silent shot.

The reverberation of the Glock's blast jangles through me, and William Bilford slumps forward onto the gurney over his friend, a spray of blood misting out of his chest. His chest and not his arm. There's a gaping hole where a heart is usually located.

Shit.

"Why did you kill him?" Sydney's eyes are wide. She wipes frantically at her cheeks, where droplets of blood spattered. "I was trying to get him to tell us what's going on here."

I scrunch my face contritely and exhale sharply through my nose.

"That was supposed to be an arm shot to stop him from pulling the alarm, but apparently my aim isn't as good as yours. I'm more of a fists or knives kind of guy."

"It's okay. I killed one, you killed one." She looks down at the two bodies. "All right. They're dead. They're dead."

"Sydney?"

She bends and starts pushing the gurney, struggling with the weight of it. "We can't leave them here in case someone comes through. And we don't know if the people ahead will be armed. We can use this for cover."

I move beside her and we push the gurney through the door.

"She's the lawyer who said she could help me get the house back," she says as we enter what seems to be another hallway, nodding her chin toward the woman's body. "She strung me along for almost a year, acting so concerned and enraged on my mother's behalf. I'm starting to wonder if all of you are evil."

"Nothing I say right now will put you at ease about that." I inhale and the smell of blood fills my nostrils. "I hope we make it out of here alive. Because I like you a lot. I want to spend some time with you that isn't us actively caught up in a web of conspiracy. I know I probably shouldn't be saying this while we're pushing dead bodies around, but life is short."

"Nothing wrong with shooting your shot in the middle of a bloodbath. If not now, when?" she asks sardonically, but doesn't reciprocate the sentiment.

We reach a bend in the hallway and turn right, slowly maneuvering the gurney and its horrific payload. We move through another set of double doors—automatic ones that haven't closed all the way.

The hallway ahead is a little dimmer, the walls painted a dull gray and many of the light sconces bulbless. We've passed into a different wing.

It's the smell that hits me first. Feces. Bodily odor.

Despair.

Large windows line the walls of the corridor up ahead—not glass, something less easy to break. Something good for keeping people confined. This looks like a lockup—it shouldn't be in the basement of an old shut-down hospital.

There's no sound except our labored breathing and the creak of the gurney wheels. The silence around us feels heavy, foreboding.

As we approach the first window, a hand slaps against it hard, and Sydney stops short and presses into me—William Bilford's body slides off the gurney to the floor with a heavy thud.

"Mrs. Payne?" She rushes past the body on the floor and presses her hand to the window.

"No, no, no. This is too much. This is too—"

Her words break off, and she just shakes her head, staring into the room.

When I walk up behind her, an older woman with matted hair and cheeks caved in from missing teeth is staring at Sydney through the plexiglass. The whites of her eyes are yellow and swimming with tears. I stare at those eyes for a long moment.

I recognize them.

"She's—I found a photo album a little after I moved here. In the garbage. She's in a lot of the pictures."

I'd wondered why someone had tossed away such precious memories like trash. This woman hadn't thrown it out. Whoever stole her home had taken care of that.

The woman, no longer the young bright-eyed girl or always-laughing young woman whose photo I had looked at countless times, slaps the plexiglass where Sydney's hand is, her hand pressing hard as if she might touch Sydney through it. I recognize the expression in her eyes—it's the same way Kavaughn looked at me.

Desperation.

A cry for help.

She points at the tubes in her arms, starts making wild gestures I can't understand.

"They said they were going to open a research center, and they have." Sydney's voice is quiet, but when she looks up at me her eyes are wide and terrified. "This is Doris Payne. The woman whose house you took."

CHAPTER 23

Sydney

I LOOK UP AT THEO, THE HORROR I'M FEELING SO OVERWHELMing that I might black out. Doris is caged. Caged like an animal. She's always been so prideful about her looks, and they have her in here looking like this.

"The day of the tour, your girlfriend was looking at the Payne house." I'd registered it as I slammed my door in Theo's face, but hadn't remembered it and what it meant until now. "It's like what Bill Bil said. They want a house, and they take it. Doesn't matter if someone else lives there."

"I had no idea about any of this."

I'm starting to wonder how it's possible for him not to know about any of this.

"Why did you even go on that tour?" I ask him, as my body shakes. I feel like every cell in my body wants to fly off in a different direction. "So Kim could play some fucked-up game? Eenie meenie miney mo, catch a brownstone by—by kidnapping and torturing?"

Doris looks at Theo, but she has no reaction to him. Not fear or anger or recognition. Her gaze drifts back to me, unfocused and awful and pleading.

She used to sell Avon products and had slipped me samples of Skin So Soft in the summer when the mosquitoes were biting. The gentle scent has always reminded me of her, but now the smell in this hallway makes it impossible to even recall.

Theo doesn't touch me, but he moves closer. "Kim told me that her dad had bought us the tour tickets and that it would be a good way to check out the neighborhood, since we were looking to buy."

I turn away from the window, away from Doris, and my gaze lands on the door beside her small room that contains only a cot and a bucket. The door has an electronic code reader on its heavy-duty lock. The chart on the wall next to the door says *Test Subject 3* and *nonviable* is scrawled beneath it in Sharpie.

I try to collate all of these facts, make them make sense, but my brain can't process this horror.

"Sydney."

I ignore Theo and stalk down the hallway, weaving from one side to the other as I inspect each room and each chart.

Test Subject 1 is a dark-skinned man I don't know who lies on his cot without moving.

Nonviable.

Test subject 2. Miss Wanda, dammit, Miss Wanda, frail and hunched over, scratching at her neck.

Nonviable.

"Sydney." Theo's harsh whisper is drowned out by the buzz in my mind.

Test Subjects 4 and 5 are strangers, a man and a woman. Maybe the woman is the one Amber mentioned, who supposedly got snatched down a subway grate. Or maybe that woman is already dead.

Number 6 is Abdul. His cell is a bit different—he's on a gurney, hooked up to machines that monitor his vitals.

I run down the hall now, heart pounding in my ears, the unfamiliar and familiar faces blending together. Stranger, slapping at his own head. Jamel Jones, who I just saw a couple of days ago, knocked out and with an IV in his arm.

The corridor seems to go on forever, the rooms and their inhabitants in various states but almost every damn room occupied. They're soundproofed, I realize at some point, so the strangled cries I hear echoing in the hallway are my own.

Test Subject 18. Mr. Perkins sits on the edge of his gurney, staring at the floor. He looks so thin compared to just a few days ago, the wrinkles on his face hanging like heavy pleats in fabric.

I tap frantically at the window and he slowly raises his head. He stares at me, no recognition on his face, but stands and shuffles toward the glass.

His movements are jerky; his head lolls to the side.

And then he lunges at me, beating his fists on the window. I can't hear him, but his mouth stretches wide in a scream and his spit flecks the window. His eyes are full of rage—I've never even seen him angry before.

A siren sounds in the hallway, but I stand there frozen. Even when arms close around me and haul me back into the recessed doorway of the room across the hall, I hold Mr. Perkins's rage-filled gaze.

The double doors that cap this wing open slowly with a prolonged *whoosh*, automated, and two white women rush into the hall, one brunette, one gray haired. They're dressed in jeans and T-shirts, but wear white lab coats. The gray-haired one, who has a short pixie cut, swipes her ID against the lock to Mr. Perkins's room, and they rush in. As they do, his wails fill the hallway, and I hate that I recognize his voice in this cry of pure pain.

Key, Theo mouths, and he slips past me, giving me a firm press back against the door that's an order to stay there. He didn't have to do that—I can't move. The horror of everything has wrapped me up tightly, strapped me down like I'm on that gurney instead of Ms. Gianetti's lifeless body.

He stalks toward the room, tucking into a crouch and then peeking around the door frame. I expect him to just burst in but he waits. And waits. Fury starts to build in me as Mr. Perkins's howls fill the hallway, but then I remember.

"My aim isn't as good as yours."

He's waiting to make a clean shot.

He doesn't want to hurt Mr. Perkins.

The howling subsides and the first woman steps through the door and back into the hallway, and then the second. Before they let the door swing shut, Theo stands up behind them and says, "Don't move."

Both women freeze, but the brunette's hand keeps going toward the bulge in her pocket. Whatever constraints were on my body immediately release as I instinctively recognize the motion—she's reaching for a weapon.

I step out from the doorway and shoot. She grabs her stomach and falls to the floor, screaming in pain, sounding not so different from Mr. Perkins.

"Oh my goodness. Julia!" the older woman calls out, and Theo rushes up to her, stripping the ID from her and searching her for weapons.

I pat down the woman on the floor and she clasps at my hand.

"Help me," she says as tears well from her eyes and course into her hair.

I shake her hand off and search her for weapons—I'm second-guessing myself, wondering if she'd gone for her phone and I'd just shot someone for no—no, it's a gun.

With a silencer. Like the one Theo took from Con Dead.

"Don't let me die here, I have a son. A husband." She grasps at her stomach and then cries out in pain.

Pity and guilt spear me, and I remind myself that all the people locked up here have families and lives, too.

"What did you do to Mr. Perkins, *Julia*? To all these people?"

"Mr. Perkins?"

"Test Subject Eighteen," I grit out.

She coughs, averts her gaze from mine. ". . . My job."

"Which is?"

She starts crying in earnest, locking her gaze on mine. "Please help me, it hurts so much!"

I want to cry, too. I did this to her. Does she deserve it? Did Ms. Gianetti? Who was I to decide? What if I was wrong?

My vision starts to swim and I suck in a breath.

"I'll help you when you tell me," I say through gritted teeth. "I don't want to hurt anyone. I just need to know what's going on here. I can't help you until you tell me."

"We're researching how to cure opiate addiction," she says quickly, hope glinting in her eyes. "We needed test subjects, and federal regulations make true progress too difficult. There's a methadone clinic near here, we picked up people there. And the others—"

"Shut up, Julia," the older woman says, then yelps as Theo tightens his hold on her.

I tug at Julia's collar to draw her attention back to me. "Why like this? You already won the bid for the new research center. Why do things like this?"

"New research center? Not new. You mean *official*." Julia's words are sluggish, and when she smiles, her teeth are sheened with blood. "And we do it because we can."

I back away from her, holding the gun, and she writhes on the floor and screams. "Help me, you bitch!"

"Go start unlocking the doors," Theo says from behind me, handing me a key card. "Start at the other end of the hall."

"But—"

He takes her gun from my hand. "Go."

His voice is hard, but not mean.

I run to the other end of the hall, frantically swiping the card over the locks and opening every door. Most people aren't in a state to move themselves, but some of them can start making their way out. At the very least they're no longer locked in. We can't call the police or an ambulance. We can't trust anyone.

As their doors open, the cries and moans of the people Veren-Tech has been using as test subjects—strangers, neighbors, and friends—fill the hall.

I want to close my ears. I want to run away from all of this. But I just unlock the doors and swing them open, one by one.

By the time I make it back to Theo there are only two streaks of blood leading into an empty room next to Mr. Perkins's.

"Do we go ahead or go back?" he asks grimly as I hand him the card.

"We can't go back," I say, even though my mind is screaming at me to do just that. "Moving those people ourselves could kill them. We can't call the police. We lose the element of surprise, and these people will get away with this. I need to end this shit."

Theo doesn't say anything. Just checks his clip, then waves the ID card in front of the sensor next to the double doors that lead out of the wing.

I step through them as they swing open.

CHAPTER 24

Sydney

"YOU EVER PLAY A FIRST-PERSON-SHOOTER VIDEO GAME?" Theo asks. "War games where you move room by room, picking the enemy off to advance?"

"I hate games like that," I say. "I can never figure out the damn controls and always freak out and get mowed down. A real gun is—"

Easier. Easier, and a million times harder because these aren't pixels on a screen. The people we've shot, we've killed, are real. Oh god, they're real and somehow I can't even make myself feel that anymore. I'm not a hardened killer—I think my brain has reached some kind of overload point and the choices are curl up or keep it moving.

I grip my gun tightly, my eyes darting back and forth as we enter a lobby space. Looking for more people we might have to shoot.

"I'm selling my PlayStation after this," Theo says darkly as he peers around.

The lobby we're passing through is a small one, with the same yellow-and-beige color scheme as the first part of the tunnel. This area is slightly nicer than what we've seen so far.

Instead of holding cages with test subjects, there are normal-looking offices behind the glass in these rooms. Plants sit on desks and hang from ceilings. Pictures of children and families are in frames of all shapes and sizes.

It could be any workplace, quiet on a Saturday night because everyone is off for the weekend. No. Two people, four people, had been working, and now they're . . . not.

Theo walks ahead of me, peering into offices. He stops in front of one, so suddenly that I'm sure someone is inside, but he doesn't say anything, doesn't raise his gun. His jaw works and his Adam's apple bobs.

When I move beside him, I look into an office that belongs to one of the people who is no longer working. A piece of patterned purple cloth that you can buy from one of the tiny Indian storefronts around Nostrand—well, you could before they got shut down—hangs on the wall. The room smells of lavender and sandalwood, and crystals of all colors and sizes sit on shelves and most available spaces. Instagram-meme-style affirmations written in calligraphy like *Rise and shine!* and *Just Breathe* and *Kindness is the key* are framed on the walls, and on the desk is an eight-by-ten of Julia laughing in a wedding photo with a slim, beaming Black guy. Beside it, a picture of her with two brown kids.

"Jesus," Theo says.

I can't absorb this. Did her husband know what her job was? How will her children feel when their mother doesn't come home? Because of me.

I look away and my eye catches on another affirmation.

The only way forward is through.

I shake my head and continue the sweep of the offices—that's what this is.

Theo peels away from the window and walks along beside me, and when I glance up at him, his expression is blank, his complexion chalky.

We pass down the corridor back to back, the glass making it easy to see that no one is inside, and no one is hiding under desks or behind doors. Interspersed with the offices are examination rooms like you might find in any urgent care center—somewhere in my head, I'd disconnected this section from the other, but the people sitting here would have seen the test subjects brought through, would have heard their cries.

They were the ones doing the testing.

Theo stops and scrubs a hand through his hair in agitation. "Do you think they were the only ones here? The people we already encountered?"

"There's the meeting," I say, trying to figure out how much time has passed since he stripped my assailant of his phone and we scrolled through the private group. Since the police started their siege of my neighborhood. It could have been minutes or hours. "Maybe that's where everyone is."

"I guess we keep going," he says flatly.

We reach the next set of double doors without encountering anyone, and swipe through; they lead us into a stairwell that's creepy as shit. A metal cage separates this level from the stairs, the gray paint peeling to show the rust beneath, but the door is ajar. The stairwell itself is concrete, dank, and dimly lit, lined with random clusters of pipes and HVAC tubes. We begin to climb, expecting to find a doorway at each landing and being met with blank wall.

"Theo?" I don't mean to say his name, don't mean for my voice to be breathy and panicked, but the dimness and the silence start to press in on me, a claustrophobic nightmare. Part of me wonders if there are any doors. Maybe we should turn back—if we do, will we find the door to the metal cage locked? Is this a trap? Maybe we should have turned back. Maybe I've chosen incorrectly, like I always do.

Theo's big hand presses into my back as we climb, right over the growing knot of tension between my shoulder blades. "Don't forget the tunnels are underground, so it's going to take time to reach ground level. There will be a door. We just have to keep climbing."

I nod.

Finally, finally, we reach a landing with a metal door. Light seeps out from the space where it doesn't meet the ground, and ugly office lighting never looked so good.

Theo tries the ID card on the scanner, and the lock mechanism whirs and releases. We crack the door and enter another level, which looks entirely different from the underground tunnels. It's clearly still under renovation, but the medical center closed relatively recently. This floor is still pretty ugly, but twenty-first-century ugly, with bright lights embedded in gray-speckled drop tile ceilings and bone-white walls.

The murmur of voices can be heard down the hall, and the scent of coffee fills the hallway, though I can't shake the smell of that first corridor we'd encountered—what would be the last corridor for people approaching from inside the building.

My insides are quaking but my hands are steady as I pull out my second gun. Theo shakes his head, leans down to whisper. "That only works in movies, Syd."

A spurt of frustration goes through me, but I tuck it away like I do the gun. He's right, and I'm used to Mommy's gun anyway.

We creep down the hallway, toward the sound of a man talking loudly. Confidently. I don't know who it is, but I know the type—the guy who expects to get what he wants, and does.

"Okay, we have some live view from the street here, via the drones and the doorbell cams," the voice says. "Look at this mess. I told those idiots to be mindful of property damage. This should have been done in the middle of the night not at the beginning of it, and it should have been done tomorrow, during the block party and leading into the parade."

Theo places a hand on my shoulder, leans down to whisper again. "Kim's dad."

I realize something. Up until now, this has not been personal for him. Yeah, Con Dead had been fucking his ex, but he hadn't walked in on them or anything. He hadn't known the cops attacking us and had barely known the people on the street.

Now it's about to get real personal.

My thoughts start racing again.

Theo is on my side. But Drea was on my side, too, wasn't she? Until money made her betray me.

Theo said he likes me, but if I keep it real, I'm his rebound hookup. He was with Kim for how long, and we've only known each other a week. I *hate* Marcus and haven't spoken to him since the divorce was finalized, and I'm not sure I could walk into a room and point a gun at him for any reason, though I've fantasized about it a lot.

I'm frozen as Theo moves ahead of me, gun at his side.

"Wait," I say, but my whisper doesn't leave my mouth, like I'm in one of the bad dreams again. I could leave, run, but I'd be caught in the melee outside and have no idea who would believe me enough to come back to the hospital with me. I might get arrested or killed, or put into one of the rooms downstairs and tested on, before I can do anything.

I want to trust Theo because he's come this far with me, but I don't. I don't trust anyone, or anything, except the fact that I have to end whatever is going on, and if I run now that won't happen.

I start walking, too, steeling myself for whatever's behind the door in this conference room. For the fact that just because Theo didn't turn on me before doesn't mean he won't now.

"The rejuvenation is not going as smoothly as planned, but if it continues as it is, then by daylight we'll have a new neighborhood under our umbrella."

"Did we really have to be so blunt about it?" another man asks. "I still think we should have moved more subtly, like with the Williamsburg and Park Slope projects."

Theo is standing beside the door now, his back to me.

"The carafe is empty," someone mutters, and gets shushed.

"Subtlety is no longer necessary. This neighborhood is ours. We had to get ahead of the other developers trying to move in," Kim's father says, voice hard. "This is no time to get squeamish. Inching slowly toward rejuvenation isn't an option anymore, and with the police, the media, and the government on our side, there's nothing to worry about. Even with any destruction and bribes, the cost of getting this over and done quickly is negligible."

A woman's voice cuts in, her tone glib. I recognize it from when she threatened to call the cops on me. "When you add the incentives we're getting from the city, this latest project will *gain* us billions of dollars to get back land that we could have paid untold amounts of money for otherwise. We totally pulled a Stuyvesant."

She laughs.

"Well, hopefully we manage things a bit better than our forebear," her father says. "On the next slide are the projected earnings for the eventual *addiction cure*. Methadone has such a negative connotation, and the new drug crisis sweeping the country calls for a hipper, funkier product. Something that can appeal to a family in the heartland and an urban millennial family."

"Our online monitoring teams have started to spot stories linking our production of opioids and our getting paid to find the solution, but nothing is sticking so far," a deeper voice chimes in, the brownnosing in his tone apparent. "They're mostly getting written off as crackpot conspiracy theorists."

Multiple voices laugh at that.

"Good. Make sure to plant some additional stories, and also even more embellished ones, like we're growing babies in tanks or something. Hell, dredge up the mole people thing, that seems to get good play."

"Speaking of vermin," someone else says, "as for the cure itself, while it's effective in mice, most of our human test subjects haven't fared as well. This one was promising, but was compromised."

"We're trying to eat here," another man says in annoyance.

I tug at Theo's shirt, but he ignores me and steps inside the room. The chatter abruptly stops.

Shit. Shit shit shit.

We were supposed to have the element of surprise, but not to just walk in and stare at them.

I grasp my gun and very carefully peek inside. Theo is standing there like a dummy, partially blocking my view. After everything that's happened, I expect the room to be filled with monsters, but no. Just a bunch of normal-looking people in rumpled suits, mostly men, mostly white. But not entirely. Goddammit. I recognize the Black man who's frozen with his napkin to his mouth, ready to bolt—a politician who's been on the scene for years. An older Asian man has his head turned toward Theo, eyebrows raised.

They're all sitting at an oval table with paper cups, plates, and stacks of documents scattered across it. A PowerPoint presentation is being projected onto a screen. It could be any old meeting, at any old company, except the slide on the screen shows a picture of Kavaughn, eyes bulging and blood crusting both nostrils. Greenish spittle has dripped from the corner of his mouth and down to his neck.

I pull my head away, press my back against the wall next to the door, and try to calm my stomach, my nerves, my soul. They killed Kavaughn. And Drea. They want to do this to all of us.

"You told us he was dead, Kimberly," her father says.

"Don't blame this on me! Erik told me—"

"Hey," Theo says sharply. "Enough. This is it. You've been caught. It's over."

"What? Oh, you really thought you would stop us?" It's the incredulous laughter in her voice that stomps all my emotions flat except for one—rage.

"You always tried to be so smart, when you're nothing but trailer trash," she says, and the tone is so similar to how Marcus would calmly tell me I was nothing. "Did you think you would waltz in here and tell us to stop and we would? Is that how this played out in your head? You really didn't pay attention at all when you met my family and their friends, did you? All the lawyers, and CEOs, and politicians?"

"You can't stop us. This is too big, and there's too much money on the line," her father says calmly. "We own the jails, shithead. They're not for people like us."

Kim's father is right. In the best-case scenario, there are some good cops in this mess, and some clean lawyers, and a jury that does the right thing. However it plays out, maybe he goes to a white-collar prison for a few years. Maybe.

I make the sign of the cross, something I haven't done since I was a teenager, and then whirl and take a step into the room beside Theo. I don't just stand there though—they've already said that nothing we can do within the bounds of the law will stop them. I get the motherfucker standing with a smug smile in front of the room's heart in my sight, and pull the trigger until the chamber is empty.

I watch his eyes, see the smug light fade from them, but I feel nothing this time. Not with Kavaughn's face up on that screen, though now it's splattered with the old man's blood.

Shocked silence fills the room. Kim, dressed in a bootleg Hillary Clinton pantsuit, jumps to her feet and stares at me.

"You—you—"

"You can see me now, can't you, bitch? Funny how that works."

I point the gun at her and pull the trigger, forgetting I'm out of bullets in my rage. She dives under the table, and pandemonium ensues. The people who've been sitting around the table in shock start to run, knocking over chairs and scattering, and Kim's father's words play in my head.

"You can't stop us. We own the jails."

I don't have time to reload. I pull the Glock I took from the cop, fumble with the safety, and start firing. This is a higher-caliber gun; the shape of it in my hand feels wrong and hitting a running target is way more difficult than hitting one standing in front of you—about a third of the people go down, but the rest of them run out of the room.

Shit!

The gun jams and I shake it, like that will fix anything, but it's messed up. I don't know what to do, so I drop it on the floor, pull out Mommy's trusty .22, and fumble for the baggie of bullets in my pocket.

The cries and shuffling of the people I clipped fills the room, and even that's muffled by the loudness of my heartbeat and my breathing and the ringing of my ears.

Bullets are spilling on the floor when I hear a gun cock next to my head.

Theo.

"Don't," he says in a barely recognizable voice. "Don't even think about it."

I thought I couldn't feel anything but rage, but sadness slices through me in a million tiny blades, like everything I've been trying not to feel compressed and then exploded inside of me. I have no one.

No one.

I see the muzzle of the gun in my peripheral vision. It's shaking almost uncontrollably, and when Theo steps past me, I follow where the gun is pointed. While I was busy reloading, Kim had stood from behind the table with a gun of her own.

"Kim, it's over for real this time," Theo says.

Her expression suddenly softens, eyes filling with tenderness even though she's pointing a weapon. "Can you really shoot me, babe? Really?"

"Do it, Theo," I urge. "She's going to kill us. She's hurt so many people."

Kim tilts her head and smiles. "You know, I'm glad you're not dead."

"Why?" Theo asks sadly, still just standing there. I can't seem to get the bullets into my gun, because my own hands are shaking, too, my body too overwhelmed by what's happening even if my mind is still hanging in there.

"Theo, please," I plead as more bullets drop to the ground.

"Because you've finally done something useful. I've been waiting for my dad to drop dead. Now I'm in charge." She grins, releases the safety on her gun. "You're big and strong, but so what? You're just a soft little mama's boy."

"Howdy Doody!" I yell at Theo. "Howdy fucking Doody!"

Theo grunts, his finger jerks on the trigger, and Kim stumbles back, blood blooming on the front of her blouse like the zinnias Mommy planted in our backyard.

I don't have time to say anything, to process anything; I hear steps running down the hall toward us and Theo is staring blank-eyed at the spot where Kim was standing. I reach for his back pocket, grab something that looks like a gun, and come away with the Taser I stripped from the cop instead.

A bullet whizzes past my head and I turn, flip what I hope is the safety, and when a laser sight appears on the chest of the man shooting at us, I fire. Two metal wires shoot out and hit him, and he drops to the ground writhing. I don't let up, watching the gun slip from his splayed fingers and the Red Sox cap slide back and be crushed as he rolls onto it.

"Fucking Drew," I say in a voice so low it rasps my throat. I finally release my finger, which is starting to cramp from willing my anger through the Taser.

I walk over to Drew and pick up his gun. I can't bring myself to shoot him, unconscious and with a piss stain on his jeans. I should kill him, but instead I slip to the floor as my legs give out without so much as a warning tremble.

Theo walks up to me. "I'm sorry I froze. I should have—I should have—"

"It's okay not to be *that* cold-blooded," I say, my teeth starting to chatter. "I'm sure as hell not. Fuck."

Theo drops down beside me and pulls me against him, and we stay like that for a minute. Holding each other in a room full of bodies and gore because if we didn't need a hug after all that, it would mean this night had broken something in us that couldn't be fixed.

"We need to get the people out of those rooms down there," I say. I don't want to give up the sensation, but there might be more Drews and there are definitely people in need of immediate medical attention. I don't know how we'll get it to them, but we have to finish this.

"Let's go," he says.

We shuffle back down the stairs—my adrenaline surge has faded and I'm fucking exhausted, and the night isn't even close to over. We each grab a wheelchair from the lobby as we head back toward that awful wing of horrors we first encountered.

When we pass through the double doors my heart stops. The blood on the floor is gone. All the doors to the rooms for the "test subjects" are locked tight, their pain locked behind the soundproof doors once again.

Two men who look barely out of college, one white with greasy black hair, wearing a T-shirt with various sexual positions on it, the other one with curly brown hair and features people call racially ambiguous, stand talking with an older white man in a blood-spattered business suit a few feet away.

"Oh, there they are," the man says, exasperation in his voice as he looks at me and Theo, completely ignoring our guns. "Perfect. Prime them, and then you can try the Feelbutrol on them. How does that sound? *Feelbutrol.* Mikel thought it sounded too much like an antidepressant, but he's gone now and I like it. Has a sci-fi element but it's still hip."

"Sounds good, Mr. Voorhies. You were always cooler than Mr. DeVries," Curly Hair says.

"Yeah, and Kim was a real bitch. Glad she's gone," Greasy Hair says, then looks at us, annoyed. "We're giving it to this guy, too?"

"Yes," Voorhies says. "I hate to say it, but Mikel was a bit racist. I mean yes, yes, superior race, whatever. He also wasted a lot of money on his whims. I'm not going to let a good strong volunteer go to waste. Use them both."

He looks past us, snaps, and makes a wrap-it-up motion with one hand.

There's a sharp prick in my shoulder and everything goes black.

CHAPTER 25

Sydney

IN MOVIES, WHEN PEOPLE GET STRAPPED DOWN TO HOSPITAL beds by the bad guys, they either develop superhuman strength or they manage to find some way to slip out. I've been strapped down against my will before. I know that no amount of wriggling, no amount of screaming, no amount of praying to God or Satan or one of their little friends will get you out.

I'm not calm as I lie on the gurney next to Theo—my heart is pounding, my jaw is locked, and I feel like if I blink too hard I might set off a full-on panic attack. I look calm compared to Theo, who, in typical white dude manner, is not pleased about being denied autonomy.

"Let us go!" he screams, writhing so that the bed he's strapped to shakes and the metal buckles of the straps clang against the rails.

The two young doctors, scientists, whatever, are in this room with us and bustle around us like they're just at a regular office job. Like Julia and her coworker, they wear normal clothes and white jackets, and both of them are sipping tea from winter holiday Starbucks thermoses even though it's summer.

The curly-haired one is power walking back and forth around

the room, opening small fridges and gathering glass bottles of chemicals. The white guy is sitting in a rolling office chair, and his hair hangs in his face as he looks over some papers and eats wings from a Crown Fried Chicken box.

We're about to get killed by some dude who probably hasn't changed his underwear in the last five days and doesn't care about getting strangers' bodily fluids in his food.

Great.

"You know what would be cool?" Greasy Hair asks.

"Letting us go," Theo answers.

"Me not having to do all the setup for once," Curly Hair says irritably. "That's what would be cool."

"Hey, I still have ten minutes in my dinner break because I got interrupted by all those suits stampeding down here. You get to go home after this *and* you got to go to the shareholder dinner and eat all the good food."

Curly Hair rolls his eyes. "It was boring as hell, I almost got *killed* at the dinner, and the food was worse than what we feed the test subjects."

"Let us go!" Theo shouts again, the tendons in his neck cording.

They're mostly ignoring him, but the curly-haired one's gaze keeps flicking over. He seems disturbed, having to do this to a white guy, even though he looks more like the previous test subjects.

Greasy Hair sucks his index finger and thumb, and then drops a chicken bone into his paper box. "I was gonna say it would be cool if there was a Whole Foods here already, so I could go to the buffet instead of eating this ghetto shit. There was one by my old job, and it was fucking—"

"Let us go!" Theo yells, and Greasy Hair grabs a syringe, stretches a lanky arm over, and squirts a liquid into Theo's face.

"Shut. Up." His voice is deadpan, like someone mildly annoyed by a cat scratching furniture that's already been shredded by three cats before it.

Theo sputters and blinks liquid that I hope is water out of his eyes, then glares at the guy. "Don't you know that you're killing people? That—"

His words are cut off because Greasy Hair picks up the used latex gloves beside his food and shoves them deep into Theo's mouth.

I gag along with him.

"Shut. Up. My rent just got jacked up. This job pays well. End of story," Greasy Hair says, then leans back in his seat. He shakes his head. "And you two just killed a bunch of people? You've got a lot of nerve judging me. At least I don't kill my own kind."

Curly Hair knocks over a beaker, swears, then heads to the medical-grade fridge humming in a corner.

"What are you doing now, then?" I ask.

"He's not one of us." He shrugs. "If he was, he wouldn't be here, would he?"

Funny how much race matters until it doesn't.

"Besides, there's no guarantee he'll die. In fact, he's gonna feel really good for a little while. Unless I overdose him on this oxy since he ruined my dinner."

"Let's do this already. He's giving me a headache and I don't want a migraine at the beach tomorrow," Curly Hair says as he walks over to me. He places his little tray of meds on the table next to me and I see the familiar setup for a medicine port from when Mommy was in the hospital.

He tightens the band around my arm, and I take a deep breath against the panic and the anger at the unfairness of this all.

It strikes me that it's pretty typical that I'd discover a goddamn conspiracy theory, infiltrate a secret research center, kill a bunch of bad guys, and still end up *not* saving the day.

I snort a laugh and Curly Hair looks at me quizzically, which makes me laugh more.

Shit, what a stupid fucking way to die. And if there *is* a hell, I certainly just earned my way in with all the blood now on my hands from this dummy mission.

What a week.

"What's so funny?" Greasy Hair asks, throwing his wings box into a garbage can with a biohazard label on it and wiping his fingers on his jeans. He takes a sip from his thermos. "Are you already high or what?"

"Nothing," I say.

"Then shut the fu—ack!" I glance over at him and he drops his cup, his hands going to his throat. His mouth is stuck in an exaggerated O shape and his eyes bug out of his head as his face turns a violent shade of purple.

Curly Hair's brow creases in concern and he puts down the port he was about to insert into my arm so he can go check on his buddy. His hand slams into the tray clumsily.

"What the hell?"

Greasy Hair drops to the floor, convulsing—I can't see him but can hear his desperate flailing and the squeak of his sneakers against the floor. Curly Hair staggers forward, and then the door opens slowly.

Slowly.

Shit, what now? I wish Curly Hair had managed to drug me before whatever fresh hell is about to go down takes place.

Fitzroy Sweeney pokes his head in, his wrinkles rearranging themselves as he smiles at us.

"There you are. Good, good." He opens the door completely and I see that he's holding a cricket bat in his other hand.

I laugh again; either I've had a psychotic break or they've given me the drugs already without my realizing because there is no way any of this shit is really happening.

Fitzroy twirls the bat easily in one hand as Curly Hair staggers toward him, then hefts it back and swings right at the researcher's head; the sound of it smashing into his skull reverberates in the room and then Curly Hair drops out of sight. Fitzroy shuffles over and lays the bat over my knees as he begins to undo the straps.

Someone glides by outside the window and then Gracie steps into the room, dressed in her church clothes and with her gray bob perfectly laid.

"What is going on?" I ask when Fitzroy's strong grip helping me up makes it clear I'm not drugged or dead. This shit is, indeed, really happening.

"What's going on is you should have listened to Candace when she told you to come inside," Gracie says tartly as she pulls the latex out of Theo's mouth with an expression of disgust on her face. "Just like your mother, always so stubborn and not wanting to ask for help."

She sucks her teeth.

She unstraps Theo's hands and chest, and he pops up into a seated position, taking deep ragged breaths. His gaze flies to the two on the floor as he rubs at his wrists. "Do-fa-do."

"I knew I liked this young man," Gracie says as she tugs his ankle straps free. "Do-fa-do means 'tit-for-tat.' Certainly seemed necessary here, wouldn't you say?" She grunts as she gives the strap one last tug to free him. "These racists never think about things like the predisposition and mood of the people who prepare their food and beverages. Much like my dear departed husbands. When you expect others to serve you, especially others who you mistreat, you should really be more careful about what exactly it is that's being served."

"How did you get in here?" I ask.

"Same way you two did," Fitzroy says, throwing his arm over my shoulder. I lean into him. "You know we watch out for each other around here. Do you really think you were the only ones who would notice something was amiss?"

Him and Gracie laugh like Theo and I are still in diapers, and even though I'm grateful to them, my anger flares.

"If you knew, then what the f—then what were you waiting for? People are dead. I had to . . . we had to . . ." My throat closes as emotion threatens to swamp me.

Fitzroy takes my hand and squeezes it. "You're right. We were trying to do things the old way, how we've handled it in the past.

But the world moves faster now, and evil moves faster, too. We were too slow."

"I think we can all agree that poison moves quite fast, thank you," Gracie says peevishly, then sighs. "Bad things happen in this world, every minute of every day. We try to stop them, when we can, how we can. We try to look out for one another. Like, when somebody recklessly buries something in a garden, we move it to a safe location."

I feel an actual pain in my body, like someone's kicked me in my chest, but I just squeeze Fitzroy's hand tighter.

Gracie takes my other hand and helps me off the hospital bed. "That's what we've always done and what we'll continue to do in Gifford Place."

"You know Candace," Fitzroy says, as if he's about to launch into one of his old man stories. "Candace's great-grandmother grew up in Weeksville. She was one of the survivors."

"Survivors?" Theo asks, attempting to stand.

Fitzroy looks at him.

"Cycles," I say quietly. "Break and build."

"They can break, but they can't erase," Gracie says. "They can build, but they can't bury us."

We're all quiet after that.

When they lead us back into the hallway, I see a line of neighbors helping to evacuate the people who'd been test subjects out through the tunnel.

We get on the end of the line.

Candace is waiting in the cellar of the bodega, holding Frito.

"Sydney."

She looks at me disapprovingly and I suddenly feel like a child again. Tears well up in my eyes.

"I'm sorry. I should have listened. I should have . . ."

She drops Frito and pulls me into a hug. "Little miss bobblehead. Let's find you a shower and some sleep."

"What about the medical center?" The weight of everything starts to crash down on me. The shooting, the bodies, the people in power. We're alive, but I've watched *Forensic Files.* We've left a trail of evidence and will likely be in a VerenTech prison by sunup.

"Oh, we takin' care of that. Let's go see."

When we walk up the steps, the scent of smoke hits my nose. Smoke and an oddly electrical smell, like a battery on your tongue.

We gather yards back from the hospital as it's consumed in orange flames, with a corona of blue at its center that brightens the sky behind it like a borealis.

Paulette comes to stand next to me, reeking of gasoline.

"Transformer," she says, more lucid than I've seen her in months. "Causes blackouts. Causes fires. Makes the sky so pretty, too. They like the dark; this is so bright that no one in the city can ignore it. If there're any of them left, and there are, that's the last thing they want. We gave them an excuse, and a warning. They'll clean up after themselves."

A hand comes to rest on my shoulder and I feel Theo's solid weight behind me.

I lean back into it, and we watch that shit burn down.

EPILOGUE

THE NEXT AFTERNOON, I WAKE UP IN AN UNFAMILIAR BED—the pullout in Candace's guest room. Arms are around me, in a bear hug, but I'm not afraid.

Theo.

He smells like Ivory soap and smoke, but not the iron of blood anymore.

The scent of coffee drifts in through the double doors that lead to the kitchen, then there's a hiss and pop of oil and the smell of bacon follows.

When I open my eyes, Miss Ruth is sitting on the arm of the couch, looking down at me and Theo.

"You move fast," she says, with brows raised and shoulders back in judgment.

I sit up, my entire body sore and my head spinning. My throat hurts from the smoke of the fire we watched and from crying it raw.

"Didn't you say you never liked Marcus? Let me live, Miss Ruth."

She leans in closer to me. "Is it pink? Down there? I've never seen—"

"Ruth, leave the children alone," Gracie calls out. "Come help with breakfast."

When I glance down, Theo is staring up at me, his expression unreadable. Everything that has passed over the last few days barrels into me.

"Good morning," I croak.

He crooks his finger at me, face still blank.

I lean down close to him and he says, "In the future, if anyone asks, you can tell them it's taupe."

I don't know how it's possible, but I start to laugh. The laughter shifts to tears so fast that I don't even realize it, and Theo pulls me against him. Holds me together.

The radio cuts on in the kitchen, which I guess is their way of giving us privacy. After a minute, I pull back, surprised to see that his eyes are red-rimmed and watery, too.

"Everything's going to be okay," he says, and I kiss him once softly on the lips even though we both know there's no guarantee of that.

"Fresh asses!" Miss Ruth calls out, and we get up, freshen up, and join them.

And back to the biggest story of the day, and maybe the year: The proposed site for the VerenTech campus has gone up in flames overnight, just weeks before construction was to start. It is believed that a transformer fire spread quickly, trapping several VerenTech employees in the inferno.

Although the new site was opposed by community activ-

ists, no foul play is suspected. The project has been canceled as the company faces major restructuring challenges. Stocks plummeted—

Fitzroy cuts off the radio as we pull two seats to the table. Jamel and Ashley Jones are here, too, looking haggard but able to move on their own. They had apparently been taken shortly before Theo and I had found them.

They nod at us, and we nod back.

Candace and Gracie bring platters to the table, not letting anyone help them, and we all dig in.

Jamel clears his throat. "Um. So y'all know I do community activist work. And I'm in some groups. It might be too soon to bring this up, but . . ."

"What is it, baby?" Candace prods, but her gaze is sharp.

"Last month, this cat in one of the anti-VerenTech organizing forums started acting real weird. A dude out in Detroit. He was saying that—that people was disappearing, and the neighborhood was gentrifying fast. He kept trying to show us all this evidence, these articles, but they just seemed like regular news, right? We all thought he was maybe going through some things. He left the group, but he sent me an invitation for a new one that he'd made. I had joined just to keep an eye out for him, but hadn't checked in in a while . . ."

"Show them," Ashley says gently.

He pulls out his phone and as it passes from person to person, their expressions drop.

When it gets to me, I hold it between me and Theo as we read.

It's a thread on a private forum, with dozens of responses. The top post is a longer version of the story Jamel told, with links; the way the page is set up we can only see the first few lines of each response in the thread, but that's enough.

Belquise Ramos (Queens, NYC): In my neighborhood, they just straight up rolled through with a tank. Arrested a man who had been going to community meetings and asking why the houses of deported citizens were getting flipped and sold for ridiculously high prices.

Sandy Smith (Jasper, AL): Oh thank god I found all of you, I was starting to go crazy. I'm white, but my town is poor. A distribution plant opened up that was supposed to bring us jobs and improve things, but I swear, everyone is disappearing, and more and more land goes to the factories.

Andrew Chen (Los Angeles, CA): Health inspectors showed up at my parents' restaurant and shut it down so they had to sell, and now it's a Panera. They'd been refusing a lot of buyout offers right before that. Lots of my childhood friends who grew up around Chinatown say the same thing—it's like someone is picking us off and just taking what they want.

Gloria Pierce (New Jersey): It was slower here and less scary and maybe it's not part of . . . this, but maybe it is. Things changed, people moved, but they suddenly upped the taxes. Overnight, all the original inhabitants of my neighborhood went from living the

American dream of owning property that had appreciated in value to having to sell because only millionaires can afford these kind of taxes. Where are we supposed to go?

The thread goes on and on, but almost every entry is more or less the same thing: marginalized people disappearing.

I hand the phone back to Jamel. My head starts to spin, imagining how many places across the country might have had nights like we had last night or were taken out by more subtle forces. How many didn't make it through.

"What happens now?" I ask.

"Now? We sit here and eat our food," Paulette says. "Always fighting to be done. Rushing won't help anything. Being strong will."

Theo grips my hand under the table, and outside a siren wails in the distance.

I don't jump.

I pat my waistband and make sure Mommy's revolver, which Fitzroy found for me, is still there.

Then I pick up my fork and eat.